Like the caffeine in a cappuccino, there are some serious points being made here beneath the froth. A light-hearted diary by an ever-hopeful, chocolate-addicted Christian.

— Veronica Heley

Not cooking chocolate, but the real thing! Christianity meets reality — with food for thought and moments to savour. A really enjoyable and amusing read.

— Liz Babbs

Also by Penny Culliford
Theodora's Diary

faith,
love &
chocolate

THEODORA'S WEDDING

Penny Culliford

Author of Theodora's Diary

 ZONDERVAN®

ZONDERVAN.com/
AUTHORTRACKER
follow your favorite authors

ZONDERVAN®

Theodora's Wedding
Copyright © 2003 by Penny Culliford

Requests for information should be addressed to:
Zondervan, *Grand Rapids, Michigan 49530*

Library of Congress Cataloging-in-Publication Data

Culliford, Penny.
        Theodora's wedding : faith, love, and chocolate / Penny Culliford.
            p. cm.
        ISBN 978-0-310-25039-5
            1. Church membership — Fiction. 2. Weddings — Fiction. 3. England — Fic-
tion. I. Title.
PR6103.U46T48 2003
823'.92 — dc21

                                                                            2003008667

Interior design by Michelle Espinoza

Printed in the United Kingdom

08 09 10 11 12 13 14 • 15 14 13 12 11 10 9 8 7 6

Contents

JULY

Monday 5 July

Well, I've done it.

I've actually done it!

Nobody thought I'd persevere, least of all me. But I have done it. I've kept up my diary for over a year. Ariadne sneered when I started. She actually sneered. 'I'll give it a fortnight,' she said. My sister, my own flesh and blood, doubting my resolve. And now I've really shown her. I shall go and wave it under her nose and say, 'See, I'm not a flash in the pan, a five-minute wonder, a here today, gone tomorrow sort of person. I have written something lasting, something that will endure. Future generations will benefit from my incisive, yet entertaining, commentary on life.'

Actually, I think I won't. I can hear the derisive snort already and, having flicked back through last year's diary, I can see that a lot of it could come under the category 'neurotic ramblings'. Besides, poor Ariadne looks so exhausted, what with baby Phoebe and getting ready to go back to work, I don't think her eyes would stay open long enough to focus. I'm sorry to say she's also letting herself go. She looks kind of tired and crumpled somehow. And she's rather plump. Perhaps she doesn't realize. Perhaps I ought to tell her.

However, I think the diary has achieved its aim. I may not have grown very much spiritually, nor am I any nearer finding my ministry, nor have I been hailed as the next British supermodel, but it has been an eventful year. I have seen friends come and go, I have a new baby niece and I have gained a fiancé, even if at times I think he is spiritually degenerate. And to cap it all, I weigh half a stone less than I did this time last year.

Tuesday 6 July

Cooking! Why on earth did Charity Hubble volunteer me to do cooking? And baking cakes, at that. She knows I hate cooking. She knows I would rather bungee-jump naked from the bell tower or enter a Michael Jackson look-alike competition than bake a cake. Just because she's the curate's wife, is responsible for a one-woman population explosion and dresses like Laura Ashley's furniture department, just because she was born knowing how to make six different kinds of preserves from fresh fruit, does not give Charity Hubble the right to conscript me into baking for the produce stall at the flaming summer fete.

Wednesday 7 July

Confessed to Kevin about my cake problem. As my future husband, I would expect a little support. Instead, he laughed like a drain as usual (and being a plumber, I suppose he should know how a drain laughs).

'How do you get yourself into these situations in the first place?' he guffawed. 'If you didn't want to make a cake, why did you volunteer?'

'I didn't . . . it just sort of happened.'

'What's it for, anyway?'

'Oh, a good cause. The village fete. The church has got some stalls there, including a home-made produce stall. Just doing my bit,' I declared proudly.

'Village fete? Bit twee isn't it? I thought your church was into preaching the gospel, fighting for justice and setting the captives free. Where do village fetes come into it?'

I couldn't answer that one.

Thursday 8 July

I have been reading an excellent book. It's called *I'm Going to be Assertive Now, If That's OK with You.* It's written by Hiram B. Jefferson III who's got just loads and loads of degrees and diplomas from all sorts of universities, so he should jolly well know what he's talking about.

'Are you a human doormat?' Hiram demands.

'Yes, I am,' I answer.

'Do you say yes when you mean no?' he inquires.

'Yes I do – I mean no I don't, I mean yes but I want to say no!'

'Then take control. You have a right to your feelings and a right to express those feelings. Use positive statements such as "I am . . .", "I will . . .", to show those who would wipe their feet on you that here's one doormat who's gonna stand up and say "No more!"'

I decided, for once, to have it out with Charity. I'm not really a coward who shies away from confrontation; it's just that she is impossible to argue with. An encounter with Charity Hubble always seems to end with her making me say the opposite to what I really think. How does she do it? How will she stand up to Hiram B. Jefferson III?

Friday 9 July

Found a box of stink bombs, knife-through-the-head headbands and synthetic dog poop in the bottom drawer of Declan's old filing cabinet today. His practical jokes used to drive me up the wall when he worked here. I wondered how he had managed to become a section supervisor when he seemed to spend so little time working and so much time playing practical jokes. But since he left, work seems a lot duller. Safer, yes: there is no danger of finding the toilet covered with cling film or discovering your coat pockets are full of cold spaghetti or standing up to find that your shoelaces have been tied together – but for some perverse reason I actually miss all that. Even the extra pay and status (ha! It's all very well being made a section supervisor but I was the only person on the section so now I'm just supervising myself) doesn't make up for it. I wonder how Declan is getting on in Manchester. I wonder what kind of priest he will make.

Saturday 10 July

I finally tracked Charity down outside the post office, with baby Methuselah in a pram and three other hamster-faced offspring in tow as she stuffed Nigel's mail into the post box.

I pounced.

'Charity, why did you put my name down for baking a cake when you know I hate cooking?'

She paused for a moment to wipe a dribbly trail of slime away from baby Methuselah's mouth and to restrain Ahimelech, who was trying to climb the pillar box, then turned to me, beaming.

'I thought it would be a wonderful opportunity to practise. After all, you'll have to cook for Kevin after you're married, unless of course you're hiring help. One never knows with you "career women".'

Her eyes twinkled mischievously, and I suddenly saw a side to Charity I hadn't believed existed. If she hadn't been so unbearably holy I would have called it 'devilment'. She was really enjoying this.

'Of course not,' I retorted, much too quickly. Once again my mouth was moving faster than my brain and I realized that unless we planned to live on takeaways for our entire married life, cooking something at some point was inevitable. And Charity knew it. She just wanted to make me suffer. I panicked.

'Kevin can cook,' I blurted. This was a lie. Kevin can *eat*. In fact Kevin could eat for England. I have yet to find something Kevin won't eat; even Kippers in Garlic Mayonnaise somehow found their way down his gullet without complaint.

But Kevin can't cook. His mum has seen to that.

'Super! Then I can put him down for a cake too.'

'No! No, he'll be far too busy, what with work and everything. B . . . besides, have you thought about the places plumbers have to put their hands? Yuck, even I wouldn't eat a cake he had touched.'

'So you can make two, one for you and one on his behalf.'

'Charity! I know you're doing this on purpose. I don't *do* cooking. When I put my name on that list to help out, you know and I know that I didn't put it under anything to do with baking, boiling, fricasseeing or any other kind of food preparation.'

'Do you know where you *did* write it?'

My brain searched the archives. No record found.

Charity reached into her enormous handbag and pulled out a neatly folded piece of paper. She opened it and waved it under my nose. True, my name was not on the list of people volunteering to bake cakes. Nor was anyone else's. My name appeared at the bottom under 'anything', a section created for people who were either so versatile that they could turn their hand to any task or so ineffectual that they had no particular talents. I definitely fell into the latter category. My indecisiveness had once again become my downfall. Charity had spotted my weakness and gone in for the kill. I bet Hiram B. Jefferson III himself would be no match for Charity Hubble.

'Well, you *did* say you'd do anything,' she said, fluttering her eyelids coyly. At that point Ahimelech made a dash for the road and Charity had to scurry off to apprehend him. Otherwise I would have told her . . .

Sunday 11 July

There was a correction in today's *Church Organ.*

It was reported in last week's publication that the Street Evangelism Team would be offensive in spreading the gospel around the village in the next few weeks. This item should have read that the Street Evangelism Team would be <u>on the offensive</u>, spreading the gospel. The editor apologizes sincerely for this error.

I have the uneasy feeling that the editor was right in the first place.

Monday 12 July

Kevin's five-a-side team is taking part in an exchange with a French club this summer. First they're coming over here, staying with English supporters, then the English are going to stay in France for a fortnight. Kevin has *asked* me (a breakthrough in itself – in our relationship so far, I've been lucky if he's even *informed* me he's going) if he can go with them.

He has also decided to better himself and learn the language. He has an ambition to be able to order a beer in twenty different languages.

I hope he has more luck learning French than my mother has had learning Greek. Despite having a love for the country that borders on obsession, her attempts to speak Greek have been little short of disastrous. My mother is enough to make the Linguaphone lady resign. The other day she informed us that Archimedes jumped in the bath and shouted, 'Euthanasia!'

Tuesday 13 July

Ariadne and Tom's for tea.

I mentioned my cake dilemma to Ariadne, who sat at the table trying to sponge a smear of baby-puke off the shoulder of one of her Versace jackets while Tom peeled the carrots at the sink. Little Phoebe was asleep for once in a sort of bouncy miniature deckchair under the table. Ariadne had one foot poised and every time Phoebe stirred or whimpered Ariadne started rocking the little chair to soothe her back to sleep.

'For goodness sake, Theodora, stop making such a fuss. Either knuckle down and make the flaming cakes or go and buy some. Just stop whingeing about it.'

I was taken aback. 'I just thought ... that as you were at home at the moment ... and you're so good ...' Something in the look she gave me told me not to proceed further down that road. Tom piped up.

'A ... actually it's not that difficult really. You just need a really good recipe book, couple of cake tins ...'

'I don't own any cake tins and I have tried before. It just doesn't work for me. I've even tried packet mixes. What a disaster! I'd have been better off eating the packet than the cake.'

'If you didn't want to make the things, why did you volunteer in the first place?' asked Ariadne, rocking the deckchair-thing furiously with her foot.

'Ah, well, that's another story.'

I decided to change the subject. Soon the kitchen was filled with the scent of shepherd's pie and we sat at the table to devour the fruit of Tom's labours.

'This looks great,' I remarked, taking a large forkful of steaming mince and potato. 'You really are a terrific cook.' Ariadne's frown told me she knew exactly what I was up to.

'No,' she said menacingly as she dug the fork into her dinner. 'Absolutely not. You got yourself into this situation, don't try to get Tom to bail you out.'

Just as she got the fork midway between her plate and mouth, Phoebe let out a wail indicating that she was awake, hungry and had no intention of waiting for Ariadne to finish her dinner before being fed. Ariadne sighed, hauled herself to her feet, disentangled Phoebe from her deckchair and shuffled into the lounge.

'I'll warm it up in the microwave for you,' Tom called to Ariadne's back.

Wednesday 14 July

Kevin was keen to practise his French phrases on me this evening.

'The beauty of this course, Theo, is that they tailor it to your needs. I don't need any of that stuff about shopping and "How do you do?" and all that rubbish. And the only day of the week I need to know is *samedi*. As in *"Quand samedi arrive"*.'

I sat incredulous as Kevin proudly trotted off what he had learnt. This, as far as I can remember, consisted of:

'C'est un jeu de deux demis,'
'Malade comme un perroquet,'
and
'Qui a mangé tous les tourtes?'

I am quite sure he is spiritually degenerate.

Thursday 15 July

Got a strange postcard this morning from Declan who, it seems, is struggling with his community project in Manchester. However, his preparation for the priesthood seems to be doing him some good. He has obviously been reading the Bible because, apart from the normal truncated greetings, he had written the verse from Psalm 102, 'My days are like the evening shadow; I wither away like grass.' He should get out more. Stuck the card to the fridge with all the others.

Friday 16 July

Rather worried about the whole village fete thing. What if Kevin is right and instead of spending time in flowery dresses and big hats on the village green we should be engaging in battle with dark forces? What do tombolas, white elephants and face painting have to do with spiritual warfare? Jeremiah Wedgwood could have told me, had he not still been in the throes of what everyone has now decided is a monumental sulk. Jeremiah is an expert in dark forces. He spots them lurking in books, films, television programmes, computers, music, fashions, hobbies, sports, just about everywhere. Then he takes great delight in warning others against them. It's difficult to find anything to do or anywhere to go where Jeremiah won't find some kind of dark force operating. Unfortunately, whereas he sees himself as a power for good, bringing light into the evil world, everyone else sees him as a bit of a wet blanket and has stopped including him. This is what brings him into conflict with the vicar so frequently. Reverend Graves is the antithesis of Jeremiah. As hard as Jeremiah tries to find the evil in everything, 'Digger' Graves tries to find the good. And to be honest, both approaches cause problems.

Poor trusting Digger looks as if he would be more at home on Bondi Beach than in the suburban commuter belt. He once admitted that he has lost count of the number of times he's had things taken from his car, which he never locks, and has lost books, clothing and other possessions which he's lent to people but were never returned. He has a trusting view of human nature too. He blurs the line between 'saved' and 'unsaved', between 'saint' and 'sinner'. He just sees them as people, loves them all and treats them all the same.

Funnily enough, both men are utterly convinced that they are doing what Jesus would do.

One thing is certain: organizing the village fete is a lot easier this year in Jeremiah's absence. Willing as he was to help out, it was a task in itself to find him a job which didn't in some way compromise his stand. He would have nothing to do with the tombola or raffle (gambling), the beer tent (potential for drunkenness and licentiousness – he obviously never tasted the beer), the country dancing (pagan origins) or the bookstall (unsuitable reading material – which in Jeremiah's view includes anything from Dennis Wheatley to Enid Blyton).

Saturday 17 July

Busy week coming up at work. We are redecorating and getting new furniture. There are benefits in being the boss (well, deputy assistant boss). We all got to choose what we wanted from an office furniture catalogue. I chose a wooden desk and a chair from a range called 'Slogbrot', 'a rhapsody in light ash with azure faux-leatherette cushioning', in keeping with my Deputy Assistant Manager status. I shall have to buy some modern art prints, cappuccino mugs and some kind of contemporary cactus.

Monday 19 July

Rather bewildering phone call from Charity. In the midst of this battle of wills about cake-making, she has just asked me to be godmother at baby Methuselah's christening. At least I think that's what happened.

The phone rang when I was in the shower this morning. Why does it always ring at the point where you've got shampoo in your eyes and the towel has run off to the far side of the bathroom? Dripping, I squelched my way into the lounge.

'Theodora! Good, you are there.'

'It's ten to seven in the morning, Charity, where else would I be?'

'How's the baking going?'

'Don't talk to me about baking! Look, is there anything I can help you with, only I'm dripping all over the carpet?'

'Well, I'm just phoning to ask a favour, really.'

If she asks me to baby-sit again, I'm leaving the country. 'And what would that be, Charity?'

'Nigel and I are trying to organize Methuselah's baptism, and to put it frankly, we're having the most horrendous problem finding suitable godparents. Obviously,

Nigel's brother Rupert will be one, now he's been acquitted, and I thought of asking Mr Wilberforce as long as he leaves that terrible dog behind, but we just couldn't think of a suitable godmother. We racked our brains, but with such a large family it's surprising just how quickly you run out of possible candidates. All of our female friends are either away on mission, engaged with their families or quite frankly not of a suitable spiritual calibre. As we couldn't think of anyone more qualified, Nigel suggested we ask you to do it. What do you think?'

'Well, I'm deeply flattered,' I said, with a sarcasm that was completely lost on Charity. 'I'll consult my diary and let you know.'

'Good. Sunday 29 August at three in the afternoon. I'll advise you about a suitable baptism gift nearer the time. Must go, Nigel needs more tea. Bye.'

And she put the phone down.

Tuesday 20 July

The cake, I'm ashamed to say, has become a matter of pride. During one of Ariadne's 'if I don't get some sleep right now, I'm going to kill something' naps, I received a furtive phone call from Tom. He whispered down the phone.

'You know, I'd help you if I could, but you know what she's like and especially at the moment ...'

He didn't need to say any more.

'I know, Tom.'

'Look, I've got a foolproof recipe, never fails. I call it my "Number of the Beast" cake.'

Curiosity completely overwhelmed me.

'Why?'

'Oh, it's nothing to do with satanic rituals – it's just that you use 666. Six ounces of flour, six of butter and six of caster sugar, plus three eggs and a spoonful of warm water. Just mix them all together, bung them in a couple of cake tins and stick them in the oven for twenty-five minutes. Perfect sponge cakes every time – never fails.'

'Thanks Tom, you're a star. You wouldn't care to provide me with a prototype, would you?'

'More than my life's worth. Good luck.'

Wednesday 21 July

Kevin and I placed a tentative toe on the first rung of nuptial commitment today – we went to see an estate agent. Kevin still lives with his mum, and my first-floor flat is too small and modest for a flourishing young couple launching themselves into married society. I felt really grown up as we sat and browsed through properties and discussed mortgages, conveyancing and amenities. I know it sounds a bit silly to say that I felt grown up – we are both over thirty (me only just) and have held down jobs and managed finances for longer than I care to think. But when you are single, there is a feeling that you're not quite taken seriously. My parents still treat me as if I'm a child. Mum will still say, 'Mind the cooker, it's hot.' 'Yes Mum,' I reply sarcastically, 'food cooks better that way.' And Dad often reminds me to check my petrol, oil and water before I embark on a long journey. (Actually, he has a point. A couple of weeks ago I had to call him out at half past midnight because I had run out of petrol. Bless him!)

As I gazed at Kevin across the photographs of 'Des. Res.' I thought proudly, 'My husband; that's my husband' – until I heard him ask if the garden was big enough to erect full-size football goals.

'But you don't even play proper football any more. Not with your dodgy knee.'

'It's for the kids,' he replied.

A rush of panic filled my mind. Kids? What kids?

10.30 p.m.

This evening, when Kevin and I sat down to eat the Cinnamon con Carne I had cooked (like Chilli con Carne but with cinnamon in instead of chilli – the pots look very similar) I tackled him, metaphorically of course.

'What did you mean this afternoon when you talked about needing a garden big enough to put up football goals?'

'Nothing, really. I just thought it would be nice for the kids.'

'Who said anything about having kids?'

'But what about the old biological clock ticking away there?' He patted my abdomen. 'We won't be able to put it off too long.'

Alarm bells started ringing (and it certainly wasn't my biological alarm clock). 'What do you know about it? What about my career?'

'You hate your job and I've got my own business now. I could work as many hours as I want to support the two, or should I say *five*,' he winked, 'of us.'

'Hang on a minute . . .' I protested, but the phone rang before I could assert my mastery of my reproductive processes. It was Kevin's friend Jez. I could hear them discussing the results of today's away match. It will have to wait until another time.

Thursday 22 July

Had a wonderful dream last night. Dreamed that Kevin and I owned a little cottage with apple and pear trees and a stream running along the bottom of the garden and a rose arch over the front gate – and not a child in sight. In my dream, Kevin and I skip hand in hand under rose arches and through a wild-flower meadow, me in a white dress and Kevin looking Byronic in a frilled shirt. We throw ourselves laughing into the long grass and I recline as Kevin reads poetry to me. Then we eat the picnic which has mysteriously appeared – smoked salmon, wild strawberries, chilled champagne . . .

This morning's post contained details of a two-bedroom flat over a chippie in Sidcup High Street and a shoebox-sized house on a new estate.

Friday 23 July

Perhaps I could ask Mum to make the cakes for me. On second thoughts, since she has been involved in this Greek catering business her oven has been so full of foil trays of moussaka, kleftiko and beef stifado I don't think there would be time or space to fit in my cakes. On the positive side, Georgie and Nicky are paying for her to go on a culinary tour of the Greek islands in October and Mum has offered to take me as her personal secretary. Better not push my luck.

Saturday 24 July

Kevin and I took his mum out for a meal tonight and the subject of house-hunting inevitably came up.

'Of course, if you two don' manage to find a place by the wedding, you can always come and live with me. I got plenty of room since mi family move out. I'll be able to cook for you and you won' have to worry about the cleaning and the shopping.'

I saw Kevin's eyes light up and nudged him firmly. I remember when Kevin's sister Deyanna first got married, she and Floyd moved in with Kevin's mum. A week later they were close to divorce, and shortly afterwards Floyd suddenly and unexpectedly got a job in Birmingham. I love Kevin's mum dearly but couldn't bear the thought of living with her.

'That's really kind of you, Eloise,' I said diplomatically, 'but Kevin and I have got our hearts set on a place of our own.'

'Of course you have. What would two young lovebirds like you want with an old woman like me hangin' around you, crampin' your style?'

This time it was Kevin's turn to nudge me and I spent the rest of the evening trying to soothe her hurt feelings.

Sunday 25 July

Had a representative from one of the main Christian aid agencies at church today. She talked about the agency's work among some of the world's poorest people. She told of refugee families leaving virtually all they possess to escape political death threats or bombs; of men, women and children

dying from or living with HIV and AIDS; of slavery, rape,
torture and murder of little children; of crop failure and star-
vation; of women having to walk many miles each day in
order to obtain water which will not kill their children ...
and I am worried about baking a cake. God forgive me. The
representative told what a difference a small, regular donation would make to the lives of these people and the vital
importance of prayer. My problems seemed infinitely small
and insignificant. I said sorry to God, took a prayer leaflet
and donation envelope and went home to bake a cake without making any more fuss.

Monday 26 July

Unfortunately fuss-free cake making didn't work.
Didn't have any cake tins so tried using microwave-proof
dishes. Sadly they were plastic and couldn't take the heat of
the oven. Had to throw the whole sorry melted thing away.
Thought about those people in the Sudan where every
grain of flour is precious ...

Tuesday 27 July

Only have a few more weeks at the dizzy heights of
Deputy Assistant Manager. They are appointing a lady by
the name of Myrna Peacock to be my new boss.

I wonder what she's like.

I wonder how Declan is.

Wednesday 28 July

Invited Ariadne round for a 'video and pizza' evening to try to entice her out of her black mood. She's been a virtual recluse for the last few weeks. She used to love going out, whether it was a rock-and-roll night at the village hall or a West End theatre. I even offered to hire a suitable video – *Nine Months* or *Parenthood* or *Maybe Baby* – whatever she wanted. Said she is too tired at the moment. I suggested that she bring little Phoebe with her but she replied, rather irritably I thought, that if she was ever, finally, going to get out of the house for an evening, Phoebe would be the last person she would want to bring with her.

Thursday 29 July

Was running a bit late today so I decided to finish getting ready on the train. If you think about it, journeys represent 'dead' time. People on trains and the underground seem limited to either reading the latest trivia in paperback form or listening to something which sounds from the outside as if a frantic grasshopper has become trapped inside their personal stereo. Either that or they sit staring blankly at their vitrified reflection in the train window. I have decided to be different. I have tried eating my breakfast on the train but have reached the conclusion that the only useful thing it is realistic to attempt on the train is a cup of coffee. Croissants are too crumbly, Danish pastries make one look a complete pig and a full English leaves one with grease stains and ketchup down one's work clothes. It is also extremely difficult to eat eggs and bacon while standing up.

Theodora's Wedding

This morning I resolved to use the time to give myself a manicure. I was going to do a pedicure as well but I was concerned that I would not be able to accomplish it in a way that would prevent my fellow passengers seeing up my skirt. All was going well with the filing, buffing and cuticle treatments, but when it came to applying the polish ('Strawberry Swoon') I ran into problems. First I discovered that I needed three hands: one to hold the bottle, one to hold the brush and one to have the polish put on it. I managed by clamping the bottle between my knees, while being very careful not to get the polish on my skirt. The second problem I encountered was the movement of the train. I hadn't realized how much it swayed, bounced and jerked along the track. Consequently it required the utmost concentration and an attempt to move in harmony with the train. So I sat there, tongue sticking out with concentration, swaying like a snake charmer and with the growing awareness that I was becoming an object of entertainment for my fellow passengers. The middle-aged woman in a raincoat sitting opposite me was swaying with me and drawing a sharp breath each time the train hit a bump. The businessman in the pinstripes next to her had abandoned his *Independent* and was watching intently. I was doing really well until the train gave a sudden lurch and the lights went out. When they came on again, I discovered that I had painted a red streak all the way up my hand. Unfortunately, the one item of my manicure kit that I hadn't brought with me was my nail-polish remover. Never mind, I thought, I will buy some at the chemist when I get to the station.

The general result wasn't too bad, considering. The polish was applied rather more thickly than normal and I was obliged to sit with my hands elevated like a pianist about to give a concert on an invisible piano. I was just congratulating myself on a constructive use of my travelling time when the ticket inspector appeared. He was a greasy, unpleasant-looking man who seemed to regard the travelling public as some kind of miscreants, to be caught out and reprimanded. Needless to say, he was unsympathetic when I tried to explain my predicament. I looked around the carriage for support. Mr Pinstripe had returned to his newspaper and Mrs Raincoat was gazing intently out of the window. I reached into my jacket pocket as gingerly as I could, trying to extract the ticket between my fingertips without touching the sides. The ticket had lodged itself at the bottom of my pocket and I had to dig deep. When I retrieved it and the inspector had given it a cursory glance, I realized that my newly polished 'Strawberry Swoon' fingernails were covered in a layer of grey fluff. I tried to pick it off but it had stuck fast. Toyed with the idea of buying a disposable razor to try to shave it off. Perhaps I could start a new fashion: 'fuzzy nails'. Eventually I had to buy a large bottle of acetone and take the whole lot off and start again. So much for efficient use of time!

Friday 30 July

Joy, bliss, ecstasy! Have just tried my holiday clothes on and they are actually too big! What a fabulous excuse to go and buy some new ones. Unfortunately, bank account doesn't agree. Saving to get married is such a nuisance. Still, have to prioritize. Perhaps I can borrow Ariadne's – she won't be able to fit into them now . . . But if I inform her of this fact, she'll kill me ... Perhaps I can borrow Charity's sewing machine and alter the clothes myself. I might even buy a pattern and try making my own outfit. I'm sure the machine would welcome the opportunity to sew things other than Charity's dreadful floral marquees.

Saturday 31 July

Tried an experimental version of the cake today. Unfortunately forgot to put the eggs in. Came out rather solid and flat with the taste and texture of chamois leather. Kevin suggested using it to clean the windows.

August

Sunday 1 August

Today is summer! After a week of drizzle, cloud and 19C, a heat wave has hit us. Suddenly children are playing out in the streets, women are wearing their summer dresses and there is a hose-pipe ban. It was even warm in church. The stone building, which usually maintains a temperature just above freezing all year round, was actually warm.

In fact, it was so hot that everyone was using the order of service as a fan and the 'peace' had a generally clammy feel. The clothes that members of the congregation were wearing intrigued me. Usually St Norbert's is pretty conservative, men in shirts and ties, women in best dresses or trouser suits and some of the younger people in casual clothes, but today's weather had brought out the strangest apparel from the backs of wardrobes and bottom drawers. Digger was wearing shorts and a kind of Hawaiian shirt with his dog-collar, Miss Cranmer sported what looked like a knitted Victorian bathing costume with a matching knitted hat, Doris and Maurice Johnson's daughter, Keely, wore a very brief black halter-neck top and shorts which exposed a small amount of bottom-cheek when she bent down, and Roger Lemarck looked like Tim Henman.

Most people were away on holiday, including the Hubbles, so the service had an exclusive and calm feeling. I sat in my summer dress with only one or two flowers on it and drank in the atmosphere. The sun gave the ancient stained glass windows a vividness which projected the familiar biblical scenes across the church and scattered fractions of intense colour on people's backs and faces. They too had become part of the pictures, like living stained glass. The words of the liturgy seemed to have a freshness in this new light, and without a shadow of a doubt, God was there.

Monday 2 August

New office furniture arrived today. It looks splendid, very cool and Scandinavian. Realized that it was the only piece of furniture I had ever had that was not self-assembly. Spent about an hour adjusting the chair then swivelled vigorously to test it until I ended up feeling slightly nauseous. Feel really professional sitting behind my desk in my chair. Pretended to answer the phone and discuss business mergers with clients in New York and Tokyo, until Gerald from Accounts caught me talking to myself and reminded me he had been waiting for some invoices that had been sitting in my in-tray for three weeks. Decided to get on with some real work before the company grinds to a halt! Must go out at lunchtime and buy some kind of modern, minimalist plant to enhance the aesthetics, perhaps a cactus or something tall and elegant in an understated ceramic pot. It will make a change from the half-dead spider-plants that seem to occupy most offices.

Wednesday 4 August

Nearly fell off my chair in shock when I opened the latest wad of house details from the estate agent. Among the maisonettes and one-bedroom starter-homes was a little two-bedroom cottage with a pleasant garden and FGCH (untested). The cottage looked homely and familiar. Then I glanced at the address and realized why. It was Miss Chamberlain's cottage. I thought about all the times I had walked past the profusion of honeysuckle and roses, knocked at that oak front door and been greeted by the elegant little lady with her white hair and antique bone-china voice. I miss her so much. But could I even consider living in that cottage that still seemed so much part of her?

My first reaction was, 'No I couldn't possibly live there,' then, 'Why not?' Still not sure. That cottage *was* Miss Chamberlain. There would be so much in that place to remind me of my dear old friend. I'm not sure I could live with the memories. Will talk to Kevin about it.

Thursday 5 August

Kevin thinks we should go and look at Miss Chamberlain's cottage but I know I couldn't get through the front door without crying. I sat and held Miss Chamberlain's engagement ring and thought about her. I know it sounds corny but she was my anchor. She never laughed at me or made me feel silly. I am not self-deluded, I know that my trains of thought can sometimes get blown off course and that I can, on occasion, get on to a wrong road. Miss Chamberlain was the one who could pull on the reins to set me back into orbit, and I miss her. Much as I loved visiting her cottage and felt at home, I just couldn't live there. Explained this to Kevin, who to my amazement seemed to understand. He gave me a hug and a peck on the forehead.

'I just want you to be happy,' he said.

Friday 6 August

6.30 p.m.

It is the village fete tomorrow and still no cake. Will just have to knuckle down and make it.

10.30 p.m.

I've done it! I've really done it. I made treble quantity, two to take to the fete and Kevin and I have polished off the best part of the other one. It was delicious! A Victoria sponge cake with chocolate butter-cream filling. It was light and moist and . . . delicious. I just bought proper metal cake tins, followed Tom's recipe to the letter, put the mixture in the oven for twenty-five minutes and out they came, risen, perfect and . . . delicious. Why did I make such a fuss? When I did it, it was so easy.

In fact, you could say it was a piece of cake.

Saturday 7 August

I have decided to use the fete as a medium of evangelical outreach to anyone who will stand still long enough to listen. I don't care that Kevin laughed at me and decided that there was a European friendly that he just had to watch on the telly this afternoon. I still have my supporters. Tom has offered to bring baby Phoebe down in her pram to give Ariadne a break. Even Kevin's mum is going to come to the fete, insisting on wearing her 'church' hat for the occasion. She didn't laugh at me – in fact she has offered to bring a cake, provided she can get the rosewater, spices and vanilla. Hang on . . . I should have asked her to bake the cake in the first place. What's the point of putting myself through all that torment when I have a mother-in-law who can bake?

Oh well, perfect sponge cakes safely tinned, (slightly) floral dress on, camera, parasol and factor 15 and off to play the domestic goddess, the village wife-to-be.

6 p.m.

Well, what an event that turned out to be! Kevin asked if we shouldn't be involved in a spiritual war – we nearly ended up with a civil war.

It had started as one of those idyllic summer days that happen all the time in film adaptations of Jane Austen novels and about once every seven years in real life: glorious sunshine, tamed by a gentle breeze. I arrived at the village green at half past nine, ready to help set up the stalls. A group of travellers had chosen the previous night to set up camp on the same village green, and when I arrived there were four large caravans, complete with sparkling chrome,

TV aerials and net curtains, parked near the pavilion. There was also a police car, two twelve-year-old police constables, Mr Wilberforce, our church treasurer who is also on the parish council, and half a dozen traveller men at the front of a large group of traveller women and children. Everyone was shouting, pointing and waving fists. Even Mr Wilberforce's dog Rex joined in by growling and snarling at a huge, wild-eyed Alsatian with fangs that glinted in the sunlight. People from the village and St Norbert's congregation were starting to amass. It was obvious from some of their faces that they would have loved to see a good fight between the travellers and the villagers. 'Spoiling for a rumble', as Kevin would so elegantly have expressed it. Years, if not centuries, of suspicion, prejudice and intolerance were in danger of exploding into something very nasty. Then Digger marched on to the green, with his hair sticking up like a scarecrow and still fastening his dog-collar. He looked as if he had overslept. He worked his way to the front of the crowd.

'Gentlemen, ladies, what appears to be the problem?'

Everyone started talking and shouting at once. I saw Digger take the opportunity to slip round to the group of travellers and slide away into one of the vans with a tall middle-aged man in a dark jacket and collarless shirt.

'What do you think is going to happen,' I asked Mrs McCarthy, who was clutching her egg-free sponge cake rather too tightly to her chest.

'I dunno. Reminds me of when they had them I-talian prisoners of war over at the old hospital. When they used to go down the village to work in the fields all the women and youngsters from the village gathered one day and started shouting and slinging stones at them. Called them names I shouldn't care to repeat.'

'What happened?'

'ARP wardens and Home Guard came and sorted them out.'

'Not much chance of that today, is there?'

The fierce-looking Alsatian had found a shady spot and had gone to sleep. The villagers had started milling around and discussing what to do. Then Digger emerged from the largest van and shook the hand of the man with the collarless shirt. Digger approached the gathering of villagers and cleared his throat.

'This is Mr William Lee. He and his family would like to stay on the village green for a couple of nights ...'

There was a mumbling of disapproval from the villagers, who were obviously hoping the vicar would be able to 'cast out' the interlopers. Mr Wilberforce scuttled off to check the parish by-laws.

'... his family's vans are only taking up one side of the green so there is plenty of room for the village fete to go ahead. In fact, they have agreed to help us set up over on the side nearest the pub.'

''Elp us set up? 'Elp themselves to our stuff more like ...' 'Wouldn't trust 'em as far as I could throw 'em ...' 'Flaming cheek, when have they paid any council tax or water rates ...?' 'Who's going to clear up after them? That's what I want to know ...'

I had the distinct impression that all was not going to run smoothly.

The scouts arrived with their marquee, which would be the tea-tent. Soon the stalls covered one half of the village green like a herd of giant nomadic deckchairs, their striped awnings flapping in the breeze. Feeling floral and domesticated, I decided to throw caution to the wind and offer to help on the cake stall. After all, I had proved I could bake a cake. The stall was manned (or should I say womanned?) by Charity Hubble, who sported an enormous straw hat and appeared to be wearing a fabric version of Kew Gardens. I took my little camera out of my bag and called, 'Smile!'

'Ephesians!' shouted Charity, the 'ee' sound forcing her lips into a smile shape, then collapsing into genuine laughter at her joke. I laughed too. Perhaps the fete would go well after all. I had intended to take some photographs of this afternoon's proceedings and submit the best ones to the church magazine (and, depending on how interesting the afternoon became, perhaps keep some for blackmail purposes).

'Hello, Theodora. Nice dress.'

'Thank you, Charity. Need any help?'

'Well, I'd never thought of you on the cake stall, Theodora. White elephant or "Bat the Rat" maybe ... but you're very welcome, come round and grab a pinny. I'm just going to get a few more doilies out of the van.' And with that she scuttled off towards her ancient minibus in the pub car park, where the words 'Repent or Perish' could just be seen on the bonnet. I was removing a particularly splendid double chocolate gateau from its tin and surreptitiously licking my fingers when Digger Graves approached, with a skinny boy of about eleven skipping at his heels.

'G'day! How's it going? I've brought you an assistant. Theodora, this is Danny. He lives in the vans.'

The boy glanced at me then shyly at the floor. His hair hung in his eyes and he was wearing faded jeans and a tee shirt. He carried an old rucksack.

Charity returned with a bundle of paper doilies and an unenthusiastic-looking Nebuchadnezzar in tow. Nebuchadnezzar (or Neb as he now likes to be known) and Danny must be about the same age, but the two boys seemed to be constructed from completely different material. Danny was dark, hard as steel, wiry and quick, while Neb was pale, soft and flaccid and resembled undercooked meringue.

'Here they are,' said Charity, slapping the doilies down on the chintz tablecloth, 'and Nebuchadnezzar has come to help too, haven't you, sweetheart?'

'S'pose so,' muttered the boy.

Danny and Neb eyed each other nervously.

'This is Danny, he's going to help us run the stall,' I said breezily.

'Looks like a Gypsy,' mumbled Neb with contempt.

'Better than looking like an arse,' snapped Danny.

Neb raised his fist.

'Now, now, boys,' soothed Charity, stepping briskly between the youngsters. 'Let's try to get along, shall we? Now, let's find you something useful to do.'

She put them to work, sending Danny to find a box to put the money in and getting Neb to write out price tickets.

'Are you sure he's trustworthy?' asked Charity in a stage whisper.

'To be honest, I'm not sure. But from the way Rev. Graves brought him over, I think we should give it a go, for the sake of *entente cordiale*.'

Danny returned with an empty ice cream tub, and a sort of peace descended as cakes were laid out and priced and customers started to arrive. Tom came, with baby Phoebe sitting in a buggy wearing a little white sunbonnet and beaming at everyone. I couldn't resist removing my little niece from her transportation and giving her a cuddle. Charity was beside herself with rapture at this little living dolly, quite different from her youngest, who looked like a miniature sumo wrestler. The boys exchanged glances and made being-sick noises. Tom looked longingly towards the beer tent. Poor Tom, he is having rather a bad time, what with the demands of new parenthood and my sister's foul moods.

'Go and have a beer, Tom. I'll look after Phoebe.'

Tom looked as if he had just won the lottery. 'Would you . . . oh, that would be wonderful, are you sure you don't . . . just a quick half.' And he disappeared into the beer tent.

I discovered early on that it was too difficult juggling Phoebe under one arm and trying to sell cakes at the same time, so I strapped her into her buggy and she soon dozed off. Neb seemed to be eating more cakes than he was selling and I was very dubious about Danny's mental arithmetic, but on the whole the number of cakes on the stall decreased and the money in the ice cream container increased. Eloise came and bought her own cake on the grounds that it was the best one there. People from the village and the travellers mingled and peace reigned. The two young policemen had stayed on, on the premise of 'crime prevention', but soon stripped to their shirtsleeves and discarded their peaked caps, joining in the fete with everyone else. The sun smiled benevolently, warming rather than roasting, and tensions faded. I felt calm, composed and . . . happy. Yes, happy. Kevin doesn't know what he is missing. Who cares if it's not spiritual warfare, it's great fun. And, I am delighted to say that *my* cakes were among the first to be bought.

Tom returned from the beer tent, relaxed but not too sedated. He had stopped on his way back to kick a football through the bandy legs of a hardboard goalie, and to his astonishment had won a large purple teddy bear.

'Tom, it's nearly as big as she is!'

Giggling, Tom removed his sunglasses and Charity handed over her straw hat and I placed them on the teddy. Tom snuggled the teddy next to the sleeping Phoebe.

'That has got to be worth a photo,' I said rummaging under the stall.

'Just don't let Ariadne see it. She'll kill me.'

'It's such a pity she couldn't come,' said Charity.

'She's very tired. I wanted to give her a break – from both of us.'

'But Phoebe's such a lovely baby and you're such a trooper, Tom.'

Tom blushed. 'Have you got that camera? She's waking up.'

'That's funny. I can't seem to find it.'

Charity pushed me aside. 'Let me look. Perhaps it got mixed up with the doilies and paper bags.'

Charity, Tom and I searched under the stall. No camera.

'I'm sure I put it under here. I can't believe I've lost it.'

'Perhaps someone's stolen it,' suggested Neb.

'It's only an old camera, hardly worth taking.'

The two juvenile shirtsleeved policemen arrived to relieve us of any leftover cakes. They joined in the search.

'I really can't believe anyone would have stolen it,' I repeated.

'Just the same, I'll report it to the station and perhaps you would like to come down and fill in a crime report. You'll need it if you plan to claim on your insurance policy.'

'Oh, it's hardly worth it.'

'Why don't we just check through our bags and pockets?' suggested Neb helpfully.

'Good idea,' said one of the policemen.

Charity began to empty her enormous straw bag. Neb, who didn't have a bag, turned out his pockets, which were empty. Tom searched Phoebe's changing bag. Then Neb suddenly grabbed Danny's rucksack and upended it. Among the sweet wrappers, string and paper tissues that tumbled out was my camera.

'You little thief,' squealed Neb.

Danny's eyes darted from Neb to the camera, to the policemen, to me – then he ran. He took off like a sprinter from the blocks, dodging the policemen and Tom.

'Well, I was never sure that he was trustworthy. I said that right at the start,' contributed Charity.

One of the policemen had set off running after Danny while the other one asked me if I wanted to press charges. I shook my head. I felt overwhelmingly disappointed. Just as there was some kind of trust growing towards the travellers. Just as they had seemed 'not too bad', this had to happen.

A crowd had gathered by the travellers' vans. Initially curious, I sensed the mood of the throng changing to hostility. I could hear angry voices. A message crackled through

the policeman's radio. He mumbled something in acknowledgement and jogged over, pushing his way to the front of
the gathering crowd. Tom and I exchanged glances and
took off, following the policeman and leaving Phoebe,
Charity and Neb behind at the stall.

'Will you keep an eye on Phoebe?' I yelled over my
shoulder to Charity.

We barged our way through the villagers. The policemen stood warily, weighing up the situation, their batons
drawn. There was Danny's father, his face red and distorted
with rage and a leather belt in one hand. With the other
hand he held the struggling boy by the collar. He screamed
words I couldn't understand and beat the boy with the belt
again and again, on the head, on the back, on the shoulder.
The boy made no sound but twisted this way and that to
loosen his father's grip and dodge the belt. All the while the
crowd bayed for blood.

'Stop!' The vicar's command rang out above the noise.
William Lee looked up in surprise and Danny took advantage of his father's momentary lapse of concentration to
break free and run. William Lee dropped the belt and
looked at the policemen.

'The boy needs to be disciplined,' he growled and turned
to walk off to his van.

'But it was only an old camera,' I called. 'I would have
given it to him if he wanted it that much.'

William Lee ignored me and carried on walking. Red-
faced, I ran after him. He turned briefly towards me.

'A thief is a thief. He has let his family down.'

And despite my pleading he marched off and stomped
into his caravan, slamming the door shut in my face.

Digger put an arm around my shoulders. 'Are you all right?'

I nodded, still too shocked to speak. The crowd had started to disperse, their preconceptions fed and their prejudices justified. Digger, Tom, the two policemen and I returned to the cake stall. Tom removed the purple teddy from the buggy and Charity started to pack up the leftover cakes.

'I knew he was a thief all along,' announced Neb through a mouth full of jam tart. 'I knew we only had to look in his bag to find the thief. Gypsies, you just can't trust them an inch.'

'Thank you, Sherlock Holmes,' said Tom, more nastily than was usual for him.

Suddenly it dawned on me. How did Neb know exactly where the camera would be found?

'Hang on a minute,' I said, my face starting to redden again. 'Who was it suggested we search bags ...'

'And who was it who knew exactly where to look ...?' began Tom.

This time it was Neb's turn to run. He wobbled off towards his parents' minibus. Charity glared at me.

'Surely you're not accusing my son of putting the camera in that gypsy boy's bag?'

'I didn't need to accuse him of anything. Looks like his conscience is doing that.'

Charity threw down her pinny and set off in pursuit of Nebuchadnezzar.

I'm sure facing the wrath of Charity would be worse than any punishment either the constabulary or I could mete out. I wondered about going to see Mr Lee to try to sort out the mess but the doors of the vans were firmly closed. I didn't want to interfere.

By the time we had dismantled the stall, counted the money and cleared up, Phoebe had woken from her nap and was very much in need of milk and a clean nappy. Digger returned to the vicarage, Tom took Phoebe home to Ariadne and I trudged my way back up the road to my flat. Not for the first time, I wished for Miss Chamberlain's wise advice.

Back home I prayed for Danny and his family and also for Neb and Charity. I wouldn't like to have been around when she caught up with him. Perhaps Danny was a thief; perhaps he wasn't. All I know was that today he hadn't stolen my camera, yet everyone still hated him. What's more, because of Neb's actions, they also hated his family and what they stood for. I tried reading the Bible, but all the bits I read – Jesus with the Samaritan woman, Jesus with the tax collector, Jesus with the adulteress, Jesus with the lepers – just served to prick my middle-class English conscience about how we treat people on the edges of *our* society.

Sunday 8 August

8.30 a.m.

Woke up early and couldn't get back to sleep so I took the film out of my camera, replaced it with a new one and set off for the village green to see Danny and try to make peace. I wanted him to have the camera. I wanted him to know that there were no hard feelings. As I rounded the corner, to my astonishment, the caravans had vanished.

Only some churned up grass and a few bags of rubbish bore witness to the fact that they had been there at all.

Whatever Kevin had said, that village fete certainly couldn't be described as twee.

2 p.m.

Jeremiah is back! I arrived at church this morning and there was Jeremiah Wedgwood, large as life, carefully blowing the dust off the hymnbooks before handing them out to the congregation.

'Jeremiah,' I blurted, 'you're back!'

He turned to face me, his familiar watery eyes regarding me impassively.

'So it would seem.'

'Great to see you.' I was about to hug him, but due to his fear of catching germs thought better of it.

'I can see this place has been going to rack and ruin while I've been away. I heard about yesterday's debacle at the village fete.'

'I thought you'd started going to the church in the old assembly hall,' I said, hastily changing the subject. 'The one where they cast out demons and juggle with snakes.'

'That place was full of darkness . . .'

'Not enough light bulbs, I expect.'

'No, spiritual darkness.'

'Oh. I see.'

'The good Lord has led me here and so here I am. Besides, I have had a long talk with the Reverend and he has seen the error of his ways.'

'Good, yes, good! Welcome back, Jeremiah. It's wonderful to have you back at St Norbert's.'

I couldn't swear to it but I thought I caught just the faintest glimmer of a smile.

Monday 9 August

Kevin rang me at work to tell me he had a surprise for me and could I meet him in the pub by the station. Spent the whole afternoon wondering what it could be. Perhaps he had booked our honeymoon. Perhaps he had seen our dream house. Perhaps he had remembered to shave and use deodorant. When I arrived at the pub he could barely contain his excitement. He was jigging up and down on the chair. He took my hand.

'Now, Theo, before you say anything, I know it was a lot of money, I know we are supposed to be saving, but I just thought of how we talked about spending more time together and . . . anyway, I bought you this.'

He stuffed a white envelope into my hand. I opened it to find a little plastic wallet.

'Er . . . what is it?'

'It's a season ticket, the seat next to me in the stands. Last year I couldn't even have imagined taking you to a match. Now I know you'll be right beside me, every home game. Oh, Theo, you mean the world to me.'

My eyes filled with tears. Three hundred and seventy-nine pounds that ticket had cost. Three hundred and seventy-nine pounds would have paid for the deposit on a honeymoon; it would have bought a living-room carpet; it would have hired wedding suits for Kevin *and* the best man. And he'd spent it on a season ticket.

He took my hand again and cleared his throat. 'I can see you're touched. You don't have to thank me; the look on your face is reward enough.'

I forced a smile. The whole season sitting next to Kevin watching football. What bliss!

Tuesday 10 August

Walking back from the station I noticed that the 'For Sale' sign had disappeared from Miss Chamberlain's garden. Must mean the cottage has been sold already. Felt a twinge of disappointment that I hadn't had the courage to go and view it. I hope the people who will be moving in are nice. I couldn't bear the idea of it being sold to developers or to someone who will rip up the roses and lavender bushes and concrete over the sweet williams.

Wednesday 11 August

Got our wedding invitations back from the printers today and very chic they look, too. Kevin and I made a list of friends and family we need to send them to. My list was about three times the size of Kevin's. Dad originally insisted that we invite all the aunts, but that would be like inviting the whole population of a small European country. Besides, most of them are too old or too eccentric to come. We settled on immediate family, close friends and St Norbert's congregation, who will be invited to the service and the evening do but not the reception. Jez will be Kevin's best man on condition that he removes his bobble hat during the ceremony. We stayed up until one o'clock writing invitations and licking envelopes. Didn't dare kiss Kevin goodnight for fear of getting stuck to him.

Thursday 12 August

The French football team is coming to stay this weekend. Apparently Pantalon-sur-mer is a small fishing resort on the northern coast. Kevin can barely contain his excitement, I can barely suppress my boredom at the prospect of spending the entire weekend in the company of a dozen amateur Eric Cantonas. Jean-Claude, the goalkeeper, is staying with Kevin and his mum. I hope Jean-Claude is good at sign language. Unfortunately, Kevin's attempts to learn French petered out after the first three weeks. Kevin's mum says she can remember a little of the St Lucian patois her mother used to speak and insists it's more or less the same thing. I have my doubts and can picture poor Jean-Claude struggling to get the most basic of his needs met while Kevin and his mum babble incomprehensibly at him. To this end I have dug my French dictionary and textbooks from school out of Mum and Dad's loft. Have reluctantly agreed to accompany Kevin, Jean-Claude and the others on their sightseeing tour around London tomorrow.

Friday 13 August, vendredi le treizième août

Brilliant day, despite misgivings. Jean-Claude is quite charming and I must admit I am quite smitten. Had a superb time doing the tourist bits around London. I feel alarmingly ignorant about the history of the sights and history of London in spite of spending the last fifteen years of my life working there. Managed to communicate adequately, even translating orders for lunch with the assistance of my trusty dictionary.

11 p.m.

Help! It's happened. I have inherited my mother's linguistic skills.

I was just beginning to gain confidence. I was starting to get quite fluent. Or so I thought.

At the pub tonight (after only half a pint of cider) the conversation was sparkling. I was surrounded by a group of both French and English players and had started talking with some authority about sport and comparing rugby and football. Now, what I intended to say was that my father is Welsh and enjoys watching rugby matches, especially when they beat the French, and that Kevin is football mad. Although he is rubbish on the field, when he goes to bed he dreams he is a great footballer. That was not quite how it turned out. Instead, I announced to the assembled Frenchmen that, 'My father, she is Welsh and is pleased to beat up the Frenchmen at rugby games. But Kevin is insane. His football is garbage on the pitch but he is good in bed.'

Stunned silence from the Frenchmen.

Dictionary is destined for the bin.

Saturday 14 August

Suffered another day with Jean-Claude's disapproving (if rather gorgeous) eyes reproaching me for murdering their language and denigrating their rugby team, not to mention embarrassing myself, my family and Kevin. I stayed silent all through the five-a-side competition, dared not speak at lunch, and through the dinner in the Masonic Hall tried to communicate only in sign language. Some of the English players tried to persuade me to speak ('Come on, Theo, give us another treat, say something in French') but I remained tight-lipped.

Sunday 15 August

Missed church so that I could go to the airport with Kevin to see the Pantalon-sur-mer team safely back on an aeroplane to France. Before they boarded, the Frenchmen handed out small 'thank you' gifts. My heart warmed a little to find that all the women, including Kevin's mum and me, were given a small box of exquisitely wrapped French chocolates. Kevin was equally delighted with his pack of a dozen French lagers. I was just wondering if it would be good or bad manners to rip open the packaging and devour the chocolates there and then when Jean-Claude detached himself from the group and came over to me. He took my hand (that solved the chocolate dilemma – even I couldn't manage it one-handed) and gazed into my eyes.

'You know, Theodora,' he oozed, pronouncing my name 'Teodora', which made my knees go sort of trembly, 'it is such a sorrow for me that you did not speak more. You were so silent yesterday, like a little mouse. Yet on Friday you were having such a clutch on the language.'

'Oh,' I said, as it was the only thing I could think of in either language. My mind raced.

'I know that you think you did not have the … finesse, but when you English girls speak, oh the accent, it is so … sexy.'

I went crimson and started to talk about the weather – in English.

Monday 16 August

Not sure whether I am pleased or disappointed that the French team has gone back. Kevin goes out to France with his supporters' club five-a-side team on Friday. I hope there won't be a French woman who feels the same way about Kevin as I feel about Jean-Claude.

Friday 20 August

Kevin and Paul, Jez and Kev 2 have opted to take his van on Le Shuttle on the grounds that you can stow far more beer in a plumber's van than you can in aeroplane carry-on luggage. I went to Ashford to see him off. In spite of the jeers from his mates, he gave me a long lingering kiss.

'*A bientôt, chérie*,' he said. I went weak at the knees.

Saturday 21 August

Why did nobody tell me? Why am I always the last to know what is going on in my own church? Just because I have spent the last week devoting myself to Kevin, so that he won't want to so much as look at a French mademoiselle.

Bumped into Miss Cranmer in the post office and am now in a state of shock. She has just told me that Digger made an announcement last Sunday to say that he is leaving St Norbert's. He is returning to Australia. He will be gone by the end of September. Apparently he approached the bishop a few months ago, and the PCC have known for weeks and are well on the way to appointing a replacement. He can't do that! Who will I go to for advice and support and comfort? Miss Chamberlain has gone. Ariadne, who at the best of times thinks I'm one sultana short of a fruitcake, has no time at all to indulge my anxieties now. Digger was my voice of reason in a sea of neurosis. What will I do? This is so unfair. I'm going to have to resort to praying, then sorting things out myself!

Sunday 22 August

Sort of subdued atmosphere at church today. Some of the people who were away on holiday have reappeared while others have left. Everyone was being really nice to Digger. Isn't it funny how everyone is very quick to tell you how much they appreciate you when they know you're going? I felt like kicking Digger in the shins. How could he leave? When he took over from old Reverend Lister, who made Malcolm Muggeridge look like an adolescent liberal, it was as if a gust of fresh air had blown through musty old St Norbert's. True, people left when Reverend Graves came, and some, like Jeremiah, should have left but stayed. But on the whole people warmed to him. I'm not sure to what extent the personality of the incumbent influences the character of his church but I know that St Norbert's will be poorer when he goes.

Wednesday 25 August

Charity phoned tonight to remind me about tomorrow's rehearsal for Methuselah's baptism. Hopped around a bit then banged my head silently against the wall. Not only had I forgotten the rehearsal, I'd forgotten all about the christening. Come to think of it, I don't even remember agreeing to be a godmother. Gritted my teeth and said of course I hadn't forgotten and what time did she want me at the church. Must go shopping at lunchtime tomorrow and buy an outfit and a present. So much for saving to buy a house!

Thursday 26 August

Digger was in 'efficient' mode today. No chat, no pleasantries, just getting on with the job in hand. He confessed at the end that he was keen to watch 'the footie' and wanted to get through the christening rehearsal as quickly as possible. Which goes to show that even the devout are not immune to the seductive influences of football.

Mr Wilberforce turned up five minutes late, which didn't help the mood one bit. He explained that he had to find someone with whom he could leave Rex with reasonable confidence that they would still have all their limbs attached when he returned. Nigel's brother Rupert couldn't be there. Apparently he was having his medication sorted out.

'Well,' Reverend Graves said to Nigel and Charity, 'I think you know the form by now. What is this? Number nine?'

'No,' replied Charity pointedly, 'this is Methuselah.'

'Of course, sorry,' said Digger. 'What I meant was that you, Charity and Nigel, are fully aware of the parents' role in the proceedings, so I will concentrate on the obligations of the godparents for the benefit of Miss Llewellyn and Mr Wilberforce.' He continued by reading the part of the service where we promise to pray for Methuselah, draw him by our example into the community of faith and walk with him in the way of Christ. He gave us both a card with our promises and 'the Decision' on it. Suddenly the responsibility seemed enormous. This wasn't just an excuse to buy a hat and have our photographs taken on a Sunday afternoon, this was taking responsibility for the spiritual welfare of a child. Suddenly Methuselah looked so small and I felt so inadequate. Perhaps Charity had been right and I wasn't 'of a suitable spiritual calibre'. I felt like crying. I didn't want to do it but I couldn't let Nigel and Charity down. I prayed hard that God would give me the ability to carry out the task.

Friday 27 August

Kevin came back today, complete with crutches and plastered ankle. Turns out he'd broken it during a five-a-side match as the result of a 'wicked tackle' on their striker. Jez had to drive his van back, in spite of having no insurance and no licence. I gave Kevin a severe telling off. First, he shouldn't have been playing football with his dodgy knee, and second, what had possessed him to let that moron drive his van? Kevin had insisted that he'd been careful with the knee and, see, it was fine (just the broken ankle, then!) and that Jez had been their best option as Paul had

brought his own van and Kev 2 had spent the whole weekend inebriated. I fussed and clucked around Kevin for a
while but it was clear that he took the whole thing in his
stride, so to speak. Of course, he'll have to take time off
work and I doubt very much he took up that health insurance plan I told him about. Still, we have savings ... I'll just
have to get married in a dustbin liner and we'll live in a
cardboard box.

Saturday 28 August

Went to Tranquil Lagoon, the local shopping centre,
which, it being a bank holiday weekend, was anything but
tranquil. What do people wear to christenings these days?
Tried the cut-price designer-wear shop but it seems everyone else had got there first. Found a dress in a sale in one of
the big department stores that will do nicely. Should I
bother with a hat? Couldn't find one that didn't make me
look like a mushroom. I'm sure Charity won't mind and
Methuselah certainly couldn't care less. Barged my way
through to Poshbabes, the exclusive designer baby-wear
boutique. I couldn't believe it; an outfit for the baby cost
more than my dress. Exited smartly and went to
Mothercare where I managed to buy a really cute outfit and
a 'baby memories' book. Looked at one which was based on
baby's birth stone and nearly bought it just to wind Charity
up. Settled on a photo album-cum-baby's first book. It had
a place for the baby's footprint and even some appropriate
Bible verses.

Shattered, I went home to contemplate my godparental
duties and nearly resigned again.

Sunday 29 August

Phoned Charity at 7.30 this morning.

'I'm sorry Charity, I can't do it.'

'Do what?'

'Be Methuselah's godmother. It's too much responsibility, I'm not capable. Surely you can find someone better.'

'Not at half past seven in the morning, I can't. Of course you're capable. If Nigel hadn't thought you possessed at least a rudimentary comprehension of Christianity, he wouldn't have chosen you. Anyway, it's not as if you really have to do anything.'

I gave a snort. 'Have you read what's on that card? I've got to renounce this, repent of that and be responsible for their growth in faith. I don't even feel responsible for my own growth in faith.'

'Have you read it properly, Theo?'

'Hundreds of times, from about three thirty this morning.'

'Then you'll know that you are not responsible for Methuselah's growth in faith, God is. You are just promising to pray for him and care for him – be his supporter, if you like. And as for the renouncing and repenting bit, it's just promising to serve Christ and him only. You can do that, can't you?'

'Of course.'

'See, you silly goose, there is no problem.'

I sighed with relief. Praying for him and promising to serve Christ. Yes, I could do that.

'Oh, I'm sorry, Charity, it all just seemed a bit heavy. I think everything just got on top of me.'

Then a thought hit. What if all my doubts had led Charity to change her mind?

'You do still want me, don't you?'

'In one sense the godparents are the least important people there. God and Methuselah are the significant ones. I'd rather be sure that God was there than you, if you understand what I mean.'

I said that I thought I did.

I went to the christening wearing my dress and carrying my present, and said my piece and had my photograph taken. Actually, it wouldn't have mattered what I said during the service, as baby Methuselah kept up a deafening wail from the first hymn until the dismissal. No one was going to speak on *his* behalf.

Monday 30 August. Bank Holiday

It is Bank Holiday Monday, so of course it is pouring with rain. I chose another good time to book three days off work to sunbathe in the garden. Roll on Friday.

September

Wednesday 1 September

Charity, for all her many domestic talents, is a complete bozo when it comes to filling in forms. I once helped her complete a passport application for Nigel when Digger hit upon the idea of buying the Communion wine cheaply from someone he knew who ran a wine warehouse in Calais. Digger, with Nigel in tow, had set out for France to negotiate a deal on a few cases of good but inexpensive wine. Unfortunately, Nigel, in the interests of good stewardship, had insisted on sampling the quality of each of the possible wines before agreeing to buy one. Nigel is not a wine connoisseur. Nigel doesn't normally drink at all. And Nigel didn't know that wine tasters don't swallow. Digger passed Nigel's unsteady gait and green complexion off to Charity as a bad sea crossing. I don't think even the gullible Charity was taken in for a moment.

To be honest, I rather enjoy being able to do something easily, even if it is only completing forms, knowing that Charity struggles. There are so few times when I feel I can get one up on Charity that I think I'm entitled to the occasional gloat.

Nebuchadnezzar has just started secondary school and Charity arrived, following a brief phone call, armed with a bundle of forms to be completed on his behalf.

Now Nigel and Charity had spent many, many months choosing the right school for Neb. They had visited, taken tests, prayerfully considered every school within a 30-mile radius. She wanted a boys' school with a strong Christian ethos that would allow what she described as his creativity (and what I would call his impudence) to be freely expressed. They visited them all in turn, Charity and Nigel with the reluctant Neb, brushed and polished for the occasion, in tow. I saw them as they passed me in the van. Charity waved, Nigel called out, 'Hello!' and Neb thumbed his nose at me.

Charity phoned me regularly with the latest school-hunting news, as if I was remotely interested. The exploits of other people's children just put me straight to sleep. Even Tom's description of Phoebe's every smile, bout of colic and percentile achieved on her growth chart puts me into a coma, though I love her dearly.

I really should have pretended to be out when Charity phoned to give me the latest update on darling Neb's progress towards the higher echelons of academia. Apparently St Rudolph's was too Catholic; Marshwood Manor tolerated multi-faith assemblies and Rowbridge School for Boys played cricket on summer Sundays and rugby on winter ones. So they had finally settled on Springmount Heath Academy, which was not perfect – there were highly suspect books in the library and the school had a *jazz band* – but the head teacher was an ex-clergyman and knew Charity's father.

The forms from Springmount covered every aspect of school life: name, address and contact numbers – no problem. Medical details, allergies, doctor's address – all OK. The problem came when we looked at the options under the heading 'religion'.

The choices, as I remember, were Sikh, Hindu, Muslim, Christian, Jewish, Buddhist, Church of England, Other or No Faith.

'Oh dear,' wailed Charity, 'what shall I fill in? Of course we're Christians, but obviously, with us being communicant members of the Church of England and Nigel being a curate, I feel that *not* to tick the "Church of England" box would be letting the side down rather.'

In the end, even with my bureaucratic skills we couldn't decide so we ticked both boxes. The school could work it out.

I must admit I was puzzled. I had always rather hoped that Christianity and the Church of England were at least compatible, if not quite synonymous.

Thursday 2 September

Kevin arranged (without consulting me) to look after his sister Deyanna's little girl Kayla for the day. Kayla is three and has the face of an angel. Unfortunately Kayla also has the concentration span of a gnat, the tolerance of a rattlesnake and the temper of a Tasmanian Devil. Kevin's mum wants her to be our bridesmaid. I have serious doubts. Nevertheless, Eloise thought it would be a good opportunity for me to meet her. Deyanna and Floyd are spending the day at a health club as they figured that they both need a rest and a break from Kayla. After today I can understand why. Considering the weather, we abandoned our first thought, which was to have a day at the seaside, and opted for a zoo-cum-theme park a few miles away. Floyd drove down from Birmingham and dropped Kayla off at Kevin's just before nine so she could have breakfast. When I arrived she was locked in a bitter dispute about the particular type of cereal she would eat. She wanted Choco-Bunnies but the best Kevin and his mum could come up with was Wheat-Bran Puffs. She even turned her nose up at Kevin's secret supply of Kaptain Krunch's Sugar Stars. As I walked in through the door, Kevin was in the middle of a valiant attempt to construct bunny shapes out of Wheat-Bran Puffs dipped in cocoa powder. Kayla sat with her arms folded and her bottom lip sticking out.

'Uncle Kevin, they are *not* the same thing.'

Kevin looked at me despairingly. I just shrugged and suggested we get our coats on and try to beat the crowds.

When Kevin got round to informing me about our 'little guest' a couple of days ago I had thought of inviting a small Hubble along to keep Kayla company. I was very glad I didn't as I very quickly realized that Kayla alone would occupy every ounce of our ingenuity and patience.

With Kevin's leg still in plaster we decided to take my car. Kayla insisted on thoroughly examining the interior. She took off her little rucksack and dumped it in the boot.

'It's not very nice, is it?'

'Not quite on a par with your daddy's Mercedes, no. But it's go in this car or don't go at all.'

'OK. I want to sit here.'

'No, that's the driver's seat. I have to sit there.'

'I want to sit with Uncle Kevin, then.'

Kevin agreed to sit in the back with Kayla, which did make it rather difficult for him to navigate, especially as he had to sit with his plastered leg outstretched. Kayla bombarded us with a constant stream of questions for the entire journey and about two miles from the park announced that she needed the toilet.

'Just wait a few more minutes, Kayla. We're nearly there,' soothed Kevin.

'But I need it *now*!'

Unable to stop 'now', I felt for the last few yards of the journey as if I had a ticking time bomb in my car, just waiting for the explosion. Fortunately, Kayla managed to hold on, and when we arrived Kevin bought tickets while I took her to find the toilet. When we got to the ladies, Kayla promptly announced that she'd changed her mind, she didn't need the toilet after all and could she have an ice cream? We found Kevin, bought Kayla an ice cream, then *all* went to the toilet. Kevin had been offered a wheelchair, which he was going to decline but Kayla insisted he accept because she wanted a ride in the 'big pushchair'.

Kevin loves the big rides with looping roller-coasters and plummeting lifts. He's just an oversized kid really. For once, I had a brilliant excuse for not accompanying him. Instead, I took Kayla on the carousel with its gently undulating, gaudy horses. Kayla pronounced it far too tame and tried to get off in the middle of the ride. I hung on to her and pinned her to her horse until the merry-go-round stopped. We returned the 'big pushchair' as Kevin refused to use it, Kayla got bored with sitting in it and it was just getting in the way.

I stood holding Kayla's rucksack and watched as she drove round a little track in a sort of go-kart. She knew exactly where she wanted to go, and woe betide any tardy tot who got in her way. She showed no mercy, almost running a little boy with spiky ginger hair off the track. I had a sort of horrible premonition of Kayla in fifteen years' time behind the wheel of a four-wheel drive . . .

We met Kevin for lunch. His ankle was rather sore, so after a burger and chips with no onion, gherkin or cheese but *with* ketchup and cola with a *yellow* straw, we took a gentle stroll round the zoo. Kayla adored the monkeys and chattered to the nimble capuchins as they swung from branch to branch. We held a competition to see who could make the best 'gorilla face', then went to the reptile house where we viewed, at a safe distance, reticulated python and red-kneed tarantula. We decided on a quick coffee, then home. Suddenly a horrible thought struck me.

'Where's Kayla?' I asked Kevin who was busy shouting instructions to a chameleon to try to get it to change colour. I looked nervously back towards the glass case that contained a boa constrictor big enough to crush a large dog.

'I thought she was with you. Weren't you counting the stick insects?'

'She wanted you to show her the Kimodo dragon. She was standing right next to you.' My heart began to pound.

'You mean you were so wrapped up in those water snakes you didn't notice she'd wandered off.'

'She was right near you. And I thought she was holding your hand.' By now I was running round the reptile house checking every nook and cranny.

'How can she, with these?' he asked, waving his crutches at me. 'I can't believe you managed to lose her.'

'Me lose her! I had her all morning and didn't lose her,' I protested.

'Oh, so it's my fault.'

'She's your niece.'

'Thanks for reminding me.' He peered into the python's case. 'D'you think she's been eaten?'

'Unlikely, but what if she's been kidnapped?' I had visions of police searches and ransom notes. This was terrible.

'They'll soon hand her back.'

I glared at Kevin.

'Look, let's just hunt around for her. She can't have got far. Besides, they've probably got a "Lost Child" place' he said.

'Right, you look around the reptile house, I'll go back to the monkeys.'

I headed back past the gorillas to the circular monkey cage. By now I was really getting frantic. I called her name and peered anxiously into cages but couldn't see her anywhere. I followed the signs towards the 'Help' point, but as I passed the penguin enclosure something caught my eye. I screeched to a halt and squinted into the sunshine. I noticed that there, among the black and white birds, was another creature, roughly the same height as the penguins but with two curly black bunches and wearing a yellow and red raincoat and green wellingtons. The creature waved cheerfully at me.

'Hello, Auntie Theodora,' it called.

I took off at a run to find a keeper, who unlocked the gate and went in to rescue Kayla. I hugged Kayla and apologized profusely to the keeper but he seemed unperturbed, as if that sort of thing happened every day. Kayla seemed unharmed and was still wearing her little rucksack and clutching her little umbrella, indignant about being removed from her new playmates. I ticked her off as my heart rate and blood pressure began to return to normal. Kayla of course had no idea what all the fuss was about. We set off to find Kevin. He looked extremely relieved to discover that she wasn't inside a snake. We went to the café and Kayla and Kevin had a "purpleberry" flavour Mr Freezy and I had a large coffee, once my hands had stopped shaking.

After all the excitement, Kayla fell asleep almost as soon as we got into the car. She stayed asleep for the whole journey, allowing Kevin and me to chat and listen to music.

'I don't know how people do this full time,' Kevin commented, looking back at the recumbent Kayla, who apart from a bright purple stain around her mouth, appeared even more angelic.

Kayla woke up the instant we got back to Kevin's house. His mum opened the door and whisked Kayla off for a bath while we unloaded her things from the car. Kayla insisted on taking her umbrella and rucksack into the bathroom, so I nipped them up to her while Eloise warmed the towels. Kevin and I were in the kitchen drinking tea when we heard the scream. I sprinted upstairs to find Eloise standing in the doorway, nearly hysterical. I pushed past her, wondering what to expect. There, in Eloise's avocado corner bath with gold-plated taps, sat one little girl and one baby penguin. The little girl was singing a song about frogs and the penguin was enjoying a splash in the bath. I yelled for Kevin, who limped up the stairs as quickly as he could manage. He muttered something about 'stripping the oil off its feathers' and grabbed the penguin and wrapped it in a towel.

'Phone the zoo,' he called, as he took the penguin chick into the bedroom to dry it off. Removed from its pool and separated from its playmate, the penguin had now set up an indignant squawking.

I found the theme park's number on a leaflet and got through to the zoo's answer-phone. It was a bit difficult to know what to say.

'Er . . . I'm very sorry about this but we seem to have accidentally taken one of your penguins home with us. Um . . . If you would like it back . . .' and I left Kevin's number.

About an hour later, the penguin-keeper phoned back, saying he'd wondered where Percy had gone. Kevin explained what had happened and apologized. We offered to take it back, but the keeper said to leave it until the morning and advised Kevin where to keep it and what to feed it. Eloise muttered something about penguin droppings in her bathroom, and we had our work cut out talking Kayla out of taking Percy to bed with her.

I drove home exhausted. In future, the only penguins I'm going to come into contact with are the chocolate variety.

Friday 3 September

It is a relief to get back to work. Floyd returned the penguin to the zoo on his way back to Birmingham. He hadn't been the slightest bit surprised to hear about Kayla's 'souvenir', and the penguin seemed none the worse for its excursion. But I'd had about as much adventure as I could take and I'm awfully relieved to be back with my feet firmly under my Slogbrot and where the most exciting thing likely to happen is a visit from the photocopier engineer.

This is my last day as Temporary Acting Deputy Assistant Manager, as my new boss arrives on Monday. Spent ages this afternoon preparing the office for her arrival. Declan's old desk looks rather shabby compared with my fabulous Scandinavian Slogbrot with its minimalist cacti and brushed steel picture frames. (I stole a picture of Phoebe looking super-cute to put in the frame.) Still, I've checked carefully for any residual practical jokes (Declan's) and removed the chocolate wrappers (mine) from the filing cabinet. I will have to get in early on Monday so I can get the coffee brewing and perhaps I'll bring some flowers – make a good impression.

Saturday 4 September

I had to drive Kevin to the football this afternoon. They were playing some northern club. Still, it was quite pleasant sitting in the sunshine. Took a magazine and read it surreptitiously while Kevin was engrossed in what was happening on the pitch.

Sunday 5 September

Popped in to Ariadne and Tom's to take Phoebe out for an afternoon stroll. Ariadne was doing her 'wrung-out dishcloth' impersonation again. Tom was ironing small frilly things. Phoebe was sitting in her bouncy deckchair, smiling and blowing bubbles.

'Why do they have to make these flaming things so small and fiddly?' grumbled Tom, catching his finger again with the tip of the iron.

'Well, they have to be small to fit the baby, I suppose,' I suggested helpfully.

'It was a rhetorical question,' said Tom, through a mouthful of singed fingers.

'Well, Phoebe looks as bright as a button this afternoon, don't you, gorgeous?'

'That's because "gorgeous" used up all her miserable grizzling and ear-splitting screaming last night, and is now all sweetness and smiles for Auntie Theodora, the little fiend,' interjected Ariadne.

At that point a hasty retreat seemed a sensible option.

It was a glorious golden afternoon with enough heat from the sun not to need a coat. I laid Phoebe in the buggy and pushed her down the High Street and along the lane that comes out at the back of their house. It took a while because the little swivelly wheels kept jamming on stones and I nearly ran the thing off the kerb several times. They should really supply pushchairs with 'L' plates. It was worse than trying to control a shopping trolley. But Phoebe didn't seem to mind.

I had hoped that she would doze off but instead she lay on her back, blowing bubbles and kicking her feet and laughing at the trees. She looked so soft and vulnerable – how could she wield so much power over Ariadne and Tom?

I returned to their house with a gurgling, smiling little bundle who, apart from needing a new nappy, had given me no trouble at all. Ariadne had taken herself off to bed and

Tom sat on the sofa with a cup of tea, surrounded by mountains of neatly ironed little frilly things.

'Ariadne's taken another fortnight off work, just to see if she can get back on her feet.'

'How did they take it?'

'Made a fuss. Made her feel guilty, on top of everything else.'

'And you?'

'I'm going to have to get something temporary. I rang up my old company. D'you know, they couldn't find any record of me ever having worked there.'

'Did you explain what had happened, that you'd given up when your wife had a baby, intending to stay at home and look after it when she returned to work?'

'Oh, I told them all that. But you're hardly arguing from a position of strength when, officially, you don't exist. Not one person remembered me. Not even the bloke I worked next to for ten years. Shows you what an impact I made there.' He let out a sigh, which seemed to come up from the soles of his hush puppies. 'I . . . I don't suppose there's anything going at your place?'

Fought back an urge to say, 'You can have my job.'

I nodded. 'I'll ask.'

Monday 6 September

My new manager Myrna Peacock arrived today. I made sure I was in early – well, 8.57 is early for me – but Myrna had beaten me to it. She stood at my desk and watched as I struggled to get my shoulders out of my jacket without dropping my carrier bags. There was no smell of brewing coffee. The flowers I bought on Saturday got accidentally left in my car; by the time I discovered them this morning they were beyond hope. I'm sure Myrna hadn't really been tapping her shoe or glancing at her watch but it felt as if she had. I don't think she had actually run her finger along her desk to check for dust but she looked as though she had a mind to. She held out an immaculately manicured hand.

'You must be Theodora Llewellyn.'

'Yes, I must be . . . er, I mean yes, pleased to meet you.'

'You may call me Myrna to my face and refer to me as Mrs Peacock when talking to others or on the phone. Now, can we run through how we are going to work together? You can start by showing me exactly what you do. Let's talk over coffee.'

'Of course. Would you like me to make you one?'

'I'm sure the company doesn't pay you your extortionate salary to have you squander your talents on making coffee. One of the filing clerks can do it.'

Studied her face to see if she was being serious. I think she was. She demanded the coffee from one of the junior clerks, who was too flabbergasted to protest. I know what sort of answer I would have got if *I* had suggested that one of them should sink so low as to make *me* a cup of coffee.

Tuesday 7 September

Astonishingly, Myrna has decided I have too much work to do on my own and is appointing an assistant for me. Can't wait to have my own underling to be superior to. I wonder if he or she will make my coffee.

Wednesday 8 September

Have put in a good word for Tom. Can't imagine him being my assistant, but he is experienced in office work and even he admitted the pay isn't too bad. He is putting in an application form.

Thursday 9 September

Kevin bought me flowers. I don't think Kevin has ever bought me flowers before. I wonder what he's been up to.

'Just to say thanks for looking after me, with the ankle and everything. All the driving and all that.' He blushed and handed me a bunch of yellow chrysanthemums.

I am highly suspicious. I'm not used to being appreciated.

Friday 10 September

Myrna came back from the senior managers' meeting with a face that looked like she had been sucking lemons. Turns out that due to budgetary constraints, my assistant won't be able to start until January. Oh well, just have to try to look rushed off my feet until then.

Saturday 11 September

Went to view a house after football this evening. The estate agent described it as semi-rural. Apparently that means that if you stand on the bed in the spare room and peer round the wardrobe, you can just about see a field. We argued as a man with an Adolph Hitler moustache and very bad breath showed us around. Mrs Hitler wore too much lipstick and carried a rather pop-eyed poodle under her arm like a set of bagpipes. Everything Kevin liked about the house I hated, and the few redeeming features, like a tiled fireplace and a picture rail, Kevin talked about 'having out' as soon as we moved in. In fact the only thing we agreed about was that we disagreed about everything. Even Mr and Mrs Hitler were beginning to exchange glances.

Kevin thought the garden was too small, I didn't like the lounge wallpaper; Kevin thought it was too far from the motorway, I thought the gold-plated taps looked pretentious. Most of all I disliked the couple who showed us round, although as Kevin pointed out, they wouldn't actually be there when we moved in. Which was a fair comment.

We didn't make an offer. Mrs Hitler looked huffy as we left and gave the poodle an indignant squeeze, which made its eyes protrude even further.

On the way home in the van, I noticed that nobody has moved into Miss Chamberlain's cottage yet. The garden she used to tend with so much care is overgrown and untidy. The cottage looks so forlorn on its own.

Sunday 12 September

Everybody's bending over backwards to be nice to Digger now they know he's leaving. People are coming up to shake his hand and tell him what a wonderful sermon he's just preached, people have complimented him on his clothes, his hairstyle, his garden. He's been invited out for dinner every night this week. Even Jeremiah is being pleasant to him. I get the feeling that if people had been like this in the first place, he would not be leaving.

Monday 13 September

Broke the bad news to Tom about there not being a job until January. Fortunately, someone from their church has offered him a few hours a week book-keeping and office work. Wonder how Ariadne will take it.

Tuesday 14 September

There is a spare place on a first-aid training course for three days starting tomorrow. Somebody has cancelled. Apparently they had an accident. Shame they didn't come along anyway and we could have practised on them. Myrna has insisted I clear my desk before I go. Perhaps she is concerned that I may not come back.

Wednesday 15 September

Didn't realize this course would be so technical. You've got to know where all the bits of the body are, what they do and which way they are supposed to bend. Still, may come in handy, especially if I want to take up a healing ministry. I know how to check if someone's still alive – may be useful during the church prayer meeting – and I've learnt what to do if someone catches fire – unlikely at St Norbert's, even during the most fervent hymns.

Thursday 16 September

We learnt how to deal with fractures and ventilation and cardio-pulmonary resuscitation techniques. I suggested Kevin should come along as a real-life example of an accident victim but he declined on the grounds that he was under the fracture clinic and 'didn't want a bunch of amateurs messing with his leg'. I thought he was being rather ungracious. Still, the CPR was very exciting, just like *Casualty*. Unfortunately I got rather carried away watching my colleagues breathing into the dummy and unwittingly found out the treatment for hyperventilation.

Friday 17 September

End of the course. Had to take an exam to see if I am safe to be unleashed on the world.

Kept watching people on the train, waiting for someone to keel over so I can practise my techniques. Didn't happen. I know it's a horrible thing to say, but after all this study it would be a pity if I never got the chance to use it.

6 p.m.

The estate agent has just rung. They have someone who would like to view the flat tomorrow. Better tidy up.

Saturday 18 September

Spent all this morning cleaning the picture rails, picking up lumps of fluff from under the bed and hoovering dead moths out of the lampshades. The towels are fluffy and neatly arranged. There are fresh flowers in vases and all the junk that might just come in handy one day but never has, has been cleared. I even removed the Christmas bauble from behind the sofa. In fact the flat looks so appealing that I don't want to sell it.

8 p.m.

That's OK because the couple didn't want to buy it. They kept talking about things like repointing, rewiring and 3/8 inch pipes. They tapped walls and stuck screwdrivers into window frames. Eventually they shook their heads and left. They didn't even feel how fluffy the towels were.

Sunday 19 September, Harvest

I'm sure the children's choruses we sing at church are getting worse. At best they are embarrassing, at worst they are so jaw-clenchingly, stomach-churningly cringe-worthy that no person, sane or otherwise, would sing them voluntarily. Half a dozen chirpy mini-Hubbles squeaked the following offering:

At ha-ha-harvest time
We ho-ho-hoe the fields
And he-he-he makes rain to fall
So ho-ho-hoe and he-he-he will make it grow for
Ha-ha-ha-ha-ha-ha-harvest time.

Then we all had to join in, sounding more like a pack of hyenas having a hysterical fit than worshippers at a harvest service. I tried to force a smile and looked around desperately for some important job that urgently needed doing. I failed. The stripy marrows, polished apples and tins of beans were all perfectly arrayed, and Doris Johnson's home-made preserves on their high shelf above the doors linking the church to the back hall glowed like stained glass in the autumn sunshine. I caught oily, slimy Roger Lemarck's eye. He did a 'being sick' mime. I knew how he felt. Charity was clapping along to the cheery tune, basking in the family moment. Nigel was videoing it all for posterity.

Suddenly there was a thud and a blood-curdling scream from the back of the church. Miss Cranmer sat clutching her head, with redness oozing out from between her fingers. Here was my moment. My first-aid course came flooding back. Airway, Breathing, Circulation. It became pretty clear from the hysterical screaming that Miss Cranmer's airway was entirely clear and that she was indeed breathing. A group of us laid her gently on the floor.

'I'm dying, I'm dying,' she groaned. 'Me life-blood's draining away.' And it appeared as if exactly that was happening. Several people comforted and mopped at her. I tried to find the source of the bleeding. She didn't appear to be cut. Just a golf-ball sized lump on her head and buckets-full of dark red liquid, which smelt strongly of . . . vinegar! I looked up and saw a gap in the line of produce on the shelf above the door. Under Miss Cranmer's chair was a jar, with its lid slightly dislodged. A jar containing Doris Johnson's home-pickled beetroot.

'It's all right Miss Cranmer,' I said. 'You're not bleeding to death, it's only beetroot.'

'Beetroot?'

'Yes, someone must have closed the door a bit too hard and dislodged the jar, which fell off and hit you on the head.'

We mopped and cleaned her, and Doris Johnson, who felt slightly responsible as it was her beetroot, ran Miss Cranmer to the hospital to get the bump on her head checked out, just in case.

'Excuse me,' came Miss Cranmer's wavering voice as Doris led her out to the car park, 'but might I keep the jar of beetroot?'

Monday 20 September

I'm sure Ariadne needs help. I don't know what to do. I'm only around at evenings and weekends, and what with planning the wedding and house-hunting and going to football to keep Kevin happy, there's little time left for helping Ariadne. I know Mum helps out when she can but, and I feel very disloyal saying this, Mum's never been particularly maternal. Mum thinks that Sheila Kitzinger used to be US Secretary of State. Tried praying about it but the only person who kept popping into my mind was Charity Hubble, and I wouldn't inflict her on my worst enemy. Ariadne has taken yet another two weeks off work.

Tuesday 21 September

A tearful Charity on the phone this evening. Neb had his first detention at school for fighting.

'Where did we go wrong?' she wailed. 'We always impressed upon him how wrong it was to fight. We always told him that if someone hit him he should turn the other cheek.'

'So what happened?'

'A boy punched Neb in the face so Neb sat on him. Badly bruised his ribs.'

I don't think that's quite what Jesus meant by 'the other cheek'.

Wednesday 22 September

It's good that Digger's replacement is starting on 1 November and we won't have a long interregnum.

Thursday 23 September

There was no point whatsoever in yesterday's diary entry except that I have always wanted to use the word 'interregnum'.

And now I have.

Saturday 25 September

Drove Kevin to another football match this afternoon. What a waste of good shopping time!

Sunday 26 September

It's Digger's last day at St Norbert's. He is flying to Australia tomorrow. Kevin came with me. I know Kevin doesn't spend much time in church but the two of them used to sit for ages talking over a pint. Kevin would never tell me what they discussed but Digger often tapped his nose and said, 'You've got a good one there, Theo love. Make sure you hang on to him.'

Theodora's Wedding

Digger was obviously trying to keep things on an upbeat note, with his sermon comparing David and Goliath to a rugby match with Neil Back and Jonah Lomu. Nevertheless it was an emotional occasion. Must admit I got a bit carried away and threw my arms around his ankles and sobbed on to his shoes.

Digger, Kevin and the organist, Gregory Pasternak, tried to prise me off in the vestry.

'Why is everybody leaving me?' I bawled.

'Strewth, Theo, I'm only going to Australia, not Mars. I'm sure I'll be back to visit sometime. Anyway, you can write or e-mail. And I'm sure the new bloke will be far better.'

Miss Cranmer brought me in a cup of tea and helped to calm me down.

Later, alone in my flat, I thought about it. It's true. Miss Chamberlain, Declan and now Digger. Why does everyone I depend on always have to leave?

Monday 27 September

Found a card pushed through the communal front door this morning. It was from Digger. He must have dropped it in on the way to the airport. The front was not much to look at, the sort of card that comes in packs of notelets or the kind of birthday card you buy for someone you don't like very much. What Digger had written inside, however, hit me like a hammer.

God has said,
'Never will I leave you;
never will I forsake you.'
Hebrews 13:5

He's right. I shouldn't be looking for security in people but in God. He won't leave me and I can always rely on him. Must write to Digger as soon as he sends his new address. Felt a bit foolish about the clinging to his ankles bit. Must try to retain a bit of decorum.

Tuesday 28 September

E-mail from my brother Ag in Peru today. He has just finished an article on the ancient civilizations of South America, and he and my intimidating sister-in-law Cordelia plan to come back to England for Christmas. He pulled my leg mercilessly about me getting married and informed me that Cordelia, who is proportioned amply and dresses flamboyantly, has offered to design the wedding dress. I e-mailed back immediately and declined. Between Cordelia trying to make me look like one of those crinoline toilet-roll covers and Charity's offer of running up something out of shop-soiled net curtains, I think I'll go it alone.

Wednesday 29 September

Got my first-aid certificate in the post today. Found a frame and now have it hanging on the wall above my desk. Feel just like a doctor. Managed to resist the urge to scatter twelve-year-old *Reader's Digests* around the waiting area.

Theodora's Wedding

Thursday 30 September

Opened the post this morning to find details of a house in Pratt's Bottom. One of my lifetime ambitions is to live there, not so much for the location, although it is a very nice place, but just for the sheer enjoyment of telling people my address. Unfortunately it was out of our price-range.

October

Friday 1 October

The estate agent phoned me at work today to arrange an appointment for a potential buyer for my flat. A distinguished-looking gentleman, Mr Singh, with a very well-upholstered wife and a nervy little mouse of a daughter, came at six this evening. He intends to buy a flat for his daughter who will be studying to become a teacher at the teacher training college a few miles up the road. She looked as if a strong gust would blow her away. I didn't fancy her chances in front of a class of children – they would eat her alive. But as far as her parents were concerned, nothing was too good for their little girl. They had recently bought her a car and now were buying her a flat. I suddenly felt deprived. My parents had never bought me a car or a flat. In fact, from the age of fourteen I even had to buy my own clothes with the money I earned from my paper round. I comforted myself that I, at thirty, was a strong independently minded woman, whereas this girl looked as if she needed all the help she could get. They questioned me at length about the lease, the neighbours, the facilities and which fixtures and fittings I would be leaving. Mr Singh was very thorough.

Saturday 2 October

Sat and got drenched at the match today. The water ran off my hat and down my back in rivulets. I couldn't even read my magazine, which had dissolved into a soggy mess. Kevin wore a waterproof arrangement made out of a dustbin bag over his plaster, which gave him a kind of down-and-out appearance. The man behind me was so rude as to ask me to put my umbrella down because it was blocking his view. As soon as he gets his leg out of plaster, I must pluck up the courage to tell Kevin that I really don't enjoy football.

Sunday 3 October

A strange woman from another church came and preached today. Her real name was Rosie Proust (as if that wasn't bad enough) but due to over-enthusiastic use of the spell-checker she was billed in *The Church Organ* as Rosé Profits, which made her sound like the earnings from a small vineyard.

She was a short, thin, plain woman with stringy dark hair and T-bar shoes.

'My text today,' she announced, 'is taken from the book of Colossians, chapter three, verse nine, "Lie not to one another, seeing that ye have put off the old man with his deeds." Now, of course, that text cannot be taken literally, like most of the Bible.'

Members of the congregation exchanged 'we're in for a good one here' glances.

' "Lie not to one another" means, of course, do not tell each other lies.' Nods all round. Nothing to disagree with there. Fairly straightforward. I'll remember that next time Ariadne asks me if a new outfit makes her bottom look big. That should help 'the peace of God rule in our hearts'.

Rosie was continuing her message. 'But what about "put off the old man"?'

Several of the male contingents of the congregation over the age of sixty started to look distinctly 'put off'.

'No, by "the old man", St Paul is not referring to a fellow of advanced years, not an octogenarian gentleman, or indeed an elderly chap of any kind or description. Aged patriarchs have nothing to fear. Father figures, whether they are birth fathers, step-fathers or, indeed, spiritual fathers, are not within St Paul's frame of reference here. St Paul himself, who was no callow youth, was not speaking to the adult males in the latter years of their life. In fact, he is referring to our unreconstituted nature, our yet-to-be redeemed selves, our souls in their former state.

'And by "put off", St Paul does not mean "tell him not to come", "rearrange it for a more convenient date" or even' – and here she gave a coquettish little giggle – '"take a rain check", but in the sense of a worn garment, cast aside. Who on a warm summer evening has not arrived home from work or a shopping trip and, with joyful abandon, shut the front door and thrown off all their clothes, skipping around as nature intended?'

It was around this point in the sermon that I lost the will to live.

Monday 4 October

Mum and I met for coffee and she explained what she requires of me when we go to Greece next week. She has a sort of vision of herself gliding from authentic Greek taverna to authentic Greek taverna, flitting in and out of the kitchens, discussing the finer points of Greek cuisine with the chefs while I trail along with a notebook to record the culinary gems for posterity. I can see that there will be conflict. I'm just hoping that there will be sufficient beach-time to compensate me. When I raised my concern, Mum told me to 'beware looking a Trojan horse in the mouth'.

Tuesday 5 October

Ariadne nearly went back to work yesterday. When I phoned Tom to ask how she had got on, he went all hush-hush and whispered that he had driven her as far as the station but then she sort of flipped and wouldn't get out of the car. He'd driven her back home and phoned Ariadne's boss with some kind of excuse about the baby being unwell. I don't understand it. Ariadne loves her job, she's practically a workaholic. This can't go on, she's going to lose her job unless she gets her act together.

Wednesday 6 October

Transpires that Mum's culinary tour is to be a week travelling around an island called Evia. I have never heard of it. No one I know has ever heard of it. Mum insists it is the second biggest Greek island (after Crete) and is just off the eastern side of the Greek mainland. A plane flight to Athens, then hop on a ferry and Dimitri is your uncle. I have my reservations.

Thursday 7 October

It is the last week of the holiday season and ours is the last plane going to the Greek holiday resorts. The weather there is supposed to be sunny, but rain is possible at this time of year so I have packed my moon boots just to be on the safe side. The flat looks like a tip with clothes and suit-cases strewn all over the place. Good job no one else wants to view it. I haven't heard any more from the Singhs and their timorous daughter.

We don't have to leave until mid-day tomorrow so will finish packing tonight to make the most of the lie-in. Dad has taken the day off work to drive us to the airport so we don't have to worry about booking a taxi. It will be funny being away from Kevin for a week. I've instructed him not to buy a house until I've seen it. I know what he's like.

Friday 8 October

On the plane 4.23 p.m.

I am facing the prospect of a week in Greece with my mother, the Greek Mrs Malaprop, who is already treating me like a lackey. Still, as I suppose as she is paying, and because I'm saving for a house I won't be able to afford a holiday otherwise, I'd better start sounding grateful.

The plane was almost on time leaving for Athens and I am currently sitting between Mum, who is dressed like

Jackie Onassis, and a huge Greek lady who seems to be eating garlic sandwiches. At least I've got my diary for company.

On the plane 6.49 p.m.

Have been re-reading my diary. If I didn't know me, and understand that I am really a perfectly sane, normal, level-headed woman, I would think that they were the ramblings of a complete neurotic.

Still on the plane 7.15 p.m.

Garlic-sandwich woman keeps looking over my shoulder and reading what I have written. Am tempted to write something unpleasant about her in VERY BIG LETTERS.

In the plane toilet 7.25 p.m.

Am now in hiding from garlic-sandwich woman, who did read my comment and appeared greatly put out. She's very big and looks as if she may well know someone in the Greek Mafia.

In the plane toilet 7.58 p.m.

People are starting to bang on the door. I'll have to go back to my seat and face her. Besides, if I stay here any longer I will miss my delicious in-flight meal.

Back in my seat 9.04 p.m.

Apart from giving me a disgruntled look as I climbed over her to get back to my seat, garlic-sandwich woman seems to bear me no malice. On reflection, if she is Greek she probably doesn't understand what I've written anyway.

On the coach 11.14 p.m.

Turns out Mum and the Greek lady had been chatting in my absence – she had even given Mum the definitive recipe for tzatziki. Discovered her name is Maria and she probably did understand what I'd written in my diary on account of her teaching English to students plus the fact that she has spent six months in England every year for the last twenty years.

The rest of the plane journey was uneventful. I prudently stashed my diary in my hand luggage and read the in-flight magazine until I dozed off. The meal when it came was a very tasty roast beef with seasonal vegetables and chocolate profiteroles for dessert. Mum muttered about 'not being able to eat this muck' but I thought it was very agreeable. Where do they get those tiny roast potatoes?

In a hotel lobby in Athens 1.37 a.m.

The ferry to Evia doesn't leave until eight o'clock tomorrow morning (or is it this morning?) so we have to sit here in the lobby of Hotel Apollyon until the coach leaves at about 6.30 a.m. Have been drinking coffee to try to keep awake and now feel slightly 'wired' from all the caffeine. Have been trying to doze off but screaming babies and the lack of anywhere comfortable to sit, let alone lie down, have reduced any chance of that to zero.

Still in a hotel lobby 4.14 a.m.

Everything has taken on a surreal quality. There seems to be a kind of satellite delay between my brain and my limbs. If I want to pick up my coffee cup it takes several seconds for my hand to receive the message and actually move.

I'm bored. Think I will go for a walk. Come on legs, walkies!

4.52 a.m.

Athens is surprisingly awake at this unearthly hour. Bars and cafés are still serving and traffic is steadily streaming through the city streets. I don't think I have ever wandered alone through the streets of London in the early hours but I feel amazingly safe here. Not logical but senses are deadened. I could have been mugged or murdered. Perhaps I have been and am too tired to notice.

Mum has been asleep in a straight-backed chair for the last two hours. How does she do it? I think I will give her a nudge to wake her up.

On a coach 6.15 a.m.

A coach turned up and everybody got on. Could be taking us to Mars for all I know or care. Mum, refreshed by her sleep, has been talking at me about her plans for visiting restaurants. I can see her mouth moving, but the words don't make sense any more. Sooo tired.

The ferry 8.20 a.m.

Sat on the harbour wall and watched the sun coming up. Dragged our luggage on to the ferry. My arms and legs have become detached from my body.

The morning sun is starting to warm the air and make little golden flecks on the sea. The gentle movement of the ferry creaking and rocking . . . the gulls crying overhead . . . the little fishing boats returning with their catches . . . rocking . . . nearly there, must stay awake . . . rocking . . .

At last ... the apartment 10.51 a.m.

I can't believe we're finally here. The entire journey, door to door, has taken over twenty hours. How is this possible? It only takes twenty-four hours to fly all the way to New Zealand!

Saturday 9 October (I think)

11.40 p.m.

Fell straight into bed the moment we got to the apartment. Mum, who wasn't tired, decided to go out to explore the surrounding villages and to look for a likely restaurant for tonight.

When I woke up, I went to investigate the apartment complex and had a dip in the pool. Standing on our balcony drying my hair, I noticed how the ground plunged away below me, terracing out to a flat area with a grid of scrubby trees, and within the squares of the grid are low white dwellings, many with large solar panels and water tanks. Beyond is the sea, extending to the horizon. The edge nearest the shore is vivid turquoise, changing to deep peacock and finally, where it touches the sky, almost dark navy. Rocks, too small to be islands and too large to be boulders carried by the sea, are strewn casually around the bay as if they had really intended to be part of the land but had become exhausted with their swim to the shore and paused there for a rest. They obviously liked it so much that they stayed.

I was just having my first Greek coffee of the evening when Mum returned, enthusing about a restaurant she had found in a neighbouring village. We got changed and phoned for a taxi. When the taxi arrived, the driver fortunately spoke English.

'Where you wanna go?' he asked.

It was then that Mum's forte kicked in.

'It's a little village up the mountain from here, must be six or seven kilometres at the most. It's got a shop ... and a taverna. I think it begins with a "P".'

I sat with my head in my hands while Mum directed the poor driver up and down unlit roads, some of which ended in cart tracks. The ones that did lead to villages did not lead to the right village. We drove along a mountain road, then into a lowland region where the narrow strip of tarmac was bordered on both sides with olive groves. Suddenly we rounded a bend and found ourselves in a small but lively village with one or two cafés and tavernas. A couple of young studs on scooters shot past us, and a group of teenage girls giggled and flirted, as the boys disappeared into the distance only to reappear seconds later and pass them in the other direction. We seemed to be the only tourists in the place. A lone donkey stood impassively watching the antics of the young people. Suddenly Mum became animated. 'Stop, stop, this is it. This is the place.'

It looked pretty much like all the other villages we had passed through tonight. 'Are you sure, Mum?' I asked.

'Absolutely sure. I recognize the donkey.'

I shook my head in disbelief but Mum was adamant.

We paid the taxi driver a very reasonable sum considering the distance he had covered to find the place, and I had the foresight to ask him to come back and pick us up at ten.

'No problem,' he said.

We found the taverna, which seemed to be in some-body's front garden, and Mum made me order half the menu so that she could try a bit of everything. She went into the kitchen and managed to communicate with the elderly lady, dressed all in black, who was responsible for cooking the meals. I trailed behind and made notes of the ingredients, seasoning and method of cooking. When we ordered the customary Greek salad or *horiatiki*, the waiter slipped off with a knife into the garden and returned carrying a cucumber. You can't get any fresher than that. The food was delicious and Mum, phrasebook in hand, thanked the cook profusely. At least I think that's what she did. The taxi driver arrived at the Greek equivalent of ten o'clock and we returned with Mum enthusing about all things Greek. Lying on my bed with a full stomach and a feeling of contented tiredness, and with the sound of the cicadas singing me to sleep, I must admit she had a point.

Sunday 10 October

Explored the resort today. The weather is still remarkably warm for October. I slapped on the factor 15, squeezed into my bikini, wrapped my matching sarong around my waist (Evia is not ready for the sight of my backside in a bikini), slipped on my flip-flops, put on my straw hat and sunglasses and set off to mingle unobtrusively with the locals. Surprisingly, the local people were not particularly friendly. I became acutely aware that I was the only tourist in the resort and consequently an object of curiosity. I quickly bought my postcards and stamps and set off for the beach, where I felt a little less conspicuous.

There were a number of Greek families enjoying a Sunday by the sea and even a group of four or five Germans. Walking back to the apartment I once again became aware of people staring. A small boy even pointed and said something in Greek, which sounded as if it could have been, 'Look, Mum, look at that funny lady. What is she doing here?' His mother drew him to one side and said something that could well have been, 'I'm not sure, but judging by the size of her bottom, she could be an English tourist.'

Perhaps I'm getting paranoid.

I talked to Mum about it.

'Well,' she explained, 'the idea of coming to Evia, rather than one of the usual tourist haunts, is to find the most authentic Greek cuisine. I wanted to go somewhere that wasn't all "Fish 'n' Chips" and "Watney's Red Barrel". This is where the Greeks come on holiday. I suppose they're just not used to us.'

'I see what you mean. A bit like finding a Greek tourist in a swimsuit wandering around Dymchurch in October.'

'Sort of, but I think the Greek tourist would soon be an elegant shade of blue.'

Tuesday 12 October

Mum is busy writing up my notes from the last couple of days. 'Aphrodite's Authentic Greek Delicacies' stand a good chance of cornering the market in chilled Greek take-aways and Mum is keen to expand the range. I'm sitting by the pool reading Mum's Greek phrase book, trying to memorize useful phrases such as 'yes', 'no', 'please' and 'thank you'. The fact that the phrase book dates from the 1960s probably doesn't help with Mum's linguistic predicament. It contains a section on 'Going to the hairdresser' which includes such useful expressions as, 'I would like some Brilliantine.' Most puzzling of all is the inclusion of the phrase, 'The water is too hot, you are scalding me.' Surely if you are lying prone in a hairdresser's chair with scalding water gushing over your scalp, the last thing you would be capable of doing is finding the appropriate page in your phrase book and screaming, 'το νερό είναι πολύ ζεστό, μέ κάψες' at the top of your voice. Perhaps it is the sort of thing you should learn in advance, just in case.

Wednesday 13 October

Spent today lying on the bed and reading. Struggled on to the balcony to write postcards for an hour then, feeling exhausted, flopped back into bed. Too much sun and far too much food has left me feeling jaded. I don't feel ill exactly, just strangely missing Kevin and, even more strangely, missing England.

Thursday 14 October

Have abandoned the bikini, sun hat and sarong in favour of tailored shorts, white shirt and make-up. Am no longer a source of attention. Mum and I booked a taxi and went over the mountains to the other side of the island. A little way inland from the beach we found a small taverna surrounded by lemon orchards, some of which had encroached on the courtyard. I sat down alone at a table for two and ordered an iced coffee. Mum had already wandered off to 'soak up the atmosphere' and take photographs. I got out my New Testament and continued reading from the Acts of the Apostles, the bit where St Paul was in Athens and talking about being able to know the unknown God. I'd hoped that being close to the place where it actually happened would make it seem sort of authentic, 'When in Rome ...', except we weren't in Rome and I was having trouble concentrating. I could smell some kind of roast meat mixed with the sweet aroma of oregano drying in the sun. I sat back and closed my eyes and felt the warm sun on my face, more content than I have been for a long time. I thought that a glass or two of retsina, the local resinated white wine, might enhance the atmosphere. Then I remembered the sheer quantity of food and drink I had consumed over the past few days and thought better of it. When I opened my eyes I saw that a party of tourists had come in – I think they were Australians – and a young woman with dark curly hair was taking their order. The woman wore jeans and a black tee shirt; she was neither plump, nor thin but had a curved shape and a friendly yet deferential manner. She laughed with the Australians, throwing back her head with joy as they attempted the Greek pronunciations. Then, making sure each one of them had chosen their food, had been pro-vided with a glass of iced water and had been shown where the toilets were, she turned to me. My eyes were drawn to the slogan on her tee shirt, 'I am no goddess but men still worship me.' She came over and took my empty glass.

'Would you like anything else?' She smiled broadly. 'We make our own retsina.'

'Oh, you're English!' I exclaimed. 'Out here we seem to be few and far between.'

'Yeah, it's my grandparents' place. I took a year out from uni to work here. That was three years ago and I never quite made it back. Besides, they find it useful with the tourists.' She glanced at the empty chairs and tables around her. 'There are a few more in high season.'

She smiled her broad smile again. I don't think I had ever met anyone who looked so ... free. Everyone in London looks sort of downtrodden – crumpled, somehow. This young woman seemed to radiate vivacity and assurance.

'Could I have a lemonade, please?' Then, on a whim, 'Would you like to join me if you're not too busy?'

'I'll just check with Yaya.' She darted through a small doorway, ducking her head under the drooping bough of a lemon tree. A few seconds later she reappeared carrying a tray with four glasses, two with iced water and two empty ones. She tugged open the door of an ancient refrigerator, which immediately started rumbling in protest, and took out two chilled bottles of lemonade and flicked off the caps. 'She'll need some help in the kitchen in a while, but I'm OK for a break. *Yammas*!' She poured the fizzy drink into the two glasses and we clinked them together.

'So are you here on your own?'

'No, I'm with my mum. She's a sort of a cook. It's a bit hard to explain, but she kind of specializes in chilled take-away food for supermarkets and that sort of thing. It's only a small range at the moment but she's keen to expand. We've come here on a sort of fact-finding mission. Mum wants to research the authentic food – as cooked by the Greeks.'

'I'll have to introduce her to Yaya, then.'

'She'd love that ... only she's gone wandering at the moment. I'm sure she'll be back soon.'

'Do you work with her?'

'No, I'm just along for the ride, really. I'm supposed to be her secretary but she complains that she can't read my writing. Now she's taking her own notes. And I'm sitting here in the sun drinking lemonade and chatting. Normally, I work in an office in London.'

'Oh,' she said as if to imply both surprise and pity. 'Do you like it?'

'It pays the mortgage. And I'm getting married next year.'

'Oh,' she said again with a similar implication.

'I'm Theo, by the way.'

'Diana, hence the tee shirt. It's sort of a "Roman mythology" joke.'

'Very witty.'

I meant it, but it came out sounding very insincere. We both fell silent for a while. I took the opportunity to refill my glass.

'What were you reading?' she asked, nodding towards my closed New Testament.

'It's the Bible,' I said, unsure of whether to add anything to qualify the statement. 'Well, part of the Bible.'

'Is it good?' she asked, as if referring to a novel.

'Yes, very good. I've been reading about St Paul in Athens. He's telling the ancient Greek philosophers about how ordinary people like us can know God who made everything.'

'Do you believe that?'

'Yes, I do. I'm a Christian.'

'It must be good to have faith.'

'It can be. It's not always easy.'

'So how do you know God exists?'

What a question! In the complete absence of anyone who would know better (just where are all the itinerant evangelists when you need one?), I racked my brains.

'Well, one answer would be that I see evidence of God in the world around us and in my own life, but ultimately it comes down to believing. God isn't physical, you can't see or touch him and you can't prove him like a mathematical theorem. If you want to know more about God, this is the best thing to read.'

She took the New Testament from me. 'So is God in here?'

'Not exactly, but it will tell you how to find him.'

'So does knowing him make you happy?'

How many more difficult questions would this girl ask? This girl whose air of happiness and contentment shone out from her more convincingly than it did from many Christians. I thought of Miss Chamberlain and tried to remember what kind of answer she would have given. Then I realized that Diana was asking me, not Miss Chamberlain.

'Sometimes. Sometimes it feels like hard work, but if everything else was taken away my relationship with God would be what is left.'

'Wow!' Her eyes were shining. I felt like the worst example of Christianity on the planet. I felt like a double-glazing salesman apologizing to a potential customer for taking up their time and convincing them that their old windows are just fine as they are. I prayed quickly, then a sudden thought popped into my head.

'What is your most precious possession?' I asked.

'My mother's wedding ring. She gave it to me before she died.'

'And what would make you give that up?'

'Nothing. There's no way I'd give it away, not for anything.'

'What about to save someone's life?'

'Maybe.'

'The thing is, Jesus is God's way of proving to us how much he loves us. God gave up his son, his most precious thing. He let him die a horrible death to save our lives. There are so many wrong things that hurt God, things that stop us coming close to him. Jesus' death and the fact that God raised him from the dead kind of proves how precious, how valuable we are to him.'

'That's amazing!' she exclaimed. And when I thought about it, it was.

'Have this.' I pushed my Bible across the table to her.

'I couldn't, it's yours.'

'No, I've got others at home, this is a spare, honest. I only brought it with me because it's small and fitted in my case. It would make my day if you took it.' I wrote my e-mail address inside the front cover. 'I'd love to hear from you sometime . . .'

'Thanks.'

Diana flitted off again, tucking the New Testament into her jeans pocket.

Without my reading material I gazed around the courtyard. There were no lemons on the trees now but some grapevines were still heavy with their late fruit. The chequered tablecloths and wooden chairs seemed to belong to another era. A canary in a cage began to sing. I thought about Diana and wondered, if she became a Christian, how she would change. If she were to come to St Norbert's the tee shirt would have to go, for a start. But it seemed so much part of her that I worried that she would somehow be forced to conform to our pale-grey suburban version of Christianity, that somehow the life force that was so evident in the way she spoke, the way she moved and the way she smiled, would be cudgelled out of her. I sat and prayed for her and thanked God for giving me the right words to say. My prayer was brought abruptly to an end when Mum returned and flopped down in the chair opposite me.

'Been busy?' she asked, kicking off her shoes.

'Sort of. Shall I order a drink?'

'Ooh, yes please.' She studied the menu. 'I'll have a glass of retriever please. I think they make it themselves.'

Friday 15 October

Fortunately the homeward leg of the journey had slightly better connections than the outward leg. Left Evia at 6.30 a.m. and walked in through the door at 7 p.m. I immediately phoned Kevin, who is now out of plaster and fully mobile again. He suggested we go out for a meal. Apart from me feeling fatter than an over-stuffed sofa, he suggested we go to a new Greek restaurant which has just opened up in the High Street. Amazingly, he wasn't joking.

'I thought you liked Greek food,' he protested.

He really has no idea.

I had treated myself to a new bottle of perfume on the plane. It contains only natural ingredients, is ethically pro-duced and not tested on animals. The bottle reads 'Blossom Meadows, organic strawberry, almond oil and vanilla body spray – capture the freshness of a summer day'. I liberally doused myself in it, as a week without Kevin had made me feel romantic. It is true what they say about absence making the heart grow fonder.

The buzzer sounded and Kevin jogged up the stairs to my flat. I stood there, sun-kissed and relaxed and only slightly corpulent, smelling like a meadow of blossom. I was initially encouraged as Kevin, instead of the perfunctory peck on the cheek, started nuzzling my neck.

'You smell lovely,' he murmured. My heart fluttered at the thought of the new Byronic Kevin. 'Just like a slice of Battenburg.'

Saturday 16 October

Kevin was at an away match, thank goodness. So I took my mum and Kevin's mum to help me look for a wedding dress. Kevin's mum liked frilly, my mum liked floaty and I liked plain. Kevin's mum liked Elizabeth Emanuel, my mum liked Suzanne Neville and I liked Debenham's. We couldn't choose between a veil, flowers or a tiara. The only thing we could agree on was that our feet hurt and we all needed a cup of coffee. Dad's chequebook is safe for another week.

I got home to find Kevin bouncing up and down with excitement on my doorstep. He told me he had sorted out a wedding car.

'Brilliant! What kind is it, a Rolls-Royce, a Bentley, is it a vintage one?'

'I'm not quite sure yet.'

'What do you mean you're not quite sure? What car did you book?'

'Well, he hasn't exactly got it in yet. He kind of gets them to order.'

'Kevin, tell me you haven't been talking to Vague Dave at the market.'

'I haven't been talking to Vague Dave.' His eyes darted left and right.

'You have, haven't you. Oh Kevin, you lied to me! How could you?'

'You told me to tell you I hadn't been talking to Vague Dave so that's what I told you. I was only doing what you asked.'

I let out a scream of frustration. 'So you're telling me that you have placed responsibility for transportation on the biggest day of our lives to Vague "As featured on *Crimewatch*" Dave! Brilliant! Honeymoon on remand.'

'You're being unreasonable. Dave's a good bloke. The engagement ring was kosher, wasn't it?'

I grudgingly had to admit it was. Also, it transpired that Vague Dave's cousin is in the motor trade and does a bit of chauffeuring on the side. He has whichever car is available on the day – Mercedes, vintage Jaguar, even a Rolls-Royce. While I was away, Kevin had been making all sorts of phone calls to try to sort it out. I gave him a big hug. Kevin's a good chap really, so what if his friends are a bit dodgy.

Sunday 17 October

Was collecting hymnbooks after the service and hoping that someone had remembered to reserve me a cup of coffee from the top of the urn, the stuff that doesn't have all the chalky crunchy ballast at the bottom of the cup, when I heard a sniffing noise coming from behind one of the pillars. I peered round the stone column to see Charity crying into a handkerchief. My first instinct was to pretend I hadn't seen her and go to claim my coffee, but something wouldn't let me leave her. I crept closer and cleared my throat. Charity jumped.

'I thought everyone had gone,' she said.

'Everyone else has.'

'I'd better go and find Nigel,' she sniffed.

'Charity, what's wrong? Is there anything I can do?' I sat down next to her.

She blew her nose loudly and looked up.

'I ... can't tell you. For one thing it's betraying Nigel's confidence and for another you wouldn't understand. You'd laugh at me.'

I felt quite affronted – I wouldn't laugh at Charity. A stab of guilt. Actually there are many, many times when I have done just that.

'OK ... Would you like me to fetch Nigel so you can talk it over with *him?*'

'Oh, we've talked.' A look approaching resentment crossed her face. 'We've talked till we're blue in the face. I know that the man is the head of the household and I know my wifely duty is to submit to him ...' Tears started to fall again. 'But when it affects me so deeply, my whole being, my identity ...' She trailed off.

'Charity ...' I began, wondering if I was getting in too deep.

'Nigel doesn't want to have any more children,' she blurted.

'I'm not surprised, you've got nine!'

She started howling into her handkerchief. 'I told you that you wouldn't understand.'

'Try me.'

Charity took a deep breath. 'Nigel wants a vasectomy.'

I tried to hide a smirk. Charity looked reproachfully at me and stood up as if to leave. I caught her sleeve.

'Sorry, Charity. Charity, sorry . . . honestly I am. Sit down.'

She sat down again. 'I knew you'd laugh. Anyone would. "Aren't nine children enough for you?" they sneer. Well, the answer's no. Nine children aren't enough. Having children – it's what I do best. It's the one thing I'm really, really good at. If I can't have babies it's . . . it's . . . as if I have no purpose any more.'

Surprisingly, I could see her point. She had poured everything she had into her family. She'd never had a career, they'd never had any money and Charity's 'soft furnishings department' dresses hid a body so stretched and inhabited so many times by little Hubbles that by now she could hardly feel it was fully her own. It would not be true to say she had sacrificed everything for her family: to Charity it was no sacrifice. She was doing what she loved with a passion, and now Nigel was threatening to take that away from her.

'Is he adamant?'

'Totally. He's booked the hospital appointment.'

'Oh Charity!'

Monday 18 October

Prayed for Diana then Charity and Nigel tonight. I really felt for Charity – much as I would rather be smeared with Bovril and be thrown to a pack of hungry rottweilers than spend time in the company of the Hubble children, I couldn't bear the thought of a barren and desolate Charity. How could I possibly feel like this? I'm worried that I may be starting to actually *like* her. That would never do. Without Charity I would have no one to complain about. I would drift through life in a sort of oblivion. Believing that Charity is wrong is the thing that makes me believe that I am right! Charity is my adversary: the Moriarty to my Sherlock Holmes, the Mary Queen of Scots to my Elizabeth I, the Elmer Fudd to my Bugs Bunny.

Thought about those hideous flowery frocks and the many, many times she has put me down and began to feel a bit of dislike creeping back in. There, that's better.

Wednesday 20 October

Reading a magazine at work (it was OK, I had hidden it inside a file so to the casual observer it looked as though I was engaged in some form of gainful employment) when I found an article all about stress. 'How stressed are you?' it inquired. It listed the ten most stressful times in a person's life. Among them were getting married, moving house, changing job and going on holiday. Only divorce and losing a close relative ranked higher. You had to mark a score against each item. Twenty or below meant you were fairly chilled. Thirty to forty marks was slightly stressed. Fifty to sixty marks was significantly stressed, and above seventy was severely stressed. I scored 110. I should be dead from anxiety. It also listed some of the symptoms of stress, which included irritability, mood swings and changes in appetite. This is wonderful news. It means I can legitimately be crabby, irrational and snappy with a good excuse. I have justification for eating five Mars bars in one sitting. No longer do I have to bite my tongue and try to be pleasant, I can snap away like an alligator with PMT and blame it all on stress.

Thursday 21 October

Took a day off work, taking leave to avoid potentially lethally boring 'Quarterly Staff Satisfaction and Personal Development Forum' and dragged Ariadne off shopping. When I arrived at the house at 9.30, Ariadne was still in her dressing gown. I took Phoebe off for an excursion down to the newsagent's to give Ariadne a chance to jump in the shower. When we returned, Ariadne looked a little less crumpled. We decided to take my car into town and it must have taken the best part of an hour to load up the car seat, the buggy and all the things a small baby needs for a day out. No wonder Ariadne doesn't get out much. Hannibal and all his elephants would have taken up less space.

I tried to make small talk on the journey but Ariadne wasn't very talkative. I told her about the stress survey in the magazine.

'Stress,' she snorted. 'Tell me about it.'

We spent the rest of the journey in silence and Phoebe fell asleep.

When we had parked, it took another hour to unload the car. Phoebe had woken up by then and started scream- ing to be fed. We found a café and Ariadne fed Phoebe while I sipped cappuccino. After Phoebe was changed and settled, I took Ariadne along to her favourite clothes shop. They had a sale on. That was sure to cheer her up; she was born to shop. To my astonishment she started to cry. Ariadne never cries.

'What's the matter?' I asked, worried that someone would see us. 'Look, they're reduced – some of them are only half price. They're by your favourite designer. Do you want me to take Phoebe while you try something on?'

'They may have been reduced,' Ariadne mumbled, 'but I haven't been. They haven't got anything bigger than a size fourteen.'

'But you're a size eight.'

'I was,' said Ariadne between sobs.

I wished the ground could have swallowed me up. How could I have got it so wrong? Poor Ariadne! Me and my good intentions. Me and my big mouth.

We spent another hour wandering up and down the High Street before Ariadne's feet got too tired. I bought Ariadne a big bunch of flowers to cheer her up and Ariadne bought Phoebe some disposable nappies and some teething gel.

Friday 22 October

Phoned Charity today to see how she was. To my aston- ishment she was sparkling and ecstatic.

'Charity, what on earth happened to you?' I couldn't understand it. On Sunday she was more down than

Leonard Cohen's clinically depressed cousin, now she's brimming over with mirth and is acting as if she has the sun shining out of every available orifice.

'Well, Nigel and I had a talk, and I explained how I felt, and he seemed to understand how important it was to me, so we went to see the doctor together . . .'

'. . . and he called it all off. Oh, I'm so happy for you, Charity.'

'Um . . . not exactly.'

'What do you mean?'

'We've decided he will go ahead with it, the vasectomy.'

'Oh, but I thought you wanted . . .'

'I haven't finished. While we were in the doctor's surgery, I got her to check me out. For the past few weeks I'd been feeling a bit . . . I thought I might be . . . but with all this going on with Nigel I didn't like to . . . so she did a test and . . .'

'You're having another baby.'

'Not *a* baby . . . triplets! They're due at the end of June.'

I sat down hard on the sofa. Just what the world needed: three more Hubbles.

'What does Nigel say?'

'We've started calling him Jacob! Soon he'll have his own twelve tribes! Seriously, though, after the triplets are born they will keep me busy enough and then, yes, I can see it will be time to call it a day. After all, one doesn't want too much of a good thing. Even if I don't give birth to any more babies, there's still the job of bringing them up, and then, who knows . . . grandchildren!'

'Neb's twelve.'

'And I had him at nineteen. That's only seven years.'

'Charity!'

'Look, thank you for your concern, Theodora. I never expected to see such kindness from someone like you. It's almost like having a real friend.'

'Any time.' I put the phone down. Charity just paid me a compliment. I think. Almost.

Monday 25 October

Tom has very sensibly persuaded Ariadne to take a career break. That means she can have up to five years off work (unpaid, of course) to care for a family member. It means Tom will have to work full time and Ariadne will be left alone with Phoebe all day; there's no way they will be able to afford a childminder. She looks totally crestfallen. I'm sure she loves little Phoebe, but deep down she is a career woman. She takes the *Financial Times* to bed with her. She knows more about the Dow Jones and the FTSE than Montessori and Mothercare. This is not what she had planned at all.

Tuesday 26 October

Got an e-mail from Diana today. She's been reading the New Testament I gave her. She sounded so excited. She sent a list of questions a mile long, which I am doing my best to answer. I e-mailed back and suggested that she try to find some other Christians in her area. She is going along to the Greek Orthodox church with her grandparents and she is finding the decoration inspiring and the music very moving, but even with her fluent grasp of the Greek language she is finding it a bit difficult to understand.

Wednesday 27 October

Went to help paint the vicarage after work in preparation for the new vicar's arrival. When I arrived, Maurice Johnson had just brought the paint in from the car to spruce up the nicotine-beige kitchen. Gregory Pasternak's brother works in a DIY store and had bought some surplus tins of paint at a discount. I put on an overall and flexed my paintbrush bristles while Maurice prised the lids off the tins with a screwdriver. I heard him gasp and went over to peer into the tins.

'It's bright pink!' I exclaimed.

It was the most vivid cerise imaginable. I peered at the label on the tin.

'It's called "Peony"! Didn't you realize before you opened it?' I asked Maurice. 'Peony flowers are usually pink.'

'I thought it would be green,' said Maurice, looking crestfallen.

'Green?'

'We've had a peony in our garden for twenty-five years. I didn't know it was supposed to flower. Ours never has. Ours has always been just green.'

I resisted the temptation to tell him to buy some Baby-Bio. 'What are we going to do? We can't possibly give the new vicar a Barbie-pink kitchen, poor man.'

'We could do the bathroom . . . or even the spare bedroom,' suggested Maurice.

'Could *you* sleep with that on the walls?'

'I see your point. Could you use it up?'

'No, thank you,' I said hurriedly.

'What about your little niece? Wouldn't she like a pink bedroom?'

I thought of Ariadne and Tom's elegant cream house and tried to be diplomatic.

'Well, they've only just decorated. Let's hide it in the shed and just give these walls a wash down. "Buff Envelope" has a sudden appeal when faced with the alternative.'

Thursday 28 October

In my new role as Agony Aunt, offering advice to troubled souls, I suggested that now she's a full-time mum Ariadne might like to take Phoebe along to the parent and baby group 'Little Pickles' at St Norbert's. I know it sounds like a chutney factory but at least she would be getting out of the house.

'That's right, rub it in,' snapped Ariadne.

Friday 29 October

I wonder what the new vicar will be like. Will he be old or young, conservative or liberal, will he wear robes and a dog-collar or will he have an open-necked shirt and play the guitar? I wonder if he'll be married and if he'll have a family. Must admit it would be nice to have a few more children at St Norbert's, although Nigel and Charity seem to be keeping the Sunday school teachers busy.

Saturday 30 October

After the nail-varnish-on-the-train disaster, I have just shelled out a small fortune on a French manicure at the local beauty salon. I flashed the result at Kevin.

'It cost how much? Looks like they've painted the tips of your nails with correction fluid.'

'But it's elegant, chic. Peach nails with white tips, all the celebrities have them.'

'Well, tell me next time. I've got some caustic solution for unblocking drains. Dip your fingers in that for twenty seconds – you'd get exactly the same effect and I'd charge a fraction of the price. Mind you, thirty seconds and you'd have no fingernails left.'

At that point, I hit him.

Sunday 31 October, All Saints' Eve

Nigel Hubble has come up with an imaginative solution to the age-old dilemma of whether Christians should allow their children to trick or treat. Jeremiah's fanatical ranting about demon possession through apple-bobbing was rather extreme for most people, but within the village community there is always a general unease which goes beyond the spiritual dimension, about the wisdom of allowing young children to go around knocking on strangers' doors and asking for sweets. It all just seemed 'unwholesome' somehow. Nigel's answer was to cancel evensong and arrange an 'All Saints' Eve' party in the church hall. He printed invitations last week and sent them to the school, inviting all the local children. The children seemed delighted and their parents seemed relieved. There were silly games, music, dancing, food and Bible stories instead of ghost stories. All the children were safe but still had fun without annoying anyone or laying themselves open to what Jeremiah calls 'dark forces'.

To my surprise, Kevin came to help out. He really seemed to enjoy being with the children and even acted as goalie for a little penalty shoot-out competition at the end. He'll make a good dad some day.

November

Monday 1 November, All Saints' Day

The new vicar arrived today.

I stood on the doorstep of the vicarage to welcome Chris Monroe. Chris Monroe turned out to be Chris for Christina, not Chris for Christopher. At seven o'clock this evening a battered red and white Mini crunched to a halt in the vicarage drive, narrowly missing a terracotta urn containing a basil plant. My first view of the new vicar was a bottom, wearing tight denim jeans. She climbed out of her Mini, rear end first, with her arms full of enormous houseplants, and staggered up the steps to the front door. Apart from the jeans, she wore a vest top and a leather biker's jacket. Blonde and Amazonian, she gave me a pillar-box red grin and did her best to shake my hand through a forest of houseplants.

'Hi, I'm Chrissie. I'm supposed to collect the key from a guy called Theo Llewellyn.'

'That's me, Theo.' I grinned sheepishly and waved the key chain.

'Funny.' Her brow wrinkled. 'I was expecting a man.'

Before I could respond, she staggered past me and dumped the plants in the hall. 'I'll fetch in the rest of the stuff later,' she said. 'Guide me to the kitchen and I'll make a cup of tea. Been waiting long?'

'Er . . . no,' I stammered.

She studied my glazed expression.

'Don't tell me . . . you were expecting a man, too! What is wrong with these people? I've met half the Parish Council. They recommended me. I've been to see the bishop twice. You'd have thought they'd have noticed.'

'I think it was just me making assumptions. Sorry.'

'No problem. I wonder how many of the rest of the congregation have made the same assumption.' She spat out an Anglo-Saxon expression that struck me as rather un-vicarlike.

'Oh well, they're bound to notice before long.'

In that top, I thought, they couldn't fail to.

We made tea in the newly cleaned vicarage kitchen. Perhaps, with hindsight, pink would have been highly appropriate. The Reverend Christina Monroe arranged her six-foot frame on a pine kitchen chair, leaned back and crossed her long legs.

'Now, Theo, tell me about the congregation. I want to know their names, their description, where they sit in church and their sensitivities. I don't want to offend anyone.' She suddenly gave a broad grin. 'Or if I do offend anyone, I want it to be deliberate.'

Tuesday 2 November

Checked on Chrissie today to see if there were any teething problems at the vicarage.

'Everything is hunky-dory,' she exclaimed. 'I even got my dinner brought to me by that nice woman with all the children.'

'Charity?'

'Indeed. Charity by name, Charity by nature. She brought me a heavenly chicken casserole, then we swapped recipes and I read a story to her little poppets – they're so sweet. Do you like kids, Theodora?'

Was very tempted to use the old W.C. Fields line that I could never manage to eat a whole one, but thought better of it. 'Mmmm,' I said through gritted teeth.

Wednesday 3 November

Myrna has given me what she refers to as a 'project' to do over the next few weeks. She insists it will help my personal development and increase my problem-solving ability. It is designed to assist in team-building and communication, skills which Myrna insists are essential to succeed in the modern office environment. She has written me a brief, which is anything but. It is forty pages long, outlining areas of concern and possible strategies for addressing them. My main area of concern is that I don't understand a word of it. We had an hour-long meeting where Myrna summarized the framework and scope of the project and described the interdependence between the departmental representatives involved. At the end, when she asked if I had any questions,

'Tell me again, what am I supposed to be doing?' would have made me look a complete idiot.

I will take the document home and study it.

Thursday 4 November

The church prayer meeting was rather better attended tonight than it has been for the past few months. For all his good qualities, Reverend Graves didn't have a lot of time for the weekly session where we prayed dutifully through the needs of the church and community. I think people would have been more disposed to attend if we had been praying for something more earth-shattering than Miss Cranmer's varicose veins and Mr Wilberforce's blocked drain.

Christina Monroe's approach was certainly a break from the norm. First, we prayed for world peace. Unfortunately, Mrs McCarthy's stage whisper could be heard ringing out, 'Of course, what we really need is a good war. That'd sort 'em all out.'

Later, we split into groups of four and had to think of one thing to thank God for and one thing to ask him for. Our foursome consisted of Gregory Pasternak, Mr Wilberforce, Charity Hubble and myself. Surprisingly, it felt quite comfortable to be in this small group and I thanked God for the new vicar. Amens followed from the other three, and then I asked him to help Ariadne. Charity asked if there was anything she could do for Ariadne, which was kind of her.

After the meeting, Christina Monroe sidled up to me.

'Um, Theo.'

'Yeees.'

'I don't suppose you're free around five tomorrow, are you?'

'I can arrange it. Why, are you having fireworks?'

'Mmm, could be.'

'What do you mean?'

'Oh, it's nothing. I just need a bit of help ... doing an inventory of the hymnbooks, and I wondered if you wouldn't mind giving me a hand.'

'OK,' I said suspiciously.

'Thanks. You're a pal.' She patted me on the shoulder then scooted off before I could say any more.

An inventory of hymnbooks? Why?

Friday 5 November

At five o'clock precisely, Jeremiah swept through the open doors of St Norbert's and strode up to Christina Monroe, who was pretending to count the hymnbooks. She shot me a glance. I had the uncomfortable feeling she had asked me to be there only in the capacity of a witness, just in case things got brutal. His watery eyes glowed with indignation as he looked her up and down, his gaze skimming quickly past her ample bust. 'And, Miss Monroe ...'

'That's *Reverend* Monroe, Mr Wedgwood, or you may call me Chrissie.'

'... and, madam, what, may I ask, leads you to believe you are qualified to be a priest in this church?'

'Well, there are many reasons I feel I am well qualified to be a priest. For instance, I have big ears for listening, big hands for helping, big knees for praying, a big heart for loving and, fortunately, I am blessed with a remarkably thick skin.'

Jeremiah bristled.

'That and my degree in theology, my ordination, my four years' curacy experience, the recommendation from the bishop, the request of this congregation ... oh yes, and the call of God.'

I resisted the urge to punch the air.

Jeremiah turned on his heel and walked out of the open door.

'Oh dear. Do you think I upset him?'

'It would be difficult not to,' I reassured her. 'I think your very existence upsets him.'

'Oh well, can't do anything about that. Seriously though, do you think he'll come round?'

'I think you will have a battle.' I admitted. 'He's only just come back after a dispute with the last vicar. You can always hope he goes again. Or disappears in a puff of righteous indignation.'

She shook her head vigorously. 'Oh no! The church desperately needs people like Jeremiah.'

'It does?'

'Yes, certainly. Our Mr Wedgwood is a passionate man. He knows what he believes in and will fight for it. He is "all out" for God. Not only that, but he is a doer. I found an old church directory when I was clearing out my desk. His name was all over it. He had been pastoral visitor and treasurer, he watered the flowers, assisted at funerals, mowed the lawns, preached the sermons, swept the paths and probably thousands of other things we don't even know about. And I'm sure he prays. I don't want to lose him.'

I just managed to stop my jaw hitting the floor.

'I know he's a bit old-fashioned. He probably finds it difficult to accept change, especially a female vicar. He probably expects to find my tights on the vestry radiator and for me to burst into tears and start throwing things from the pulpit once a month. But deep down, I can see he's a sweetie.'

I had never heard Jeremiah called that before.

Saturday 6 November

Decided to be straight with Kevin about not enjoying football. Obviously I don't want to hurt his feelings by telling him that his favourite pastime is marginally less interesting than sitting in a twenty-mile tailback on the M25.

'Kevin,' I wheedled.

'What?' enquired Kevin, looking up suspiciously from his newspaper.

'You know I'm supposed to be going to football with you this afternoon.'

'Yes, the crunch game of the season,'

'I wondered if you'd mind if I just gave it a miss this once. It's freezing cold and I really need to go shopping.'

'Is that need as in "I have no food and will starve to death if I don't buy some", or need as in "my already over-stuffed wardrobe will suffer if I don't buy another outfit to add to the hundreds of others I bought but don't wear"?'

'Cynic!'

'Anyone would think you didn't really like football and were only going along with me because I spent all that money on a season ticket.'

'Well ...'

Before I could finish the sentence, Kevin briskly folded up the paper and flicked it into the magazine rack.

'No problem, love. You go shopping and we'll grab a takeaway for tea. It would be a shame not to use the ticket, though.'

'Tom ... he's always saying that he would like to go to a match. He's a bit down at the moment, stuck at home with Ariadne ... This is the perfect opportunity. I'll ring him now.'

Rang Tom, who was trying to feed Phoebe, who was trying to feed herself.

'Well, it's a very kind thought, Theo, and it would be a relief to get out of the house and get some male company ... not that your sister's not good company ... Oh dear ...' Tom's voice trailed off as if he had uttered a heresy. 'Look, Theo, it's enormously kind of you to offer but you know that football's not really my thing.'

Oh Tom! Don't let me down. I couldn't face another afternoon on those hard plastic seats watching a couple of dozen blokes run from one end of a field to the other. 'Yes, that's right,' I said loudly enough to make sure Kevin heard me, 'there's a spare ticket and I think you deserve an afternoon off.'

Kevin started to look suspicious.

'I'm more of a quiet pint down at the pub sort of bloke,' said Tom.

'Going out for a drink afterwards? I'm sure Kevin would be game for that.' I covered the mouthpiece of the phone. 'Kevin, Tom suggested going down the pub afterwards. What do you think?'

'Yeah, great,' said Kevin, his suspicions abating.

'Good that's fixed then Tom, Kevin will pick you up at about two.'

'Oh. . . er. . . okay, if you insist.'

Just one problem, convincing Ariadne.

8 p.m.

Ariadne was a pushover. All I had to do was offer to take Phoebe out for the afternoon so that she could put her feet up. She really didn't seem to care less where Tom was.

We wrapped Phoebe in a pink nylon cocoon and I pushed her buggy into town. Shop doorways are just not designed for buggies. I hit so many people's ankles with my swivelly wheels that I felt I should have kept a tally on the side of the pushchair in the manner of First World War fighter pilots.

I bought a new outfit . . . it was a bargain, just better not mention it to Kevin. I also bought Christmas cards and a book for Ariadne, the latest one by her favourite author. Miraculously, Phoebe slept right through. We stayed until the shops closed, then we went home. Ariadne was still asleep when I rang the doorbell. Kevin and a slightly glowing but much-cheered Tom followed us in a couple of minutes later.

'That football match,' enthused Tom, 'what can I say? Utterly brilliant!'

I think this afternoon was a success.

Sunday 7 November

The Reverend Christina Monroe preached her first sermon today, the like of which has never been heard at

St Norbert's before. The church was packed with people from the village as well as St Norbert's regulars. Alfreda Polanski from the post office peered at the new vicar, proclaiming dejectedly that, 'She's nothing like 'er off the telly – you know, that Dawn French.'

Christina Monroe then managed, in the course of a twenty-minute sermon, to instruct her congregation eloquently and faithfully from the scriptures. She also managed to relate her tenets to everyday life, making reference to, as I recall, football, the construction of the box-girder bridge, slimming, *Star Wars*, model railways, golf and greaseproof paper. Old and young, cynical and convicted, flippant and serious, there was something in her sermon for everyone. In short, she knocked 'em dead.

Everyone, that is, except Jeremiah Wedgwood, who sat next to the organ, shaking his head and making copious notes. After the episode over the hymnbooks, I have the ominous feeling Jeremiah was not there for spiritual edification.

Monday 8 November

Have read my work project outline from cover to cover and still don't understand what I actually have to do. I am supposed to start it today. Perhaps I'll ask Tom this evening. He's good at that sort of thing.

He's found a job: nothing special, routine office work, but at least they have some money coming in.

Tuesday 9 November

So worried about Ariadne that I have asked Charity to come and see her. I have tried everything else to entice her out of her black moods but nothing works. I've tried chocolate, pizzas, copies of *Investors' Weekly;* not even a life-size cardboard cut-out of Mel Gibson I persuaded the man in the video shop to let me have would make her smile. Nothing has worked. Tom has tried to persuade her to go to the doctor but she stubbornly refuses. Her health visitor hasn't noticed anything wrong. Baby Phoebe continues to thrive but Ariadne seems to be ... well, fading away. Charity agreed willingly. Have I done the right thing?

Wednesday 10 November

Accompanied Charity to see Ariadne tonight. I know Tom is doing his best but I am getting desperate. Ariadne didn't appear to mind that I had brought the human equivalent of a horticultural propagator around, complete with three little seedlings germinating internally. In fact, Ariadne hardly appeared to notice we were there and seemed too low and tired to care about anything. Phoebe had just been bathed and was sitting in her pyjamas, propped up with cushions and surrounded with toys. She waved her arms and blew bubbles. I started to clear away the breakfast things and other clutter from the floor and coffee table. Evidently Tom was still at work.

'She's growing fast. She looks happy enough. Is she a contented baby?'

Charity knelt on the floor and spoke gently to Ariadne while looking at Phoebe. Ariadne raised her dull eyes but did not answer.

'How about you, Ariadne? Are you all right?'

Again Ariadne didn't answer, but a tear began to trickle slowly down her cheek. I am ashamed to admit that at this point I exited to the kitchen to make coffee. I did not feel equipped to cope with the strength of emotion in the room. Like a child who cannot bear to see a parent cry, I felt off kilter. The world was not as it should be. My emotional foundations were being shaken. Ariadne had always been strong for me, but I was shocked to find I had no capacity to feed it back to her when she needed it. I had run away. Those few feet to the kitchen might just as well have been a hundred miles.

When I returned with the pot of coffee and mugs, Charity was sitting on the sofa cradling Ariadne and rocking her like a baby as she wept. Phoebe, feeling left out, began to bawl. This emotion I could cope with, and I lifted her from her nest of toys and cuddled and rocked her too.

Charity spoke as if Ariadne wasn't there, which I suppose in one sense she wasn't.

'She needs to see a doctor now. Do you have a number.'

'Now?' I glanced at my watch. 'It's nearly half past seven. Is it that urgent?'

Charity gave me a look that indicated that it was. I handed her Ariadne's phone and address book. After a brief conversation, Charity bundled Ariadne into her coat and steered her out of the front door.

'You'll be all right with Phoebe?'

I nodded and Charity and Ariadne went. I had, it seems, done the right thing.

Thursday 11 November

Writing this with my eyelids held open with match-sticks. Tom returned from work shortly after Charity and Ariadne had left. He came into the lounge to find me holding Phoebe, and looked bewildered in the manner of earthlings in those science fiction films where aliens have performed body-swaps on their unwitting human victims.

'Charity's taken Ariadne to the doctor's,' I explained.

Tom ran his hand across his forehead. His face looked a mixture of anxiety and relief.

'I knew something was wrong. I just knew it. I told her to see a doctor. But would she listen to me? You know your sister!'

I knew her only too well.

'How did she take it? Did she protest?'

'Like a lamb. Just let Charity lead her out. Do you want some dinner?'

I tried to deflect the subject from Tom's guilt to something more mundane, like Tom's stomach.

'No, that's OK. You can go if you want to.'

I didn't want to. Tom and I sat talking for the two hours Ariadne and Charity were at the surgery and the two and a half hours after they returned and Ariadne was put to bed.

According to the doctor, Ariadne is suffering from post-natal depression. She has been given some tablets and an appointment in a fortnight's time, and has been recommended to rest as much as possible. Charity has kindly offered to pop round for a few days to see her.

Thank you, God, for friends like Charity.

Did I just say that? Must go and have a lie down.

Friday 12 November

I contemplated the 'Buff Envelope' walls of the vicarage kitchen as I hugged my mug of tea.

'Seriously, Chris, what made you decide to become a vicar? It can't have been easy, being . . . you know, a woman.'

'It's the outfit. That's what did it. Obviously designed with women in mind. Well, of course, the cassock – let's face it, it's basically a dress. Long and black, couldn't be more slimming if you tried. Long sleeved to cover up chubby arms, fitted to accentuate the waist and nice and warm round the ankles on chilly days. The surplice – designed to flatter any figure, hide all the lumps, bumps and spare tyres. No danger of visible panty-line in that. And the stole – a different colour for each season and you can get some with beautiful embroidery.'

She saw my face and let out a roar of laughter.

'I'm sorry. Seriously?'

I nodded.

'I just always felt that's what God wanted me to do. Simple as that! Ever since I was a small child I've wanted to be a minister. My parents were farmers. We always got taken to church at harvest and I felt so at home there, you could hardly drag me away. I used to sit in the pew with my little legs dangling – obviously I was a lot shorter then – admiring the stained glass windows, breathing in the flowers-and-furniture-polish smell, scrutinizing the vicar as he thanked God for the harvest gifts, and thought, yes, that's what I want to do. Of course, at first everyone laughed because I was a girl. But I stuck to my guns. I was sure the feeling came from God, and nothing, no amount of persuasion or careers advice, would make me change my mind. It seemed impossible but I held on and kept on believing, and gradually things changed. First came the arguments and debates and the campaigns, then finally women were being ordained. And ... here I am!'

She took a sip of her coffee and looked hard at me.

'Theodora, what does God want *you* to do with your life?'

I shook my head and stared into my empty mug. She had to ask. She just had to ask.

Saturday 13 November

Kevin's mum is away with her church choir for the weekend so Kevin and I decided to surprise her by tidying up the garden. Since Kevin's dad died she has had trouble keeping it under control. Kevin doesn't usually have time to do much more than steer the mower over the lawn occasionally and the whole thing had become overgrown and messy. Kevin is not exactly Alan Titchmarsh and I'm hardly Charlie Dimmock, not by any stretch of the imagination. Even so we managed quite a transformation.

Kevin's team was playing away and he was determined not to miss a second of the action so he had the earphones of his radio plugged firmly into his ears under his woolly hat. That made conversation impossible. This didn't matter as we worked in silence, punctuated only by the occasional 'Ooh!' or 'Ah!' or 'Yeeees, nice one my son!' from Kevin.

The morning had started crisp and bright, with the dawn frost still on the grass and spiders' webs decorated with diamonds of dew. By mid afternoon, a foggy darkness was descending. Our breath came out in frosty puffs. I remembered as a child walking home from school on winter evenings, playing 'dragons' and frightening the life out of little Ag with my 'smoke'.

I pruned the roses while Kevin mowed, clipped and dug. One bush was still putting on a valiant display of red roses. Obviously it hadn't been told that it was no longer summer. Kevin dug up a huge elder tree that was taking over one of the flowerbeds by the front gate. I cut down huge amounts of some kind of weed with twirly stems and white flowers that seemed to be trying to strangle all the other plants. We put it in a big pile so that Kevin could have a bonfire next weekend. He loves setting fire to things, bless him. He also cut back the ivy that was hanging over from next door. We were just finishing off and Kevin had written his mum a list of the jobs we had completed so that she could let us know if she wanted any more done. I went round to the front garden to collect the secateurs I had left under the rose bush. Suddenly I felt a presence behind me and I spun round to see a huge man in an overcoat by my left shoulder. I screamed and Kevin came racing round to the front of the house. He smiled and took a step forward, and shook the man respectfully by the hand.

'I'm here to see Eloise.'

'I'm afraid my mother is away for the weekend. She's with the choir.'

'Of course. I forgot. Would you tell her I called?'

'Certainly, I'll tell her, Brother Moses.' Kevin spoke deferentially. The big man walked back down the path. 'That's Brother Moses,' whispered Kevin, 'one of the elders at

Mum's church. They don't call him Moses for nothing. His word is law. He's been seeing rather a lot of Mum lately. Perhaps he's sweet on her. Come on, let's put this note inside and we'll get a curry on the way back to your place.'

Removed large unsightly elder from front garden
Cut down weed – will help you burn it later
Got rid of ivy hanging over from next door

Sunday 14 November, Remembrance Sunday

And everywhere, across the field, a sea of scarlet poppies spread,
Harsh-wrung from devastated earth where devastated bodies bled.

Monday 15 November

When Kevin came round this evening, it took several minutes before he could speak, he was laughing so much. Between gasps for breath, he told me that he had just been home to check on his mum – he had gone to work by the time she got back from her choir weekend. She had arrived to find Brother Moses on the doorstep again. She invited the church elder into the kitchen to make him a cup of tea. While the tea was brewing he had obviously caught sight of the note.

'"Eloise,"' Kevin boomed, in frighteningly accurate impersonation of Brother Moses, '"I never thought you were that sort of a woman. Burning weed – I would have expected better of you. And if that's what your family think of me, that I'm unsightly, better I just go and leave you alone."'

'And at that, Brother Moses got up and left! Mum just stood there, open-mouthed. It was only when we read the note again that we realized what had happened. Poor Moses! She had to telephone him to explain. The poor man thought he'd had his chips.'

I could imagine it. Brother Moses, so polite and digni-fied: it would take a lot of pouring oil on troubled water to restore that friendship. And I bet if Ivy from next door read the note, she wouldn't be too pleased, either.

Wednesday 17 November

Myrna has asked for a progress report on my project. Slight feeling of panic. Read it again. Must look up 'ceiling', 'leverage', 'ring-fencing', 'quorum' and 'outsourcing'. I have no problem with understanding the words in between, such as 'in' and 'the' and 'of' – which is good.

Thursday 18 November

Spent the evening with Ariadne so Tom could go out to his computer course. I left him my project outline and he has promised to do his best to help. Ariadne is still crying a lot and she seems to spend every spare moment asleep. I don't know what I expected. Depression isn't cured instantly, I know that. Even the doctor said it would take several weeks before we would see any real effect. It's just that with all the praying we are doing, it would be encour-aging to see a bit of a change.

Friday 19 November

From what I've heard, Chris Monroe seems to be shaping up admirably as the new vicar despite a few initial concerns from some more conservative corners of the parish. She wowed them at the children's party with her juggling skills and her impromptu leading of sixteen verses of 'The Wheels on the Bus', which included several verses I had never heard of before, such as 'the bell-ringers on the bus' who apparently go 'ding dang dong' and 'the vicars on the bus' who don't, contrary to popular belief, go 'hatch, match, dispatch'. At the Ladies' Golden Hour, which is supposed to be a Bible study-cum-tea party but is in reality a forum for the most malicious and improbable gossip in the parish, she appeared sympathetic and genuinely interested in Miss Cranmer's varicose veins and Mrs McCarthy's wartime reminiscences. Her sermons are sincere, practical and entertaining. She sings, bakes, paints, acts and is currently rewiring the medieval circuitry in the vicarage. Are there no ends to this woman's talents? Her energy seems endless and her enthusiasm boundless. I mentioned this to Ariadne, who muttered rather cynically over a mountain of baby-gro's, 'Well, she's not married.'

Monday 22 November

Clearing out junk from the dark recesses of cupboards in the flat, I have just found an unopened pack of Easter cards. I remember buying them last February, with good intentions. I can't remember whether that was in my evangelist phase or my missionary phase, but I was going to spread the gospel through sending Easter greetings. I even made sure the cards had pictures of churches or daffodils, or preferably both, rather than cuddly bunnies or Easter eggs. Unfortunately, I had decided to put them somewhere safe. Obviously, somewhere *so* safe it has taken me nine months to find them again. This is where my sister and I differ. If Ariadne had bought the cards, they would have been written and handed out three weeks before Easter. With me, they might just get there in time for Christmas.

Tuesday 23 November

Charity Hubble phoned me this evening in a terrible state again. She was cleaning out their budgie, Solomon, when Nigel came home, seven minutes earlier than expected, and the budgie flew out through the open door. Charity, Nigel and several of the Hubble children pursued Solomon up the street. Solomon, who is supposed to be extremely intelligent (according to Charity a sort of member of budgie MENSA), decided in his wisdom to fly up to the top of a huge oak tree and refused to come down. They called to him, waved millet at him, offered to buy him a new mirror, but to no avail. Solomon stayed at the top of the tree. With the amount of cats in the neighbourhood, not to mention owls, and considering the sharp frost that was forecast, nobody fancied Solomon's chances of making it through the night.

'What should I do, Theodora?'

I paused for a moment. Was I suddenly an ornithology expert? I looked across at the settee for inspiration, but Kevin was asleep in front of some kind of quiz programme.

'Well,' I said. You could try leaving a window open tonight and have his cage, stocked with his favourite birdseed, next to it. If he's as intelligent as you say, he'll know which side his bread is buttered and choose a warm cage over a frosty night in a tree.'

'Good thinking, I'll try that. Do you think it would be a good idea to put a "missing" notice in the newsagent's window?'

'Good grief,' I said. 'I know he's clever but I didn't know he could read.'

Wednesday 24 November

Tom phoned me at work about the project outline.

'Theo, I've read it from cover to cover and it is complete rubbish. It's full of jargon and has no clear objectives or ways of measuring outcome.'

'What am I going to do, Tom? She wants an interim progress report on Friday.'

'You seem to have two choices. You can either write a report which is equally incomprehensible and meaningless and hope she's so blinded by the jargon that she doesn't notice, or you can come clean and admit you don't know what she expects of you and ask for clarification.'

I groaned. I would have to bite the bullet. What's the worst thing that could happen?

Thursday 25 November

To Ariadne's for tea. She is finally starting to look better but, more importantly, she is talking now. I don't just mean the odd comment, but she is saying how she feels. It sounds odd but she tried to explain it to me. She said that she couldn't have asked for help because she couldn't put into words how she felt. Not only that, but she didn't actually *know* how she felt. It was beyond words. Her ability to communicate had completely ceased. She couldn't even talk to God; she just didn't have the words.

'But what about the people from your church? Didn't they help?'

'Not really. You're not allowed to be melancholy at our church. You must be "full of the joy of the Lord" at all times. Which is fine when you are. If they suspect your "joyometer" is not filled to the brim, you get prayed for. If that doesn't work, it must be demonic and you get delivered. If you're still not grinning like a Cheshire cat, you must be backsliding and they suggest you go off and get right with the Lord. As for depression, Christians are not permitted to get depressed. They'd have me throwing my tablets away and praying for "divine Prozac".'

I suspect she didn't mean it. I guess there was a lot of distress and the tail end of depression speaking, but I can't help believing there was an element of truth. If you are unhappy, anxious or worried, it's almost as if you're letting God down. 'Cast your burdens on me.' But if it's not working – and you can't say Jesus isn't working – it must mean there is something wrong with the person who is depressed. Double the guilt and anxiety!

Poor Ariadne!

Friday 26 November

The worst thing that could happen is that Myrna could sack me, that I could end my career in ignominy, that I would be unemployable, lose my home and family, take to drink and spend the rest of my days on a park bench conversing with pigeons. Help me, God.

4 p.m.

I am sitting here trying to drink coffee and stop shaking. At two o'clock I joined Myrna in the small interview room.

'Sit down, please, Theodora. Now would you like to take ten minutes or so to relate to me how you are progressing in your project?'

I took a deep breath. 'Well . . . the thing is . . . I'm sorry, Myrna, I'll have to come clean with you. I have read the outline a dozen times, I have asked the advice of friends, I have looked things up in manuals and office guidelines and I couldn't for the life of me work out what I was supposed to do. I know I should have come to you before now and asked for help but . . . I wanted to see if I could do it by myself. I'm sorry. Shall I clear my desk and fetch my coat?'

To my astonishment, Myrna grinned broadly. 'Well done, you have successfully completed the project.'

'What? But I haven't done anything. I don't even understand it.'

'Can you remember what I told you the aim of the project was?'

I cast my mind back. 'It was to do with team-building, problem-solving and communication.'

'Precisely! And the problem that you had was that I, as your line manager, had given you a task to do that you didn't understand. You have come to me and communicated this. I am now able to build the team by encouraging you and letting you know that you can always come to me to discuss anything which isn't immediately clear to you.'

'So the project outline . . . ?'

'Rubbish, tosh, gobbledegook, jargon, balderdash, complete twaddle! I'm impressed that it took you less than three weeks to work this out and admit you didn't understand it. The record is seventeen months. One employee kept writing "progress reports" every month that were just as incomprehensible as the original document. He eventually left to pursue a career in journalism.'

'This was all a sort of . . . test?'

'And you passed with flying colours. Remember, communication is the key. Here' – she handed me a little book – 'a souvenir. Why don't you go and get yourself a coffee? And well done.'

I left the little office, shutting the door firmly behind me. All of this had been a monumental wind-up. I looked at the book that Myrna had given me. It was *The Emperor's New Clothes.*

Saturday 27 November

Called in to the church office this morning to find the vicar looking uncharacteristically preoccupied. Her immaculately plucked eyebrows were furrowed and her glossed lips were pursed in an expression of bewilderment.

'What do you make of this?' She handed me two sheets of white notepaper with a tirade of personal abuse aimed directly at Chrissie and more general abuse aimed at the female sex. The writer had quoted 1 Corinthians 14:34.

Let your women keep silence in the churches: for it is not permitted unto them to speak; but they are commanded to be under obedience, as also saith the law.

The letter was unsigned but I recognized the handwriting immediately.

'Jeremiah Wedgwood,' we said in unison.

'What are you going to do about it, Chrissie?'

'Well, you can't deny it. Even though *we* take account of the historical context and interpret the passage differently, to Jeremiah, it is there, in black and white, in the Bible. "Women should remain silent in the churches ..."'
Suddenly she became animated. 'Theo, I've got an idea. Will you promise me that you'll go along with it, however daft it sounds?'

'Of course,' I said.

'OK then. We're about to give Jeremiah exactly what he wants.'

And she told me her idea.

Sunday 28 November

Most peculiar service this morning. Couldn't help wondering what God made of it. When Kevin heard about the plan he begged me to let him go to the service, saying it sounded like 'a right laugh' but I refused. You don't go to church to enjoy yourself!

The proceedings started with Chrissie opening the service with a little wave of her hand rather than the usual welcoming liturgy. Mr Wilberforce proceeded to give the notices as if they contained absolutely no punctuation whatsoever. As far as I can remember they went something like this: "Smorning's service is a normal Sunday service with Sunday schools and young people's work and we warmly welcome any visitors and would invite you to join us after the service for a cup of coffee in the hall only don't spill none 'cos that carpet's a beggar to get clean now this week's meetin's kick off with the normal Monday prayer meetin' only because of the WI annual get together will be 'eld on Tuesday instead ...' (here he paused for breath) '... and the meetin' for parents what want their little ones baptized will be held on Wednesday at the vicarage on Thursday and it bein' a third Friday the Scouts will be meeting at the usual time which is ...' (he paused briefly to study the notices sheet) '... well, at the usual time and if you usually go you'll know when that is.'

He made the banns sound like a free-for-all. I'm still not sure exactly who was marrying who – and, more worryingly, nor were the couples who were getting married. This was followed by the first hymn, indicated by the vicar in semaphore. 'And Can It Be?' sounded rather odd with only the men singing and with Gregory Pasternak valiantly trying to sing the women's part falsetto.

The peace was indeed far more peaceful than normal. The men shook hands noiselessly only grunting in acknowledgement. The whole affair was accomplished in a tenth of the usual time and without the usual hubbub. Jeremiah stood in the pulpit to preach. He explained that the vicar had dropped him a note indicating that she thought she might be coming down with laryngitis and would he please preach the sermon, based on whichever passage in the book of 1 Corinthians came to mind. Not surprisingly (and fortunately for Chrissie's little scheme) he had chosen chapter 14 verse 34. He gave his interpretation of this verse and went on to back it up with other scriptures, which, rather than enforcing his opinions of non-involvement of women in church, seemed to indicate what an important role they had in Jesus' life and ministry. During the sermon, he was interrupted several times by escaped toddlers who were being frantically beckoned back to the crèche by soundless but desperate-looking ladies.

Starting with the Virgin Mary, without whom, he grudgingly admitted, Jesus wouldn't have been born, Jeremiah proceeded to advocate that as Jesus had no female disciples, there was no place for them in the church, except perhaps making the tea, but certainly not preaching the sermon. He chose to ignore the facts that Jesus had many female followers – Martha and Mary to name but two – and that it was to the women that he first chose to appear after his resurrection. Despite Jeremiah's bias, the evidence in the book of Galatians points out that there is no distinction of gender, race or status in Christ. The many women St Paul refers to in his letters as backbones of the early Christian community didn't get a mention, nor did any of the great women of the Old Testament such as Esther, Ruth or Miriam. I was beginning to feel rather cheated and I longed to call out (something I had never done before) or at least whisper my criticisms to Mrs Cranmer, who was sitting next to me – something I had done frequently. But I stuck to the letter of the verse and Chris's instructions and kept silent.

Maurice Johnson stood up to lead the intercessions and prayers. Doris, who was due to do them, he explained, had been suddenly and inexplicably struck speechless. Maurice's brave attempt caused jaws to drop, especially when it came to praying for the sick. He gave far more detail about people's ailments than was strictly necessary, and I couldn't help but feel sorry for poor Jeremiah. Who wants the details of their haemorrhoids shared with seventy of their closest friends?

Monday 29 November

Visited Chrissie to see what kind of fallout there had been from yesterday's act of insurrection. She said that she had called Jeremiah to apologize for setting him up and to call a truce. Throughout the phone conversation, Jeremiah had been calm and dignified, which worried Chrissie even more than if he had been abusive. She provided me with a stunningly credible impersonation of Jeremiah's strangled voice.

'"Miss Monroe" – he always refuses to use my title "Reverend" – "I know not what you hoped to achieve from that debacle, that . . . travesty of what passes for worship in the House of God these days, but be assured, madam, that the bishop will be hearing about this."'

(Rumour has it that the bishop has a special file for letters from Jeremiah. Digger once suggested that there would soon be enough to justify their own filing cabinet.)

'Theo, do you think I went too far?'

I looked at Chrissie as if over an imaginary pair of glasses. 'We'll just have to see.'

Tuesday 30 November, St Andrew's Day

Today is the feast day of St Andrew. I looked him up on the Internet. Of course, St Andrew was a fisherman, one of the first disciples to be called by Jesus. Apart from the accounts in the Bible, there is a great deal of legend and tradition surrounding his life and death, which may have been in the form of crucifixion on an X-shaped cross, hence his flag. The relics of St Andrew, including his disembodied head, continued to travel widely and may be at the root of the connection with Scotland. Yuck! It doesn't inspire me to sainthood.

December

Wednesday 1 December

Myrna and I have spent the afternoon standing on chairs and hanging Christmas decorations. Apparently 'celebrations are good for morale'. I put down newspaper so that her heels wouldn't damage the light ash finish of my Slogbrot and moved my cactus to a safer position. By four o'clock my arms were aching, I had broken two nails and I never want to see another piece of tinsel as long as I live.

Thursday 2 December

Strange phone call from Nigel Hubble this evening. Apparently Charity is extremely upset because she has just received a Christmas card from their budgie Solomon, who went missing just over a week ago.

'Don't be daft. How could a budgie send a Christmas card?'

'It's not the budgie! It's someone's idea of a sick joke. Charity's a sensitive little thing and this sort of prank causes her a great deal of distress.'

'I don't see what I can do about it.'

'You mean it wasn't you?'

'Of course not! Why would I do a thing like that?'

Nigel was immediately apologetic. 'Well, if you do hear of anything, you will let me know? I can't bear to see Charity so troubled.'

Began to wish I had done it. 'Sensitive little thing' and 'I can't bear to see Charity so troubled.' Yuck, pass the bucket.

He put the phone down and I smoothed my ruffled feathers. What on earth could have made Nigel think I was behind the budgie's Christmas card? I'm not that clever.

Friday 3 December

Jeremiah has left the church again. No one is particularly surprised. At least he left quietly this time. There was no *High Noon* shoot-out with the vicar in front of half the village. He just wrote an eighteen-page letter outlining the faults of the church in general and its incumbent in particular, packed his bag, locked his front door and disappeared. Alfreda Polanski from the post office reported seeing his red sports car disappearing off towards the A20. That was on Wednesday and nobody has seen him since. I think the only reason he came back to St Norbert's in the first place was to leave again.

Saturday 4 December

Pre-Yuletide de-junk. Took some boxes of books, clothes and ornaments to the charity shop and had a good dust around all the bits that don't usually get dusted. Eloise would have been very impressed. I even tidied the airing cupboard. Went off to make a coffee and returned to find the most enormous spider I have ever seen, crouching just outside my bedroom door. I am not normally arachnophobic but the sight of this menacing creature, which must have crawled out from under the hot water tank, was enough to make me squeal with shock and send me scuttling back to the kitchen. I peeped around the doorframe. The spider was dusty, and what must have been lumps of old web combined with fluff made it look as though it was wearing heavy boots. There was something defiant in its stance. I tried shouting and waving my arms at it – after all, spiders are supposed to be timid creatures – but this audacious arachnid refused to budge an inch.

I decided to do what any modern independent woman would do in this position, and phoned Kevin. Fortunately, as his team was playing away, he was working in the next street, and he had just finished the job when I rang. I heard him telling the householder with great delight that he had to go round to his girlfriend's now, as she was scared of a spider. He was still chuckling when he jogged up the stairs to my flat.

'Go on, then, where's the poor little thing?'

'It's outside my bedroom door, by the airing cupboard. It won't go away, it's like it's . . . squaring up to me.'

'Probably paralysed with fear, more like,' he sniggered. The smile soon disappeared from his face when he saw the spider.

'Blimey, that's big!'

'I told you. Do something about it.'

'What do you want me to do?'

'I don't know, chuck it out of the window or something.'

'If you think I'm going near that thing ...'

'All right then, kill it ... No, don't kill it, that would be cruel ... Yes, kill it. I just want it out of here.'

Kevin disappeared into the lounge and returned with my copy of *The Complete Works of William Shakespeare*, which he promptly dropped on the spider.

'What did you do that for?' I squealed incredulously.

'You wanted me to kill it. What was I supposed to do, play it your Dire Straits albums and bore it to death?'

'But squishing it like that seems so ... barbaric.'

We both stood in silence, staring at the book.

'Do you think it's dead yet, Theo?'

'I'm not picking up the book to check. You do it.'

'I'm not picking it up. Dropping a book on it like that might have enraged it.' He withdrew to a safe distance.

'For goodness sake, it's a house spider, not a Siberian tiger.'

'If you're so brave you pick it up.'

'Look, one of its legs is sticking out ... Oooh, it's moving!' I joined Kevin in the kitchen doorway. 'We can't just leave it. That would be cruel.'

'More cruel than dropping a book on it?'

'We ought to put it out of its misery,' I said decisively.

Kevin took two steps backwards, ran down the passage like a long-jumper and leaped, landing heavily with both feet on the book.

'There, that's fixed it. No more spider.'

The noise was enough to bring Mrs Barrie scurrying up from the flat downstairs.

'Are you all right? I heard a noise.'

'Fine, thank you, Mrs Barrie. Just a spider.'

'A spider? What were you doing, teaching it to pole-vault?'

We left the defunct spider under the book and went out Christmas shopping. This must be a sign of our new 'engaged couple' relationship, Kevin agreeing to come shopping with me without having his arm twisted up his back. The only problem occurred when we passed the television shop in the High Street. I'd got to Woolworth's before I realized Kevin was still standing in front of the window watching football. He genuinely doesn't know he's doing it.

When we returned home, I bribed Kevin with some chocolate biscuits to lift up the book. There underneath was a fragile, dried-out little scrap, like a broken twig or blades of grass. That was all that was left of our fearsome spider. I felt sorry and ashamed. Kevin laughed at me as I hoovered it up with tears in my eyes.

We sat cuddled up on the sofa watching the late film. I noticed that Kevin kept glancing towards the cupboard where I kept the vacuum cleaner.

'What's the matter with you?'

'Theo, you don't think it could sort of ... revive in there?'

Sunday 5 December

Lunch at Mum and Dad's. Mum was trying out her Cretan Christmas range and we were treated to Hortosoupa followed by Kotopoulo Kokinisto with Tzatziki and Melitzanosalata, then Vasilopitta, in preparation for New

Year, and all washed down with tiny cups of coffee served glykos. No idea what we ate but it all tasted very nice.

Over lunch, Kevin told Dad about the spider incident.

''Course you have to watch out. Can be very expensive getting rid of spiders.'

'How come?' I asked.

'Well, you remember Auntie Blodwyn?'

'No, who's she?'

'You know Auntie Blodwyn, married to Uncle Clifford, they had a farm over Beaumaris way? She had everything beige in her house.'

'Yes,' I said, even though I still didn't have the faintest idea who he was talking about.

'Auntie Blodwyn cost Uncle Clifford £500 all because of a spider.'

'What on earth did she do?'

'Your auntie was on her own in the farmhouse one afternoon. Uncle Clifford must have been getting ready for the afternoon's milking. She'd dozed off in the chair, right, and woke to find a huge spider hanging from a web from the ceiling right above her face. She screamed – well, you would, wouldn't you? – and kind of limbo-ed herself out from under the spider. Then she called for Clifford but he couldn't hear her, see, on account of his being down in the bottom field. She was so shook up by the experience that she didn't rightly know what she was doing and she got Clifford's twelve-bore, the one he used for shooting rabbits, from inside the grandfather clock and blew the little blighter to kingdom come. Trouble was, she brought the farmhouse ceiling down with it. Clifford had heard the bang and came running up the house to find Blodwyn standing there in a state of shock, covered in plaster, with the smoking gun still in her hand and a great big hole in the farmhouse ceiling. Well, she tried to tell him about the spider, but of course he had her certified. Things were never the same at the farm after that. "Five hundred quid for a ruddy spider," he used to mutter. But he kept the gun locked up after that, I can tell you.'

Monday 6 December

It is becoming apparent exactly how many different 'behind the scenes' jobs Jeremiah did. The vital work of snuffing the candles after the candle-lit carol service (and sometimes during the service if the flames came too close to one of Miss Cranmer's floral festoons, with their trailing ribbons and tinder-dry pine cones). Jeremiah handed out the hymnbooks, he organized the carol singing, made the Christingles and phoned the garden centre to order the colossal Christmas tree to stand at the front of the church. Chris had decided to allocate Jeremiah's former jobs among other members of the congregation. On the whole the system worked fairly well, except when some bright spark would interject, 'Oh, Jeremiah used to do it that way,' or 'Jeremiah always did it like this,' and then duck to avoid the imaginary right hook which should have followed. By and large, most things got done. Maurice Johnson snuffed the candles and the garlands did not burst into flames. The hymnbooks got handed out at the door accompanied by a greeting a good deal friendlier than Jeremiah himself ever gave.

I discovered the only slight drawback in the system when I arrived at St Norbert's to help Chris prepare for

Sunday's carol service and to drop in the Christmas tree she had asked me to collect from the garden centre on my way home from work. (I wasn't very popular on the bus, I can tell you.)

For a short while we had a verger called Mary to help prepare the church, but she only lasted a few weeks. Pleasant enough young woman. She and her husband, Mike, were living in temporary accommodation in the village while their house was being extended. She was second assistant verger at St Pollock's, a neighbouring church. She and Mike attended the relatively lowbrow St Norbert's rather than travel the eight miles or so to their usual church. Mary was expecting, and the old ladies were rubbing their hands with glee at the prospect of a new baby in our church at Christmas time. However, the couple were able to move back to their own home sooner than expected and the old ladies were cheated of their opportunity to admire and coo. I heard later that the verger Mary had a baby boy, the verger Mary had a baby boy, the verger Mary had a baby boy . . .

When I walked into the church I was struck with the impression that I had just entered a Scandinavian pine forest. The entrance, by the font, was blocked with trees propped up against the pew-ends. The whole church smelt of pine and I had to battle my way through the prickly branches to get up the aisle. I counted them: one, two, three, four . . . including mine, five trees. Was Chris trying to set up a sanctuary for lost, strayed or abandoned Christmas trees? She must have heard me coming because I was suddenly aware of a murky figure on the other side of the forest.

'What's all this for?' I asked, peering at the vicar through the branches.

'What?'

'All these trees.'

'Ah, you noticed.'

'Noticed! You need a machete to get to the altar.'

'Bit embarrassing, really,' she confessed. 'You see, Jeremiah usually ordered the tree. So I left Maurice a note asking him to do it. Doris found the note and, thinking Maurice had forgotten, ordered a tree. Only ...'

'Maurice hadn't forgotten.'

'Right. Also, Jeremiah apparently had an agreement with the nursery and they rang to ask me to collect St Norbert's regular tree. I couldn't really refuse to pay for it ...'

'That's this one?' I indicated my spiky ward.

'Yes.'

'That accounts for three of them. Where did the rest come from?'

'Well, Mr Wilberforce donated one and I couldn't really turn it down, could I?'

'And the fifth one?'

'Ah yes. I sort of bought that one in case everyone else forgot.'

'I see. What are we going to do with them all?'

'Well, we can't keep them.'

'But which ones do we get rid of? People will get very touchy if you don't use their tree. They'll see it as a snub.'

'I know. I don't want to upset anyone.'

'Hang on!' The thought struck me like an express train. 'One tree is pretty much like another. If we don't tell anyone,

everyone will assume it's their tree, and no one will be any
the wiser and no one will get upset.'

'Brilliant!'

We lined them up like a sort of tree identity parade and
examined them carefully for any distinguishing features.

'Hmm. That one's a bit bent over at the top,' I said,
peering like Sherlock Holmes.

'That's my one,' offered Chrissie. 'That'll do for the vicarage. I've paid for it, anyway.'

'Good. The rest look fairly similar.'

'This one can stay at St Norbert's. I'll just thank everyone separately for their tree, and as long as they don't all
get together and discuss it, I think we can get away with it.
Now, what's left? That one can go in the church hall for the
playgroup.'

'Worthy cause . . . and Doris already knows there are
two trees.'

'And we can give this one to the school.'

'There's still one left.'

'Have you got a tree yet, Theo?'

'No, but . . .'

'Take it – it's yours.'

'Well, thanks, but . . . Thanks.'

I wrestled the tree home and set it up in the lounge of
my little flat. The only space big enough was the centre of
the lounge, and even then you had to walk sideways, half-
sitting on the furniture, to get around the room. Watching
television was only achieved by peering through dense
woodland.

'Excellent tree!' exclaimed Kevin when he called in
later. 'It's so . . .'

'Big?'

'Brilliant! You need more than those few scrappy decorations. Hang on a minute.'

He disappeared off downstairs to the van, appearing again a few moments later with arms full of tinsel and garlands and baubles.

'I was going to use them in the van,' he explained. 'But you can have them.'

We spent the rest of the evening giggling like children, decorating the tree and sometimes each other. When we had finished, we sat down together on the sofa and looked at the tree. Although, to be honest, it was difficult to look at anything other than the tree. It did look magnificent.

Just think, this time next year, we'll be married with a place of our own.

Tuesday 7 December

Spent this morning with Myrna planning our Christmas party. This year, the divisional director has decided to assign each department a budget and let them decide what kind of party to have. The thinking behind it seems to be that the company will avoid having to close down entirely for a day for one giant booze-up, as usually happens. Instead we will stagger the parties, each department choosing its own date and venue, while the other departments continue working efficiently and all the punch-ups, fumbling behind filing cabinets and being sick into the fax machine can be avoided. A good idea in principle, the only problem being that the department I work in consists of only two people, Myrna and me. I tried to point out to her that it wouldn't be much of a party and suggested that we join forces with Accounts, but Myrna would have none of it.

'Why should we let them cramp our style? We have been given a free rein to do exactly what *we* want to do. We could go to an art gallery, have a meal, blow it all at the pub – whatever we like.'

I tried to point out that I didn't like any of them and was all for pocketing the cash and going home early, but Myrna was determined.

Wednesday 8 December

Myrna and I have decided what we want to do for our Christmas party. Yesterday we both sat and imagined our perfect day. Then we discussed it. Myrna's really into arts and culture and wanted to visit a gallery. She makes me feel like a real plebeian. She asked me what I thought about the French Impressionists and I said that, in my opinion, nobody had come close to Rory Bremner and she laughed at me. So I had a brief sulk disguised as a coffee break. Then we talked some more. My perfect day would involve staying in bed all day and eating chocolate. Decided not to share this with Myrna but instead talked about relaxing, being somewhere warm and eating wonderfully cooked, beauti- fully presented food. Myrna said she wanted something to stimulate mind and body and to promote her personal growth. We decided that a trip to Hawaii was out of the question, and a jog round Highgate Cemetery incorporating a tour of Karl Marx's grave would be no fun in December.

This morning, Myrna arrived brandishing a leaflet for a local health spa, Viscount Court. She had booked us a

'Pamper Day' each. It was expensive and we would have to make up the shortfall out of our own pockets, but I had to admit she had come up trumps. The day includes a sauna and massage or facial, use of the gym, swimming pool and jacuzzi. Lunch in the bistro is also part of the package. The walls seem to be made of marble, with plants and murals between the decorative fountains and waterfalls. The leaflet showed slim, attractive women in bikinis or fluffy white bathrobes lounging or standing around. It is booked for next Wednesday and I must admit I am rather looking forward to it.

Thursday 9 December

Of course, going to a health farm rather than sitting down for a blow-out lunch will carry the advantage of being an excellent kick-start for my pre-Christmas diet. Going to Greece in October, especially on a so-called 'culinary tour', has played havoc with my thighs. I look as if I am permanently wearing jodhpurs. I will be able to swim in the pool and, if I'm feeling very keen, use the gym. Feel a bit guilty that I last went more than a year ago. I don't think my 'pecs' ever fully recovered. The food is bound to be delicious yet healthy. Viscount Court is noted for its excellent cuisine, or so it says in the leaflet.

Saturday 11 December

Went Christmas shopping. So did the rest of the world. Managed to buy most of the main presents plus the obligation presents and some reserve presents for anyone who unexpectedly gives me a gift, so that I am not socially embarrassed by being unable to reciprocate.

They looked rather swamped under my mammoth Christmas tree. Toyed with the idea of wrapping up large empty cardboard boxes, just for show, but that seems a bit dishonest.

Monday 13 December

Bought a bag of chocolate Christmas decorations on the way home from work but accidentally ate them before I got as far as hanging them on the tree. Must buy some more tomorrow before Kevin finds out.

Tuesday 14 December

Having just examined the state of my swimming costume I am about to embark on an emergency shopping trip to purchase something which doesn't look as if it has been parboiled. The sad soggy grey item would have accommodated a fully grown elephant, it had stretched so much. All the fluffy white bathrobes in the world would not have compensated for that outfit. The shops will still be open for Christmas shopping so I will nip out before dinner.

9.30 p.m.

Have you ever tried to buy a swimming costume in December? Several shop assistants laughed at me. Eventually I really lost my rag in the department store that boasts that it sells everything, and had one of those conversations with the world in general that makes people stare at you and leave at least a 10-metre gap around you.

'Does nobody ever go swimming in December?' I asked no one in particular. 'Do all the swimming pools close for the entire festive season?' I was warming to my subject. A woman pulled a small boy into her skirts. 'Perhaps there's an unwritten law which says that swimming costumes never wear out during winter. Is there?' I glared at a group of teenage girls. 'Where oh where can I go in the whole of this town to buy a swimming costume, or do I have to swim in my bra and pants?'

An elderly man who was braver than the rest chipped in. 'Have you tried the sports shop, love?'

I thanked him politely and proceeded to the sports shop, where I managed to buy an extortionately expensive professional costume. Still, it would do my image as an athlete some good.

Saw the same man as I was coming out of the sports shop. 'Did you get one, love?' he enquired.

'Yes, thanks,' I said cheerily. 'I had to get a one-piece, though. Couldn't find a bikini anywhere.'

'I had exactly the same problem myself,' he confided. Which was a worry.

Wednesday 15 December

Arrived at Viscount Court Country Club and Spa at ten o'clock, clutching my new costume and my best towel, the one without holes in and still roughly the same colour as it was when I bought it. Myrna was already there, sitting in a sort of palm court dressed in a white towelling bathrobe and sipping a cocktail. She looked like Basildon's answer to Greta Garbo.

'Morning, Theo dahling, can I get you one?' She nodded at the red and orange creation in a tall glass that was bristling with fruit and paper umbrellas.

My constitution struggles with alcohol at any time of day so cocktails before elevenses were definitely out of the question.

'Just a coffee, please, Myrna.'

'Certainly, dahling.' She waved at a waiter in a white jacket and ordered my coffee, which arrived promptly in a large silver coffee-pot. Beside the gold-rimmed cup were two wafer-thin almond biscuits. I made a mental calculation as to their calorific value. They were so thin, surely there was hardly room for any calories in them.

'Is there anything else I can get you, dahling?' asked Myrna as she ordered herself another cocktail. I fervently wished she would stop calling me 'dahling' in that affected way. She never did it at work and it was beginning to drive me insane.

Coffee and cocktails finished, we went to the changing rooms to prepare for our swim and jacuzzi. To my dismay, the ladies' changing room was communal. Myrna slipped her robe elegantly from her shoulders to reveal her black one-piece with gold-coloured chain straps and a little gold chain belt. I was still fully dressed; in fact I hadn't even taken off my coat. I glanced around for somewhere discreet to change. Even the showers were open to view. I couldn't cope with the vulnerability of being naked in front of my boss so I grabbed my bag and nipped off to the ladies.

I emerged to find that Myrna had acquired me a bathrobe and had staked her claim on two sun-loungers near the pool. She had also obtained another cocktail. I decided to start as I meant to go on and slid elegantly into the pool. I was very contented with my forty lengths, although my legs felt a little wobbly when I got out.

'Coming for a jacuzzi?' I called to Myrna. I hoped she'd say no as I didn't relish the prospect of sharing a puddle of bubbling water with my boss. There is such a thing as personal space.

'You go ahead, dahling,' she replied in a slightly slurred fashion. So I did. Then I went in the sauna, then the steam room. Meanwhile, Myrna lounged on the lounger, seemingly relaxed, watching the world go by. Several other guests at the spa wandered past, wearing the white uniform of fluffy towelling bathrobes. They were all women, ranging in age from late twenties to early seventies.

I got chatting to a woman who had recently recovered from a nasty operation and had come to the spa to recuperate. She told me how the doctors hadn't expected her to survive and how she was so grateful for every day. A buxom blonde called Lynda had been given a 'Pamper Day' as a birthday present and was having a break from her four children. Thought about Ariadne – perhaps a day being pampered would be just what she needs to help her get over her post-natal depression.

Ordered another coffee and joined Myrna on the sun-loungers. I lay back in the tropical warmth and thought of the grey foggy day outside. My watch said 11.45. I thought of all the Christmas shoppers bustling along the High Street. I thought of Ag and Cordelia preparing to fly back from Peru. I thought of spending Christmas with my family. I thought of Phoebe's first Christmas. I closed my eyes for a moment and began drifting off in the heat. Then my coffee arrived. Myrna had one too and we lay there, in companionable silence, sipping our coffee and pretending to be somewhere exotic.

'So how are you spending Christmas, Myrna?' I asked, just to be sociable.

'Alone, as usual,' she sighed.

'Oh, I thought you were married, I thought you were Mrs Peacock.' I blurted, realizing that after working with Myrna for over three months I knew next to nothing about her.

'Divorced,' she answered bitterly.

'I'm sorry, I didn't know.'

'No reason why you should. I don't talk about it. Some things are better left unsaid. I just try to forget about my ex-husband – the swine.'

'I wasn't prying, honestly,' I said, back-pedalling frantically.

'I know you weren't. It's just that sometimes the secrets, the silence, the concealment becomes too much . . .' Myrna turned her head away.

I know that my track record in counselling had not been exactly first class but here was my opportunity to make amends. Here was the chance to put into action my sympathetic, caring side. I figured that it would do my career prospects no harm and maybe God was giving me a second shot at a 'listening' ministry.

'If it helps to talk . . .'

'Oh, I wouldn't like to burden you . . .'

'I've got broad shoulders,' I said, and indeed they looked extremely broad in my racing-cut swimsuit.

'Of course, I wouldn't want it to go any further.'

'I promise I will be the soul of discretion.'

'I know you will.'

We both lay back on our sun-loungers and Myrna began to tell me her story.

'I first met Mike in 1985. He was in the Royal Navy and had just come back on leave. He looked so handsome in his uniform . . .

'. . . so you can see why things are so difficult for me today.'

I sat up with a start.

'Yes, yes, of course I can, very difficult indeed.' I glanced at my watch. It was nearly a quarter to one. My right foot had gone dead. I stifled a yawn.

'Not tired, are you?'

'No, not at all.' That was the truth. I had just spent the last hour asleep. Myrna's secret was safe with me – very safe. I had nodded off and hadn't heard a single word she had said.

It was time for lunch. We changed out of our damp costumes, put on our white bathrobes and went into the bistro. We had a lovely lunch. I had warm bacon salad served on a bed of endive and wild rocket and Myrna had smoked salmon. It was rather strange to be sitting there in a dressing gown in the middle of the day with no underwear on.

After lunch Myrna opted for a facial which left her looking rather flushed and shiny. I had a neck and shoulder massage. The masseuse pummelled and kneaded me with her strong fingers.

'You're carrying rather a lot of tension in your shoulders. Is there anything in your life at the moment that might be causing you stress?' she asked.

Where do I start? With my punctilious boss who has just confessed her deepest darkest secrets but I don't remember what they are? With my depressed sister struggling to keep her life and family together? With my church and family, which are supposed to be places of respite and harmony but seem more fraught than my work life? The fact that I am trying to sell my flat and buy a house? The fact that I am getting married in 136 days and I haven't even bought the shoes yet?

'Oh, just everything,' I said.

Thursday 16 December

Myrna didn't mention the secret that only she and I shared. I was hoping that she'd sort of drop a hint so that I could sound knowledgeable if it ever cropped up again. When I mentioned this to Ariadne, her theory was that God, knowing my character and weaknesses so intimately, deliberately and supernaturally put me to sleep so that there was no possibility of me blabbing. Pretended to be outraged at the suggestion but secretly realized that both God and Ariadne know me too well.

Friday 17 December

Took a day off work so Mum and I could collect Ag and Cordelia from the airport. We got there early and stood in the Arrivals area craning our necks as plane after plane disgorged their weary, suntanned contents. First a planeload of exhausted-looking families trudged through, the children clutching their newly acquired Donald Ducks, Goofies and

Mickey Mice. Orlando, I thought. Next was the Fort Worth plane. It was strange to see so many British people wearing Stetsons.

'Those hats will go straight to the back of the wardrobe when they get home,' commented Mum.

Finally the flight from Lima flashed up on to the board. Mum and I must have looked like two eager giraffes as we stretched our necks to catch a glimpse.

Ag looked taller and more handsome than ever. I could hear Cordelia several minutes before I could see her. She looked even more voluptuous than the last time I had seen her and was wearing an extremely tight red dress with green and yellow ruffles around the bottom, reminiscent of a flamenco dancer's costume. They both had Peruvian suntans. After we exchanged hugs and greetings, they gave Mum a poncho and me a model llama. I was surprised to see that Ag and Cordelia were still holding hands. Disgusting – they've been married for over six months! Their Peruvian project involved Ag writing a series of articles for the *Guardian* and Cordelia filming a documentary on lost civilizations for the Discovery Channel. They have now agreed to settle in England for a while. I wonder if they'll start a family. If they do, I'm sure Cordelia will have it videotaped for Channel 4.

Saturday 18 December

Took Cordelia to spend the day last-minute shopping in Oxford Street. It nearly killed me, what with the crush of the crowds and Cordelia's overbearing personality.

Everything was either 'exquisite' or 'loathsome' according to Cordelia. We ended up buying nothing.

So much for the season of goodwill! I have been sworn at, trodden on, poked with umbrellas and squashed into tube trains. Next year I'm doing all my Christmas shopping on the Internet.

Sunday 19 December

Carols by Candlelight service. All my family, except Dad, came. Even Kevin put in an appearance with his mum. They all wanted to see our lady vicar do her stuff, and I'm delighted to say she didn't disappoint. I had to restrain Cordelia from giving Chrissie a round of applause at the end of the sermon. Although how she managed to get Frank Sinatra, washing machines, the virgin birth, adenine, guanine, cytosine and thymine, the best way to grow delphiniums and the story of grace and redemption into a twenty-minute sermon, I'll never know.

As usual, I managed to sit behind a string of Hubbles. To my amusement, twelve-year-old Neb was singing all the wrong words to the old carols. Charity was either pretending not to notice or so genuinely caught up in the festive celebrations that she was oblivious.

'While shepherds watched their flocks by night . . .' the congregation warbled.

'While shepherds washed their socks by night . . .' rang out Neb's treble tones.

Kevin nudged me and grinned. He was enjoying every minute. Neb's brothers and sisters were starting to giggle and shift in their seats. Ag and Cordelia just sat gazing into each other's eyes.

'We three kings of Orient are . . .' chorused the assembled throng.

'We three kings of Leicester Square, selling ladies' underwear . . .' crooned Neb.

'He's going to get caught in a minute,' I whispered to Kevin as Neb belted out in his choir-boy voice, 'Star of wonder, star of night, Jesus caught his pants alight.'

'Charity will hit the roof if she hears him. You know how obsessive she is about scriptural accuracy in the carols.'

'Well, you do something,' muttered Kevin.

I reached over the pew-back and poked Neb with my rolled-up carol sheet. 'If your parents catch you, you'll be in deep trouble,' I hissed. He gave me a look of such utter contempt that I battled with the desire to shop him immediately to Charity, but the next carol had started. The organ reverberated out the first chords of 'Hark the Herald Angels Sing'. The first verse was begun with great gusto, especially by Neb. Unfortunately, at the precise moment Neb decided to replace the words 'Glory to the new-born King' with 'Elvis Presley's still the king', his voice dipped two octaves. His treble tones were no longer concealed among the voices of the other worshippers and the words boomed out in a magnificent baritone.

The singing stopped.

The organist hit a discord.

Charity's head swivelled round and her mouth hung open.

Neb went scarlet.

Nigel extracted himself from his seat with the choir, took his son by the collar and marched him down the aisle in front of the silent congregation. I'm sure Neb Hubble will remember the moment his voice broke for the rest of his life.

Monday 20 December

Nobody has been round to view my flat for two and a half months. The estate agent blames Christmas. I don't know why. It's not as if it's a surprise, it comes around at the same time every year.

Saturday 25 December, Christmas Day

Eloise, Ag, Cordelia, Kevin, Ariadne, Tom, Phoebe and I all had lunch at my parents' house. Didn't make it to church this morning as I didn't manage to surface until eleven. Still, I had been to the midnight service. It seemed strange sleeping in so late on Christmas day. Not that many years ago I would have bounced into my parents' bedroom at five thirty to open my presents.

We all helped out with cooking the Christmas lunch – at least that was the idea. Mum, rather rashly I thought, invited us all while in a particularly good mood (I suspect initiated by one glass too many of ouzo) and then couldn't or wouldn't back down. We all brought a contribution to the lunch with us. Tom brought some herby roast potatoes, Kevin provided the crackers, Eloise prepared some yams and sweet potatoes, Mum excelled herself with roast turkey (Greek style) and I made a chocolate Victoria sponge cake, because I can.

The small kitchen became overcrowded as we all jostled for space to serve our offerings, and tempers started getting frayed. Eventually we ended up with a rota system, which worked quite well. Cordelia insisted on sitting next to Kevin at the table and Ag just smiled indulgently as she flirted outrageously with my fiancé. She squeezed his cheeks so that he looked like a Cabbage Patch doll.

'Isn't he lovely?' she said, 'just like a young Bob Marley.'

They're going to see Cordelia's parents tomorrow, thank goodness.

Sunday 26 December, Boxing Day

Particularly pleased with the presents that I received this year. They struck a nice balance between useful and pointless, and the chocolate count was up on last year's record by one box and two bars.

Wednesday 29 December

Visited Miss Chamberlain's grave this morning. As I cleared away a few weeds and left a bunch of flowers, I still can't imagine her in the cold earth, she was too much alive. Thought I caught a glimpse of Jeremiah Wedgwood's car when I arrived but I may have been mistaken. Nevertheless there was already a small bunch of pink carnations on her grave.

Friday 31 December

There is going to be a fancy dress party at the vicarage tonight and the theme is 'Cops and Robbers'. Kevin is a fan of the American cop shows from the seventies and once even had a red car with a white stripe painted up the side. He is going to carry one wooden ski and the star from the top of the Christmas tree, and I will have a cardboard box, made to look like a rabbit cage, and borrow one of Phoebe's toy rabbits. I wonder if people will guess who we are.

January

Saturday 1 January, New Year Holiday

Everyone groaned at our 'Starsky and Hutch' outfits at the party, but it was a great success. Just managed to drag myself out of bed to find that Ariadne had stuck a Post-it note on my fridge door with a little poem on it.

'For some reason this made me think of you,' she'd written.

I made my resolutions on the last day of December
And wrote them on this Post-it note so that I would remember
To eat more fruit and vegetables and fewer chocolate bars
To hoover every evening and clean inside the car.
I resolved to cut out boozing, no more wine and no more beer,
I resolved to go out jogging twice a week, not twice a year.
I said I'd read my Bible and sit in quiet to pray.
I kept my resolutions ... to the end of New Year's Day.

Why should it make her think of me?

Monday 3 January, Bank Holiday

Resolutions on hold as I have come down with a streaming cold. Sat in bed feeling sorry for myself in a sea of paper tissues. Didn't go to church yesterday and Chrissie rang me to find out why. I explained but she was far from sympathetic.

'Ugh, keep your virusy carcass away from me, then.'

I can see why she delegates the pastoral visits.

Tuesday 4 January

Struggled into work today to look virtuous. Myrna got so fed up with my sniffing that she sent me home. Spent another day in bed. Kevin was conspicuous by his absence. He can't stand being around me when I'm ill. Perhaps I'll stamp on his foot when it gets to the 'in sickness or in health' part of the wedding service and see how he likes it.

Wednesday 5 January

Woke up feeling a bit better today so I decided to go back to work. Met a now enormous Charity on the way to the station and she offered to pray for me. It seemed churlish not to let her although it felt rather peculiar having what appeared to be a two-woman Revival meeting outside the newsagent's. After rather more 'casting out' and 'rebuking' than I would have opted for I actually felt a lot better.

Thursday 6 January

Starting diet today in preparation for wedding. I know the wedding is less than four months away and I haven't even started looking for a wedding dress in earnest, but whatever size would fit me now, I want to get married in a dress that is at least two sizes smaller. By starting the diet now it is a realistic possibility by the time I walk up the aisle.

Sat there at lunchtime psyching myself up to eat the cottage cheese and grated artichoke salad I had carefully prepared at 6.30 this morning. After the train journey and several hours fermenting in a centrally heated office, it looked less than appealing. Myrna passed on her way to do something vitally important and sneered at my salad.

'There's more to healthy eating than cottage cheese, you know. Dairy products make mucus. Why don't you try the health food shop? I'm sure they could suggest something.'

Healthy eating, who said anything about healthy eating? I just want to get thin.

Friday 7 January

I was reading a magazine article on the train entitled 'Vitamins – Your Tiny Allies'. The article explained the health benefits of vitamins and listed the types of food that contain them. I was particularly interested in vitamin C, which can apparently help to prevent colds. The article recommended eating as much citrus fruit as possible.

Hmm, I wonder how much vitamin C there is in a chocolate orange.

Saturday 8 January

Kevin has just finished a big plumbing job and received a bonus from the contractor for finishing on time and within budget. Bless him, he's offered to take me out for a slap-up meal to celebrate. After shivering in the stands all afternoon, the prospect of being wined and dined seems a hundred times more appealing than the healthy alfalfa and mung bean salad I was intending to prepare.

We arrived at the restaurant to discover that one of Kevin's ex-girlfriends, Dolores Armstrong, was working there as a waitress. A smile sprang to Dolores' lips as soon as she saw Kevin and just as quickly froze, then vanished, when she saw me. She sashayed off to the kitchen and a small man with bulging eyes and a wide grin showed us to our table. Kevin seemed to have developed a nervous cough and kept swivelling his head towards the kitchen.

'What's the matter?' I hissed.

'Nothing,' coughed Kevin.

'It's her, isn't it?'

'Who?'

'What's-her-name Armstrong! All hair extensions and legs up to her armpits.'

'Oh, Dolores. Is she here?'

I kicked him under the table.

Frog-man returned to take our order. I requested fish and Kevin went for the steak. I ordered some red wine and we held hands across the table. Our tryst was suddenly interrupted when Dolores brought the food. She leaned over Kevin so that her bust was at his eye-level and placed the plate seductively in front of him.

'You must be the beefsteak,' she said as she shimmied past Kevin.

She crashed a plate down in front of me with such force that it nearly broke in half.

'And you're obviously the trout.'

Kevin looked as if he might be about to laugh so I kicked him again to be on the safe side.

'Hey, what did you do that for?'

'For looking at her like that.'

'Me? I've done nothing. Dolores and me, that was finished years ago.'

'She doesn't seem convinced. She's flirting outrageously with you.'

'Really,' said Kevin, swivelling his head to face the kitchen.

'Why did you break up, anyway?' I asked sulkily.

'You've seen her. She's scary.'

'And I'm not?'

'Your brother isn't seven foot tall with metal teeth and doesn't head up the Sidcup Gangstas in his spare time, when he's not strangling cows at the abattoir.'

'Oh, I see.'

'And if you think she's scary, you should meet her mother.'

I saw his point. I concurred that the relationship between Kevin and Dolores had probably run its course.

The rest of the meal passed pleasantly enough, with Dolores stopping only briefly to glare at me or to squeeze past Kevin.

Dolores reluctantly served us the dessert.

'Your sweet, Kevin,' she simpered. Straightening up, she contemptuously thudded my Tarte au Citron down on the table. 'And you,' she sneered, 'must be the tart.'

Monday 10 January

Ariadne did it. She went back to work today. She seemed a bit shaky as we stood on the platform and waited for the train. For a moment I thought she was going to lose it and bolt, but she took a deep breath and arm in arm we got on the 08.14 to Charing Cross. I gave her a hug before we went to our separate offices, Ariadne declining my offer to meet for lunch.

'No,' she said, 'I'm all right. I'm going to make it.' She took a deep breath and we turned back to back like combatants beginning a duel. I looked around after I had walked a few paces but Ariadne had disappeared into the crowd.

I thought about her and prayed for her all day. Myrna inquired as to whether I was 'off with the fairies'.

When we met up on the station platform after work Ariadne was full of it. She had slipped back into her office as if she were putting on a familiar jacket. She even criticized me for carrying my lunch and book in a carrier bag rather than a briefcase. I wouldn't have minded but it was a Harrods carrier bag.

'It looks so . . . unprofessional. Don't you want to make a good impression?'

It was wonderful to have the old Ariadne back.

Tuesday 11 January

Just as I was going out for tea at Ariadne and Tom's, I bumped into Charity coming up the path. She was wearing what appeared at first sight to be a tarpaulin but I think was some kind of maternity raincoat. She looked as if she should have a sign hanging down her back saying 'Wide Load'.

'Come in a moment, Charity.'

'But you're about to go out . . . I should have rung first.'

'Don't worry, I was just going to my sister's. Tom's promised to do me a low-cal Chicken Chasseur . . .'

'How is the poor man, having to cope with all the household responsibilities now your sister is back gratifying herself at work?'

The hairs on the back of my neck started to rise but I managed to stay calm.

'He's fine. He's having a great time. He's given up work and Ariadne has finally gone back to a job she loves and excels in, and she'll be home to see Phoebe before she goes to bed every night. They just do things differently from you, Charity. And . . .' I added with relish, 'of course we shouldn't judge others.'

'It's not natural for a man to be at home with the children. He's the hunter, he should be out in pursuit of food to provide for his family.'

'Running round with a spear like Nigel does, you mean?'

'That's not the point,' she said, looking a little flustered. 'Anyway, I came to show you this. What do you make of it?'

She handed me an envelope. I pulled out a small piece of paper and a photograph. The photo showed a blue budgie wearing a paper crown with a party blower to its beak. In the background was a line of people doing a conga. The slip of paper read, 'Happy New Year from Solomon and all his new friends.'

I concealed a smirk.

'Oh, I know it's supposed to be a joke but I find it really hurtful. Either someone has kidnapped Solomon and is subjecting him to all sorts of inappropriate company or poor Solomon is dead and they have used a stand-in budgie to double for him. Oh poor, poor Solomon . . .'

Charity started sobbing into a handkerchief. I put my arm around her and directed her up to my flat. I made her a cup of tea and sat with her until she calmed down. The Chicken Chasseur would have to wait.

'Charity, I have no idea who is doing this or why, but I'll do my best to find out. Meanwhile try not to worry. Remember Jesus' words in Matthew's Gospel: "Are not two sparrows sold for a penny? Yet not one of them will fall to the ground apart from the will of your Father." So I'm sure God's got an eye on Solomon.'

Wednesday 12 January

Today was quite possibly the worst day of my life.

It started badly when I discovered that an overnight power cut had left the display on my clock radio flashing at 03.28. It was in fact 08.43, approximately three-quarters of an hour after I should have left for work. Toyed with the idea of phoning in sick but Myrna (who, I keep reminding myself, is really a very nice lady) is keeping a close eye on my absence record. I rushed my shower and cleaned teeth and brushed hair at the same time. Very difficult as one is up and down and the other is just downwards. Ended up looking like a haystack in a hurricane with toothpaste down my jacket. Spent the journey trying to think up a plausible excuse for being late.

Failed. Decided to tell the truth. Sounded as if I had made it up anyway so needn't have bothered. Myrna obviously didn't believe me. As she gathered up her papers for a meeting I heard her mutter something about good organization being the key to efficiency.

Resolved to tidy my desk to impress Myrna with my efficiency but unfortunately muddled up the out-tray and the in-tray. I ended up doing one lot of work twice (shows how much attention I pay to my work) and spent the whole afternoon on the phone explaining why yesterday's work was still outstanding. I am not finding efficiency very efficient.

The new temp started today. He is younger, cleverer and already more popular than me.

To compound my misery, I just found Declan's emergency supply of trick rubber biscuits,which were hidden in a box-file in case he got the sudden urge to play a practical joke on a visitor.

I can't imagine Myrna serving anyone fizzy sugar, dissolving teaspoons or rubber biscuits.

I really miss Declan.

Thursday 13 January

Have been doing some research into the new temp while he is away on his induction course. Managed to bribe

Carole in Personnel with a packet of bourbons and she let me see his file. He is called Covenant Blake. He is twenty-two and has just moved into the area. He is extremely well qualified and experienced, and I have discovered that he is earning more than me even though he is officially my junior. Have a feeling that he and I are not about to become best buddies.

Saturday 15 January

Dad is helping me to be environmentally friendly with my gigantic Christmas tree. I took down the decorations on Twelfth Night but the monstrous fir tree has been maliciously shedding needles all over my living-room carpet ever since. I'm expecting a post-Christmas boom in the housing market and I do not want potential buyers to be confronted with a towering, naked tree. As we struggled down the stairs with it, Dad embarked on one of his stories.

"Course, your Auntie Myfanwy was into all this "green" stuff.'

'Who is Auntie Myfanwy?'

'You know, lived down near the bakery at Porthmadog. Terrible facial hair; had to shave twice a day.'

'I'm sure you make up half of these aunts.'

'I can show you photos.'

'If she's got that much facial hair, I'd rather you didn't. Anyway, what about green Auntie Myfanwy?'

'Well, you see, she used to go on these marches in the sixties, like. Ban the bomb, save the whale, you know the sort of thing.'

I nodded through the branches.

'Well, once she went on an anti-whaling march. She'd made her own banner and everything. Now what she had meant to say was "STOP THE SLAUGHTER" but one of the "S"s must have dropped off in the train. Poor Auntie Myfanwy ended up marching along carrying a banner that read "STOP THE LAUGHTER". Of course, it had just the opposite effect. Everyone fell about. That was the end of Auntie Myfanwy's campaigning. After that the poor old whales just had to fend for themselves.'

Monday 17 January

I have just discovered that Covenant Blake is a Christian, and not just an ordinary Christian but one of the super-spiritual sort, the sort whose first words were not 'Mama' and 'Dada' but 'propitiation' and 'predestination'. He's the sort who would have his own healing ministry at the age of four and a half. In fact he's probably already got his invitation to heaven in copperplate script with gilt edging sitting on his mantelpiece. I've been watching him. He has just said grace before drinking a cup of coffee and I notice he's stuck a little shiny fish symbol to the back of his office chair. Just think, I'm supposed to be his line manager. I have the horrible feeling that if I suggest anything he doesn't agree with, he'll have me cast out.

Tuesday 18 January

Kevin will be working away for most of this week. He was recommended for a job close to Portsmouth and is leaving tomorrow morning. It's a holiday cottage belonging to a bloke called Zippy. Kevin did some work on Zippy's London flat and received a personal recommendation. Zippy is part way through renovating the place and intends to hire it out as a luxury holiday home. It is in a pretty village, close to the sea. Kevin will be sleeping in the cottage while the work is going on and is taking Jez, who is a carpenter, and Kev 2, the electrician, to complete the renovation. The three of them are planning to spend the evenings fishing. I pretended to sulk because I was not going.

'It's work, love. True, we'll have a few beers and that in the evenings, but even if you could get the time off work you'd be dead bored.'

'I could be your "mate". Hold your spanners and bend your pipes and all that.'

'No, thank you,' said Kevin, a little too quickly.

He's coming round for breakfast before he leaves tomorrow.

Wednesday 19 January

Had to buy some sugary breakfast cereal especially for Kevin. As I munched through my healthy bowl of what Kevin kept referring to as 'hamster food', he poured out his third helping of Kaptain Krunch's Sugar Stars.

'Have you seen what's in that stuff?' And I proceeded to read out the list of ingredients. 'What on earth are "mono and diacetyltartaric acid esters of mono and diglycerides of fatty acids" when they're at home?'

'Dunno, but they taste good.'

'And have you ever read the nutritional information?'

'No, but I'm sure you're going to tell me.'

'This is per 100 grams . . . Did you know it has 380 calories? And look at this: protein 9, carbohydrate 75, fat 5, fibre 5 . . .'

'. . . but fibre goes through on aggregate!'

Does he ever think of anything else?

Thursday 20 January

On a whim I called into the pet shop on the way home from work. They had several blue budgies, bright-eyed and twittering, in their aviary. I chose the wisest-looking one and bought it, along with a cage. I will decide later whether to tell Charity the whole truth or whether to make up a rather inventive little story, designed to make me look heroic and, at the same time, explain how the bird that used to be able to recite the Nicene Creed was suddenly unable to say 'Good morning'. The story would involve me gallantly rescuing Solomon from the clutches of Mrs Barrie's moggie and how, tragically, the shock of the encounter had made him lose the power of speech.

I hung the cage in the kitchen and wished the budgie goodnight.

Friday 21 January

Was still considering the ethics of the budgie-switching scam when I had another visit from Charity and several little Hubbles. I hustled them into the lounge and shut the kitchen door. I didn't want potential Solomon II to reveal his presence. That would have been too difficult to explain. Seated on the sofa, Charity showed me a postcard of

Nelson's ship, HMS *Victory*. There, clearly visible in the rigging, was a small blue bird wearing an eye-patch. The card read, 'Kiss me, Hardy. Who's a pretty boy, then?' and was signed 'Solomon'. Charity was beside herself.

I have a visit to make on Sunday.

Saturday 22 January

Viewed a house on my own this morning. It was a dreary little box on a depressing estate. It was cold, smelt strongly of dog and had a motorbike parked in the hall. I didn't make an offer.

Went home to my nice warm comfortable flat and told the budgie all about it. He didn't seem very keen, either. It has just occurred to me that I seem to communicate better with a dumb bird than I do with my fiancé, which is a bit of a worry.

Sunday 23 January

Arrived at Kevin's house at 8.30 this morning. Eloise let me in and I waited in the hall. Kevin was still in bed; he'd only got back from Portsmouth at two o'clock this morning. I made a cup of tea while Eloise shouted up the stairs. Kevin emerged a few minutes later looking sleepy and dishevelled.

'Theo, it's lovely to see you so *early*.'

'Have you missed me?'

''Course I have. I was going to ring you but I got back really late, you know.'

'So what sort of things did you get up to with the other two "musketeers", then?'

'You know,' he yawned. 'Lots of work, bit of fishing . . .'

'Any sightseeing in Portsmouth?'

'Maybe . . . What are you getting at?'

I picked up the tray of tea and went towards the dining-room door. 'Let's just take our tea in here, shall we?'

Kevin flung himself in front of the door. 'Er, no . . . let's go into the kitchen, it's warmer in there.'

I thrust the tea tray into his hands. Eloise gave him a reproachful look as she elbowed him aside and opened the door to the dining room. I marched in and drew the curtains. A blue budgie in a cage popped its head out from under its wing and blinked its bleary little eyes.

'I . . . I can explain . . . it was just a joke. I didn't mean any harm.'

Eloise stood with her arms folded and tutted her disapproval.

'Have you any idea how upset Charity is? You must have been listening when she was telling me he had flown away. Solomon meant the world to her. That was a cruel and insensitive thing to do.'

Kevin hung his head.

'I take it that isn't the real Solomon?'

'Bought it in a pet shop in Sidcup. I suppose you want me to go and make it up to Charity.'

'You can try. I don't know how she'll take it.'

'I'll go now.' He shuffled out to the hall to get his coat.

'Hadn't you better take this?' I held out the cage containing Solomon II.

4 p.m.

Charity accepted Kevin's apology and the new budgie with more grace than I would have expected. She commenced elocution lessons for 'Ignatius' immediately, which involved sitting by the cage and repeating the Lord's Prayer twenty times. She also intends to play him Billy Graham tapes to counteract any 'influences' to which he may have been subjected while in Kevin's care.

Monday 24 January

Everybody is laughing at Covenant Blake because he is a Christian. Everyone at work knows that I am a Christian and no one has ever laughed at me because of it. How come he is being persecuted for his faith and I'm not? It's just not fair!

Tuesday 25 January

Covenant has started handing out tracts at work. Disturbingly, although I agree with almost everything that is in the leaflet, I had an almost overwhelming desire to shove it up his nose. He doesn't seem to realize I'm a Christian too. What a horrible thought! If he finds out that I'm on the same side, he'll want me to join in with his office evangelization scheme. I've worked here for nearly fifteen years and have never yet evangelized anybody. Yes, I've been happy to talk to people when they've asked me, and when Margaret in the canteen lost her husband we prayed together, but on the whole I've left well alone. Covenant is definitely not of the same mind. If he knew I was a fellow pedestrian through this 'vale of tears', life would be even more unbearable than it is now. (Actually, can something become more unbearable? Surely it is either bearable or it isn't? Oh, I know what I mean.)

To avoid the possibility of anyone letting slip, I have just been round and begged them all not to let Covenant know about my faith. As a guarantee of compliance with my request, I have threatened to shred the pay records of anyone who lets on, so I think I've got it covered.

Wednesday 26 January

I'm getting quite attached to the budgie. I've never really had a pet before. When we were children, Dad insisted that all animals were either workers or wildlife or, failing that, food. He resented spending his hard-earned cash on feeding another mouth. He said that he already felt as if he lived in a zoo. The nearest we got to having a pet was when Ag brought home the school gerbil for the half-term holiday. He'd left the cage open 'to give it some fresh air' and Gordon had escaped. We searched high and low for the rambling rodent but to no avail. Ag was distraught when we had to return the empty cage to school. Gordon's whereabouts were only discovered six months later when Dad went to put on his wellington boots. Needless to say, it didn't make him any more amenable to the idea of having pets in the house.

Thursday 27 January

Had a bad dream last night. I dreamed that I had arranged the wedding service but had forgotten to tell Kevin. I had also forgotten to book a car or buy a dress. In my dream, I had to wear jeans and go to the church on the bus. The bus was late and when I arrived at the church, all the guests had got fed up and gone home. I woke up in a cold sweat and didn't stop shaking until I got to work. Must make a list and tick things off as I do them so that nothing gets forgotten on the real day.

Friday 28 January

Went armed with a list of things to do for the wedding when I picked Kevin up this evening. Just as Kevin was searching for his keys, Eloise came down the stairs wearing a beautiful black dress, make-up and jewellery and a hat with a feather in it.

'Well, well, who is this glamorous lady? I didn't know Diana Ross was in town.'

Eloise blushed and giggled. 'Get off with you. Jus' because a girl wants to make an effort once in a while . . .'

'Honestly you look fantastic. Are you going somewhere special?'

'Not really, just the prayer meeting.' Just then there was a ring on the doorbell. Kevin opened the door.

'Ah, it's my chauffeur. I'll just get my handbag and I'll be right there.'

'Good evening, Brother Moses,' said Kevin. 'I hope you are feeling well.'

'Fine, just fine, thank you for asking.'

The stilted conversation continued while Eloise checked her lipstick, adjusted her earrings and smoothed her hair. Finally she was ready. She took Brother Moses' arm and he led her down the front steps.

'Just you have her back by midnight,' called Kevin to Brother Moses' broad back. I could detect the hesitancy in his voice, unsure of how the big man would take the joke. Moses turned and grinned the broadest grin imaginable at Kevin.

'Well, well,' I remarked after Kevin closed the door, 'looks like ours may not be the only wedding on the cards.'

He nodded.

'He's very different from Dad,' mused Kevin. 'Dad was such a quiet, mild man and Moses is so . . .'

'Scary?'

'Exactly. And Mum's been on her own for so long. I hope she knows what she's doing.'

'I think she's old enough to look after herself.'

Saturday 29 January

My list has 272 separate items on it, all of which need to be done before we can get married. Felt so depressed last night when I got home that I resorted to sticking my finger into the tub of cocoa powder and licking off the concentrated comforting chocolateyness. I woke up this morning feeling a little more positive, and by ten thirty had reduced the list to only 238 items.

Monday 31 January

Got cornered near the lifts by Covenant Blake at lunchtime. After years of evading Charity Hubble, anyone would have thought that I would have mastered it by now.

'Ah, Theodora, I've got you at last. Anyone would think you've been avoiding me.'

I smiled weakly, willing the lift to come. 'As if!'

'Well, now I've found you,' he said, 'I would like to take the opportunity to give you this leaflet. Have you thought about your eternal destiny?'

My eternal destiny seems to be standing here waiting for this lift, I thought. I shrugged noncommittally.

'Well, if you could find the time to cast your eye over this little leaflet ... and you know if you have any questions, you can always ask me.'

I smiled again and took the leaflet. Mercifully the lift arrived and I stepped in. I waved a cheery little wave to Covenant as the door closed. Unfortunately the lift was going up and I wanted to go down, so I ended up travelling from the first floor up to the thirteenth then all the way back down to the ground. I was mortified when it stopped again on the first floor and the doors opened. Covenant was still there so I waved again, brandished the leaflet as if to say, 'I'm enjoying reading it already,' and pressed the button frantically until the doors closed again.

I met up with Ariadne for lunch at Gianni's Café.

'What's that?' asked Ariadne, pointing at the crumpled leaflet I was still clutching. I handed it to her and she read aloud, ' "Wondrous ways of God", "victorious living", "eternal refuge" – and what's this? "Stand before the judgement seat"?'

'Covenant Blake – he's a sort of super-Christian. Works at our office. I think he's trying to convert me.'

'With this?' snorted Ariadne. 'It's full of the most appalling jargon and clichés.'

'He doesn't know I'm already a Christian and I intend to keep it that way. Isn't it a pity that the truth about Jesus is hidden by all this . . . language?'

'I suppose every group has its specialized language, whether it's trainspotters or world religions.'

'I'd like to rid the world of Christian jargon. That way people could see what really matters.'

'I know what you mean,' Ariadne agreed. 'The terminology can be confusing. When I was little, I used to think Jesus was a tortoise.'

'What?' I exclaimed, wondering if Ariadne's juvenile confusion could have been the product of an over-ambitious object lesson.

'Well, just before the Lord's Prayer, the vicar always says, "As our Saviour tortoise, so we pray . . ." '

February

Tuesday 1 February

Had another worrying dream last night and woke up feeling totally exhausted. I've been reading about Joseph (without his Amazing Technicolour Dreamcoat) in the Bible and I'm now wondering if *my* dreams contain a message. What if God is trying to tell me something?

Wednesday 2 February

Tea with a much happier Ariadne and Tom tonight. She really is back to her old self now that she has returned to work, and Tom is blossoming, being allowed to run the house and family and look after Phoebe without Ariadne's constant criticism. While Ariadne changed Phoebe and Tom finished getting the Spaghetti Bolognese, I decided to broach the subject of dreams.

'Ariadne . . .' I wheedled.

'Yeees.'

'Do you think dreams can have meanings?'

'Yeees,' she replied, wrestling Phoebe's arm into her pyjamas while pretending to eat her pudgy baby fingers.

'Do you think I should buy a book about interpreting dreams?'

'Well,' interjected Tom, 'I read a little about the meanings of dreams when I was going through my parapsychology phase.' Ariadne shot him a withering glance. 'Of course, that's before I met your sister.'

'Go on, Tom,' I urged, 'what did the book say?'

'Well, it depends a lot on whether your dreams are one-off or recurring. The recurring variety has more significance.'

'Mine are definitely recurring.'

'Good. Then, the dreams can be grouped. Do any of them involve being chased by animals or being naked in public?'

'Er . . . no. Should they?'

'Not really, just that mine did – related to feelings of insecurity, apparently.' Ariadne sent him another withering look. 'Don't have them now, of course. Wouldn't dare feel insecure.' Ariadne threw a cushion at him and they both laughed.

'Would it be easier if I just told you about my dream?'

'Go ahead. I'll see if I can remember anything about the meanings.' Tom leaned forward in his chair with his fingers steepled like a yuppie Clement Freud.

'Well, the dream usually starts at home. I'm late for something and I can't find my handbag or my keys or my shoes. I'm looking everywhere and it's getting later and later but I can't leave the house. Sometimes I've forgotten to do something really important and only remembered when it's too late. Then sometimes I'm trying to catch a bus or train but I get held up and I just see it pulling away but I still need to get to where I'm going and I try to ask people but nobody will help me and I've got no money . . .' I paused for breath. 'Do you think there's a hidden meaning in all this? Is God trying to tell me something?'

'Hmm,' said Tom, thoughtfully.

'I mean, do you think it relates to my life?'

Ariadne could contain herself no longer and let out a roar of laughter.

'What's the matter with you?' I huffed. Tom still looked deadly serious but Ariadne was howling like a hyena at the Comedy Store.

'"Do you think it relates to my life?" My dear sister, it *is* your life. You are dreaming that you are always late because you *are* always late. No analysis needed.'

I looked to Tom for support but he just shrugged. I wish I'd said I dreamed about being chased by gorillas or going to church naked, I would have felt less humiliated.

Thursday 3 February

Just read back through yesterday's entry and realized that I inadvertently put Clement Freud when in fact of course I meant Sigmund. Is that what they call a Freudian slip?

Friday 4 February

Walking back from the station, I rounded the corner to see Kevin's van parked outside my flat. He was practically bursting with excitement.

'I've found it, I've found it – the perfect house!' he blurted. 'I've made an appointment with the estate agent to see it straightaway.' He practically pushed me into the van. 'Hop in. You can look at the details on the way there.'

I settled into the van's passenger seat and squinted at the photocopied sheet. I had to admit the house did look very promising. It was in a suburban area, further into London than we had been considering but close to the station. There was parking for the van and my car, and the house itself, part of a long Edwardian terrace, looked clean and cared for. It had two bedrooms, a nice big lounge, fitted kitchen and double glazing. It also had central heating (vital on cold winter mornings) and a compact back garden with a patio area. It sounded ideal and was within our price range.

'It only came on the market this morning,' enthused Kevin. 'It's my . . . er . . . our dream home.'

Kevin seemed to be taking a strange route to get to the house. Up the motorway, through a tunnel, across a housing estate . . . I was sure we'd gone a long way. When we finally pulled up outside the house, the road looked rather familiar.

The house was indeed lovely. It was too dark to see the back garden properly but the owner, a single man in his early forties, spoke of his love for the house and his reluctance to sell it. Unfortunately his job was moving to Oxfordshire and he would have to move with it. He described the house as handy for all local amenities and possessing a magnificent view. As he said this he winked knowingly at Kevin. Kevin pretended not to notice. The man, who was called Geoff, described the neighbours; a single man called Tony on one side and recently divorced

Derek on the other. He said there was a little shop on the corner that sold fifteen different brands of beer and giant-sized packs of pork scratchings. When I asked about the nearest hairdressers he just shrugged. It was all I could do to stop Kevin making him an offer there and then. He stomped out to the van in silence.

'Yes, I agree it's the best we've seen by far, but we shouldn't rush into it. We haven't even seen it by daylight. The roof could be falling off for all we know ... Look, I don't want to be negative but we must approach this logically and professionally. Why don't you give him a ring when we get home and say that we'd like to see it again ... say, tomorrow afternoon?'

'Match,' said Kevin sulkily.

'Oh, and of course buying a house isn't more important than football,' I said sarcastically. 'OK, tomorrow morning.'

Kevin grunted his agreement.

I opened the van door and started to get in. 'Oh,' I said. 'I've just remembered, I've run out of bread. I'll just nip up to that little shop he told us about on the corner. I won't be a minute.'

'No!' screamed Kevin getting out of the van and rushing round to stand in front of me on the pavement with outstretched arms to block the way.

'Why on earth not?'

'Er ... too dangerous!'

'Dangerous, round here? What dark perils are awaiting me between here and the corner of the street?'

'You never know ... a woman alone at night. Anything could happen.'

'Get out of the way, you daft thing.'

'I mean it,' he said menacingly.

'If it's that dangerous, I certainly don't want to live here,' I said, starting to climb back into the van.

'Well, maybe it's not that dangerous. I'd just rather you didn't go on your own.'

'You come with me and protect me, then,' I said.

Kevin suddenly yawned and looked at his watch. 'Goodness me, is that the time? We're missing ... *Coronation Street*. Quick, let's go.'

'But you hate *Coronation Street* ...' I tried to look him in the eye but he kept glancing away. 'Kevin, what are you hiding?'

He hung his head. 'Well, you were bound to find out sooner or later. Come on, I'll take you to the shop.'

We walked past the rest of the neat little Edwardian terrace and stopped outside the shop. The houses ended abruptly as just around the corner loomed a monster of an edifice. A gigantic fence painted bright scarlet stretched as far as I could see into the gloom that surrounded it. Part way along the fence was a bank of turnstiles. Giant floodlights sprouted on poles above the stands. They were dark now but when they are lit up it must be like the land of the midnight sun. I stood with my mouth hanging open. That's why the road looked familiar. That's why we had approached it by such a bizarre route. That's why all the neighbours were single men. That's why Kevin was so eager to make an offer. I couldn't speak. Did Kevin really think that I wouldn't notice, or if I did that I wouldn't mind?

'Sorry, love, I wasn't trying to keep anything from you ... I just thought if you saw the house first and fell in love with it that you might ...'

Obviously, something in my look told him that further attempts at explanations were undesirable and he shut up. We drove home in silence and I didn't invite him in for coffee.

Sunday 6 February

Kevin came to church with me this morning in what I suspect was a feeble attempt to make up for the house next to the football club. He tried once more to raise the subject but I stood my ground. There are some issues upon which one simply cannot compromise.

Monday 7 February

In the interests of self-improvement (and as a result of the humiliation I suffered over the dream interpretation at the hands of Tom and Ariadne) I have decided to tackle my lateness problem. Last night, I set my alarm clock to go off ten minutes earlier than normal and put my wristwatch five minutes fast. I have decided to streamline my morning routine by applying my make-up after I arrive at the office, and I will catch the train that departs eight minutes before the one I normally catch.

7 p.m.

Unfortunately, new punctuality regime did not work according to plan. Alarm went off as predicted but got so confused that all the clocks were telling different times that I didn't dare have any breakfast, not even a coffee. Caught the train but discovered that although it left eight minutes earlier, it stopped at every homestead and hamlet between

here and London and actually got me there eighteen minutes later. Rushed into the office pale-faced with wild bed-
hair, and attempted to dart straight into the ladies before
anyone saw me. Unfortunately, it was not before Myrna
had seen me and I had to hide in the cubicle making retch-
ing noises.

I returned to my desk.

'My goodness, you look terrible!' Myrna observed. 'Look
at you, all pale and with those enormous dark rings under
your eyes. And is that some kind of boil on your forehead?'

I sat there, nodding dumbly, stomach rumbling and suffering from severe caffeine withdrawal.

'You poor thing. You'd better go home, dear.'

She called me 'dear'. She'd never called me 'dear' before.
I gathered my coat and handbag and hauled myself out of
the office trying to look as sick as possible. As soon as I was
out of sight I dived into the nearest café, did a miracle
transformation with some concealer, a streak of eye-liner
and some lippy, then ordered an obscenely large fry up and
plotted how to spend my day off.

I will *never* leave the house without make-up again.

Monday 14 February, St Valentine's Day

Kevin wrote me a love-poem (I think it's actually more
of a love-limerick) in my Valentine's card.

I'm in love with a girl, Theodora
She's so quaint that you cannot ignore her
She's bouncy and fun
She's my number one
I want all to know I adore her.

I'm not sure I like the 'bouncy' bit. Is he thinking golden labrador or pneumatic lingerie model? Feel sort of obliged to reciprocate.

Kevin, Kevin, oh my Kevin
Being with you is just like heaven
I've known you since we were eleven
How I wish that there were seven
Of you, my one and only Kevin
You're even more worthy than Aneurin Bevan
If I'm the dough, then you're my leaven
Oh, Kevin, Kevin, Kevin, Kevin.

Eat your heart out, Lord Byron.

Tuesday 15 February

'ANGELO HEISENBERG WILL CHANGE YOUR LIFE,' alleged the poster on the staff notice board. Covenant Blake has invited the whole department to a crusade meeting in a nearby school hall. It takes place after work on Friday. Tried to think of a good excuse for not going, but nobody else from the office will attend and I feel a bit sorry for Covenant and a bit guilty about criticizing him. Kevin is going up to Birmingham to see Floyd and Deyanna on Friday and Saturday so I will be on my own. I've been going to church for so long that I must be pretty immune to religious brainwashing. (Not that I'm implying that the Church of England brainwashes anybody – although I have been to some highly suspect harvest barn dances.) I'll go . . . to support Covenant.

Wednesday 16 February

The estate agent phoned this morning. Mr Singh has finally decided to make an offer for my flat. They are willing to pay the full asking price. They want to arrange for a survey next week. Did I accept?

'Of course I accept.'

'The only snag is, Mr Singh would like his daughter to move in at the end of March.'

'But I don't get married until April.'

'Are you saying that would be a problem?'

'No, no. I'm sure I can sort something out. Stay with my parents or something.'

I've just sold my flat!

Thursday 17 February

Had a celebratory drink with Kevin, Mum, Dad, Eloise and Ariadne this evening. I stand to make a few quid on the deal, and with Kevin's savings we have quite a substantial deposit for a new house together. Felt a little nomadic. Can't say I'm looking forward to going back to my parents' house. Dad didn't seem to be relishing the idea, either.

'Honestly, thought I'd finally got rid of you lot and you start coming back. Like flamin' homing pigeons.'

'Charming,' I said, pretending to be deeply offended.

''Course, you heard what happened to your cousin Huw, Auntie Angharad's son, when he tried to go back to live with his parents?'

'No, but I'm sure you're going to tell me.'

Kevin looked skyward.

'Well, young Huw, he'd taken a year off before going to university to go on his travels, see, all round the Far East, Laos, Burma, Thailand, all that. Anyway, he's gone for a year, gets home tired and dusty off the flight from Bangkok, knocks on the front door; Auntie Angharad answers the door, sees Huw, and faints away, there on the doorstep. Well, when she comes round, she explains to him, like, how she fainted on account of the fact she thought he was dead. Young Huw naturally couldn't believe what he was hearing. Anyway, still in a state of shock she lets him in and he goes up to his room with his cases, only to find another bloke in there. He recognizes him as Wynn Lewis, a lad he was at school with. Wynn's lying on his bed, wearing his clothes and listening to his music. Well, Wynn legs it as soon as he sees Huw. Off he goes, through the front door like a rabbit in a greyhound stadium.'

'Oh yes, and why had Auntie Angharad let this Wynn stay in his room?' I asked incredulously.

'Well, about six months after Huw had left for Laos, they had a phone call from the embassy there to say that there had been a terrible accident and Huw had been killed in a shark attack while swimming. Apparently a brave young Welshman had battled to save him, knocked the shark on the head and tried to pull the boy out, but it was too late. Huw had been eaten. All that was left was the boy's wristwatch.'

'Yuck, gruesome!' I winced. Eloise's mouth hung open in disbelief. Mum just shook her head.

'Anyway, this young Welshman promised to bring the watch back to Huw's grieving parents, which he did. He told Angharad and Mike about the story and gave them

Huw's mangled watch with the engraving still visible, "To our darling son Huw on his 18th birthday". Wynn told them how he was so traumatized about what had happened that he'd lost his job and had nowhere to live. They immediately invited him to stay with them – after all, they had a spare room – and Wynn moved in and became like their son.'

'Hang on a minute,' piped up Ariadne. 'How could he get eaten by a shark in Laos? It hasn't got a coast, it's completely land-locked.'

'Exactly,' said Dad. 'If only they'd looked it up in an atlas.'

'But what about the watch?' asked Eloise. 'Was it a fake?'

'No. As I said, it was Huw's watch right enough. Huw and Wynn were at school together and both in the same rugby team. Wynn swiped it from the changing room and gave it to his Alsatian dog to chew, make it look like shark bite, see. Huw knew his parents would be upset if they realized he had lost the watch, so he didn't tell them.'

'So it was all an elaborate hoax,' said Kevin. 'Sweet!'

'But didn't Huw send any letters home all the time he was out there?' asked Eloise.

'Of course, for the first six months they wrote to him and he wrote to them as normal. After his "tragic demise", of course, they didn't try to contact him, and after Wynn moved in he was able to intercept the letters before Angharad and Mike found them. Young Huw thought he would surprise his parents by turning up on their doorstep.'

'He did that all right,' laughed Kevin.

'Did they ever catch up with Huw's so-called friend who'd lived rent-free in the lap of luxury for six months?' I asked.

'Yeah, turned out his family only lived round the corner, but because he hadn't tried to get any money out of them and even returned the watch, there wasn't a lot they could do.'

'What did he say when they confronted him?'

Dad thought for a moment. 'I think he said, "Oh well, you can't Wynn them all!"'

We took it in turns to pelt Dad with our beer-mats.

Friday 18 February

I arrived early at the school hall and helped Covenant, who was still setting out the chairs. We went for a quick coffee, which we drank gratefully, after of course saying grace. Covenant, with zealous eyes shining, explained to me his hopes for this evening, which as far as I could work it out seem to be to convert the whole world to Christianity. A very noble ambition, I thought, and a very earnest young man.

'We're hoping to plant a church here as a follow-up to this crusade,' he said.

'But there's already a church here, we passed it on the corner. St Mark's or something.'

'Yeah, but that's only an old Church of England. All that outdated liturgy and stuff.'

I remembered the 'Workers' Lunch' group they had started at St Mark's to provide a place where office workers could eat their sandwiches and have a chat over coffee. There were friendly pastoral workers and the opportunity to ask questions about faith. I felt a pang of guilt that I hadn't been to the meetings recently, although I had dropped a few coins in the collection boxes members of St Mark's held, when on a bitter December day they stood out on the street collecting for a charity to support homeless people.

Angelo Heisenberg, short, tanned, well-dressed and confident, arrived shortly after we returned to the hall. Covenant made his excuses and took Angelo off, no doubt to find somewhere to put down his enormous Bible. 'Would you mind very much showing in the worship band and the lighting and PA people when they come?' I nodded and found a chair. I was alone in the hall, and for all Covenant's enthusiasm and the professionalism and slick organization of the event, I couldn't help thinking back to those people, mostly elderly, standing outside St Mark's on that bitterly cold day . . .

The hall filled up, and the meeting started with a prayer and some rousing modern praise and worship songs. Perhaps it wouldn't be too bad after all. Then Covenant introduced Angelo Heisenberg, who began to deliver his evangelical message – a real tub-thumper.

I became aware that the rest of the room had melted away and all I could see was his lips moving. The words he spoke seemed aimed only at me. I had experienced this feeling before and it meant one of two things. Either God was using this man to speak directly to me, or I was about to embark on a guilt trip. If it was the latter, I had the feeling it would be the full luxury guided tour, complete with air-conditioning and toilet facilities and with places of interest pointed out.

'Are you saved?' he boomed.

I was pretty sure of that one.

'Are you really sure?'

Well, yes, I was absolutely, definitely a Christian. That would be the box I would tick on the Afterlife Admission form.

'Can you name the date and time – nay, the very second – you surrendered your putrescent existence to Jesus Christ?'

I swallowed hard. I hadn't the faintest idea.

'For if not, brother, sister, perhaps it is that you are not saved at all.'

All aboard! And the guilt trip commenced with engines screaming and horn blasting.

Saturday 19 February

So it's true. I'm not really a Christian at all. I have just been deluding myself all this time. Hoped that God had been deluded too. Repented of that hope. Tried to think back and remember the second that I had become a Christian. Failed miserably, couldn't even remember the decade with certainty. For as long as I could remember, I'd always believed in God. Accepting that his son Jesus had died for me and wanted to be the central person in my life seemed a natural progression from that. All my prayers and words seemed earnest enough. I know that I love Jesus, but that's the problem: I don't remember *starting* to love him, so according to Angelo Heisenberg I can't be a Christian. He had gone on to say how we all needed to turn from our wickedness and start again, putting all our former life and relationships behind us.

Seeing as I was definitely considering myself as a Christian by the time I was six, there was very little scope for major lifestyle change. Yes, I could have tidied up my Barbies a bit quicker and not given in to the temptation of pinching my baby brother Ag, but I had never exactly been a Hell's Angel. Perhaps it would have been easier if I had been. I envied all those people and their wonderful testimonies, how they had stopped using drugs or turned away from lives of crime and prostitution. It's not fair. Jesus even said that those who have been forgiven the most would love him the most. What chance do I stand? Copying the answers in a spelling test and driving at thirty-four miles an hour in a thirty-mile-an-hour zone are about the limit of my crimes. What can I do, go out and rob a bank this afternoon, repent first thing tomorrow and all will be well? Surely not. I have ordered a copy of Angelo's book called *How to Guarantee Your Salvation*. Just hope I don't get run over in the next couple of days before the book arrives, otherwise, to quote Angelo Heisenberg, I'm 'hell-bound with a full tank of gas and no brakes'!

In the spirit of my new honest relationship with Kevin, I have decided to discuss my problem with him. Perhaps I will invite him round for tea tomorrow.

Sunday 20 February

Church service didn't help much. Chrissie was away on a conference and Nigel Hubble gave a dreary sermon about eternity, which was roughly how long the sermon itself lasted.

This morning I woke up in a cold sweat, having dreamed that I really did have to fill in the application form for admission to heaven. In my dream, I had died suddenly. I stood outside the pearly gates while St Peter tapped his foot impatiently. 'You're late!' he said.

I didn't have a pen and had to borrow one from the holy doorman, who looked heavenward in exasperation. Actually, as we were already in heaven, I don't see how he did that. Still, it was only a dream.

'Date of salvation?' inquired the writing on the form in accusing black letters.

'Um . . . I'm not quite sure about this bit.' I showed St Peter the section that asked me to provide 'exact date of conversion to Christianity DD MM YYYY'.

'Well, what is it?' said St Peter impatiently. 'When were you born again?'

'I . . . I'm not exactly sure. I don't remember exactly when I became a Christian.'

'Sorry.' St Peter shook his head and pointed towards a door labelled 'Hellfire and Damnation'.

At that point I woke up crying.

I phoned Mum after the service. She seems to have a photographic record in her memory of every little peccadillo and blunder that I ever made as a child, so surely she would remember something as important as this. 'When did I become a Christian, Mum?' I asked.

Mum paused. 'Well, to be perfectly honest you've always been a funny little thing, a bit religious. I never could work out where you got it from. As soon as you were old enough to go out on your own you would take yourself off to Sunday school. I'd hoped it would make you behave yourself a bit better. In fact I used to threaten you that I wouldn't let you go to church if you were naughty. Worked, too. Mind you, for your brother and sister, church was a punishment, but not for you.'

I thanked Mum. Encouraging, but it didn't really help. According to Angelo Heisenberg, I am still quite firmly among the heathen. Kevin is still in Birmingham so I will have to postpone the discussion until tomorrow.

Tuesday 22 February

Cooked Kevin bangers and mash for dinner tonight. The sausages tasted fine once I had extinguished them. Even so, it didn't stop Kevin referring to them as 'carbon-based life forms'. I got so fed up with buying sausages that kept bursting into flames every time I tried to cook them that I once complained to the butcher.

'No one else has that problem, madam,' he said condescendingly.

Over the washing up I decided to talk to Kevin about my problem. I explained that I had been to an evangelical meeting, at which point Kevin raised his eyebrows. I went on to tell him about Angelo Heisenberg's principle and how it was causing me so much uncertainty.

'I just can't give a date for certain,' I complained.

'Fourteenth December, about half past six in the evening, when I was sixteen. I'd just started my apprenticeship, so that was about, ooh ...' and Kevin proceeded to start counting on his fingers.

At this point I left the room. Kevin can name the time to the hour when he became a Christian, and there was me thinking he was spiritually degenerate.

Wednesday 23 February

Started packing in earnest today and threw away a whole sack of old clothes. Ariadne popped round in the middle of it and there followed a tug-of-war over my moon boots, which I maintain are practical, warm and comfortable but Ariadne insists are the fashion equivalent of addressing the Queen as 'ducks'. We took two boxes of books, photographs and ornaments round to Mum and Dad's house and Ariadne helped me manoeuvre them into the loft. The flat is starting to look empty. I hope Kevin and I find somewhere soon.

Friday 25 February

Of course, if I'm not a Christian perhaps I should make the most of it. The frightening thought is that if I stopped being a Christian (or never was one in the first place), would it actually make any difference to my life? Would anyone notice? I thought of my friends who didn't profess Christianity but who are still pretty nice people. They wouldn't leave you stranded on the motorway in a blizzard. They give to charity and don't commit crimes. They are not drunken adulterous moral degenerates. The only difference to my lifestyle I can see at the moment is the fact that I will now have a couple of hours to wash my car on a Sunday morning.

Sunday 27 February

Despite being a heathen, I decided to go to church anyway; the car would have to stay dirty. I thought perhaps they would have an 'altar call' and I would be able to go forward and become a Christian and sort of start from square one. I'm not sure what all the people who have known me for so long would make of it, but it might be a bit of excitement.

There was no 'altar call', but after the service I asked Chrissie for a chat. We sat in the vestry and I began.

'Thing is . . . I'm not a Christian.'

'What are you, then? Buddhist, Hindu, Taoist, perhaps?' Chrissie laughed.

'No, I'm being serious . . . I went to an evangelist's meeting in a school hall . . .'

'Why?'

'I . . . I don't know. I was supporting a friend. And the preacher there said that unless I could name the date I gave my heart to the Lord then I'm not actually a Christian at all.'

'Did you find that helpful or unhelpful?'

'I don't understand.'

'Well, did it increase your faith or decrease it?'

'It made me think that I didn't have a faith at all. That I'd been living a lie.'

'Do you think that what your preacher said counts as "building up"?'

'No, but Jesus said that we must be born again.'

'Do you remember being born the first time?'

'Of course not.'

'Oh well,' said Chrissie, leaning back in her chair, 'that means you probably were never born at all. What a shame. I was just about to suggest we go down the pub, but since you don't exist I'd better go on my own.'

'Chrissie, don't laugh at me. This is serious.'

'Look, I could take you through the "sinner's prayer". We could kneel down here and if you would feel happier we could say it and you could write down the date and your preacher-man friend would be satisfied. But it wouldn't be true. It would be like cancelling out all that has gone before, a lifetime of faith. Being a Christian isn't about reciting some magic words. Your relationship with Jesus isn't about pressing the right button, it's about living the life. Your faith and your genuine love for Christ have been evident to me for as long as I have known you. I don't know when it started but I know it when I see it and so does God. Accept that you have belonged to him since before you remember and thank him for that. Of course we all need to assess our priorities, make a fresh start from time to time, but don't throw away his love. It will be the thing that will keep you going even if you lose everything else. Remember that.'

I nodded and tears filled my eyes. The reason I didn't remember Jesus coming into my life is that he'd always been there.

'Well, after that speech, I'm definitely going to the pub. Are you coming, non-person?'

Monday 28 February

Received the contract to sell my flat this morning. My hand was shaking as I held the pen. My nest, my womb, my refuge will soon belong to somebody else and I will be homeless. 'Foxes have holes and birds of the air have nests, but the Son of Man has no place to lay his head.'

Tuesday 29 February

A whole extra day ... pity I can't think of anything useful to do in it.

March

Wednesday 1 March, St David's Day

Following his third pint of Australian lager, my father announced that he saw no reason on earth why the Irish should have all the fun celebrating their saint's day when the nearest the Welsh got to wild jubilation was to stick a daffodil in their lapel. I pointed out that at least the Welsh were fortunate enough to have their national flower growing on their national saint's day. St George's Day is in April and roses don't grow in England in April. We have to buy expensive imported roses, whereas the Welsh only have to go out into the garden and pick their daffodils. The discussion was showing signs of degenerating into a nationalistic slanging-match until Mum intervened and said that unless Dad and I showed some signs of helping with the washing up, we would both find ourselves wearing our national flowers up our noses.

'Besides,' she said, 'I think the Greeks have the right idea. Each island has its own saint and, boy, do they know how to celebrate. One island even keep their saint's mummified body in the church and get it out and parade it round the streets on his special day.'

I quite liked that idea. After all, why should a minor detail like being dead stop anyone from joining in the party?

Thursday 2 March

The church secretary is retiring next month, and not a day too soon. She is going to live with her sister in Brighton. A vacancy notice appeared in *The Church Organ*.

Required – Church Secretary

Must be acccurate trypist 30 – 50 worms per minuet

Good reception skills – must be able to tell people where to go

Good telephone manor

Must be able to deal diplomatically with difficult people.

Will be working directly for the vicar.

Will have sole responsibility for the Church Organ (editing it, that is, not playing it)

Please apply to the vicar or call in at the Church Orifice

As I said, not a day too soon.

Friday 3 March

Met up with Ariadne for dinner in the West End. Took clothes, make-up and a pair of high-heeled shoes to work, intending to change in the loo without needing to go home. As it was a surprisingly clement spring evening, I decided to forgo the tube and walk (or considering the heels, stagger) to the restaurant. As I tottered through Leicester Square, I suddenly found myself in the middle of a huge crowd that had gathered for a film première. I was already late, having spent far too long applying some new 'juicy lips' lip gloss, then spending a similar amount of time un-gluing my lips so that I could actually speak and eat. I elbowed my way through the throng of cinema-goers just as the film stars were arriving. I felt a tap on the shoulder. I pivoted round to find myself face to face with a middle-aged man with bad breath, clutching an autograph book.

''Scuse me. Are you famous?'

I didn't know what to say. I felt simultaneously flattered and irritated. If I *had* been famous, I would have been utterly insulted by this question.

I tried to balance elegantly on my shoes and pouted my 'juicy' lips. 'I am famous to those who know me,' I drawled and swivelled back to my original course, leaving the man standing looking puzzled.

Elaborated the story of 'being mistaken for a film star' a little to impress Ariadne.

'I think he must have mistaken me for Gwyneth Paltrow,' I said, smiling in what I hoped was a Paltrow-like manner.

'Unlikely,' mused Ariadne, 'as the film they're showing is a sequel to *Planet of the Apes*.'

Saturday 4 March

Chrissie phoned me. The church secretary couldn't wait to see out her month's notice and has rushed off to the exotic climes of Brighton this weekend, leaving Chrissie rather in the lurch. The church committee is due to meet this week and there is no one to type the agenda or take the minutes. Even though it would probably involve an Act of Parliament to become part of the Parochial Church Council when you haven't been elected, Chrissie asked me to agree to be co-opted on as secretary, pending the election of a new committee in April. Against my better judgement, I agreed. As least I couldn't be any worse than the last secretary. Also, she left in such a hurry that she hasn't finished putting together this week's *Church Organ*. Chrissie begged me, with the promise of a big box of chocolates, to come into the church office this afternoon to finish typing and photocopying it. Not my idea of a scintillating Saturday afternoon but better than going to football.

6 p.m.

Well, I got it finished. It looks a bit sparse but I've checked the spelling and added some clip-art to pad it out a bit and make it look a little more attractive. I moved the quote from Psalm 100, 'Enter his gates with thanksgiving and his courts with praise', away from the notice that read, 'Due to repeated vandalism, the gates will be kept locked unless a service is in progress.'

Even though the back page is blank, I think I did a pretty proficient job.

Sunday 5 March

Chrissie was as good as her word, presenting me with a large box of chocolates before the service. I grinned humbly as several people patted me on the back for stepping in and producing *The Church Organ* at the last minute. My glow of self-satisfaction was only slightly dimmed when Doris Johnson apologized during the notices for the fact that today's edition of *The Church Organ* had no backside.

Monday 6 March

I am determined this year not just to use Lent as an excuse to feel pious about giving up chocolate, but I am going to use the time for self-improvement and spiritual growth. Must call into the library on the way home from work tomorrow.

Tuesday 7 March, Shrove Tuesday

Ariadne and I had a chocolate feast this evening. Trying to cram six weeks' worth of chocolate into three hours wasn't that easy even for a confirmed chocoholic like me. Went home feeling faintly sick. Stood on the scales and discovered I had gained twelve pounds since this morning. Nearly fainted until I remembered that I was still carrying a bag full of library books.

Wednesday 8 March, Ash Wednesday

Intended to start reading one of the library books tonight. I borrowed *Revelation of Divine Love* by a chap called Julian from Norwich, St John's *Dark Night of the Soul* and several books of essays by C.S. Lewis. I was determined to settle on the sofa with *The Problem of Pain*. But the phone rang and I got up suddenly, dropping the book on my toe.

As I hopped around in agony, whoever had rung me having rung off before I could get there, I decided to leave the book for another night. I knew all I needed to know about pain for one evening.

Thursday 9 March

Spent an hour trying to convince Kevin that church wardens do not issue parking tickets to members of the congregation who spend too much time sitting in one pew, nor do they have the power to clamp people for sitting in the wrong place. I think he's trying to wind me up.

Saturday 11 March

Called at the vicarage to drop in the PCC agenda and minutes. Walked up the drive just as Chris and two other women were tottering down the front steps. All three were wearing short skirts, glittery shoes and small, tight, sparkly tops. Chris, to my consternation, was wearing false eyelashes with little glistening jewels on the ends. My jaw must have dropped. The two other women giggled.

'Oh hi, Theo, is that my agenda? Did you remember to include the notes on diocesan policy on children and Communion? Only I've got an update from the bishop's office.' She patted her skimpy skirt. 'Oh never mind, I must have left it in my cassock. I'll let you have it later.'

The encounter was starting to take on a surreal quality.

'Going out?' I asked, as nonchalantly as possible under the circumstances.

'We're goin' clubbin',' replied one of the women. I dismissed a sudden vision of the trio culling baby seals.

'Oh, night-clubbing, I see. How ... um ... contemporary.'

'Wanna come?' invited the other woman, indifferently.

'Er, I'm a little busy at the moment. Perhaps another time.'

I smiled weakly and pushed the minutes into Chris's hand. Another side to our vicar. What would Jeremiah have said?

Sunday 12 March

Chrissie pulled me to one side after church. I grabbed a cup of coffee and she bundled me through to the vestry.

'What's the matter, Theo? You've had a face like an undertaker sucking a lemon all morning. Never seen a vicar go to a night-club before?'

'Well, frankly, no.'

'Do you disapprove?'

I tried to be honest. 'I'm not sure. I suppose I do a bit. I mean ...' I dredged my mind back to the last night-club I had been to while on a training course in Sheffield, about five years ago. The pounding, mesmerizing music, the sweat, the too many glasses of overpriced wine, the heat, the creep who had offered to sell me – no, tried to force me to buy – some pills which he said would make sure I had 'a good time'. I shuddered at the memory. I had felt uncomfortable. 'I mean, the drink, the drugs ... the men! There are some real creeps around. Once some loathsome, drunken lobby-lizard tried to put his hand up my dress while we were waiting for a taxi.'

She let out a squawk of laughter. 'Can you imagine me needing to rely on drink or drugs to have a good time?'

I laughed too. Ha, ha, ha. How could I have even entertained such a notion?

'As for the men, whenever I tell them that I'm actually the local vicar they never seem to bother me. Funny, that.' She hijacked my coffee and took a swig. 'What is it with most Christians? Are you afraid of being contaminated? That going somewhere other than a church meeting might suddenly lead you to rip off all your clothes and initiate an orgy? Some Christians are so obsessed with keeping their noses clean that they're afraid to get their hands dirty.' She paused and took another slurp of my coffee. 'I love being with young people . . . I love young people. God loves young people, but not many of them ever set foot in a church. I take the church to them.'

I was still dubious.

'But what do you do there?'

'What do you think I do? Dance, have a good time, mostly, but I also make it known that I'm available if anyone wants to just talk.'

'And do they?'

'Some do.'

'Isn't it a bit loud?'

She hooted with laughter again. 'There's the toilets or the lobby, and I've found a quiet office the staff let me use sometimes if it is getting a bit heavy.'

'Don't the staff mind?'

'They seem to quite like it. When a bar worker's mother was ill, she asked me to pray for her. Just like that. I didn't have to push or anything. But it's mainly young girls who want to talk – boyfriend trouble, exam pressure, eating problems, problems with parents, that sort of thing. Sometimes we discuss faith. There's so much need out there. So much!' She sighed. 'And if I find a youngster the worse for wear, I help her call a cab and make sure she gets in it safely. And I protect them from "loathsome, drunken lobby-lizards"!'

Monday 13 March

Finished reading the first of my library books. That Julian was a funny bloke. He thought God was a woman and that everything was a hazelnut.

Tuesday 14 March

Spent one of the most tedious evenings of my life as secretary of the St Norbert's Parochial Church Council. The high spot for me was when the committee looked into a motion to let the young mothers' group use the church hall for their weekly meeting and Mrs McCarthy proposed that we should give them our wholehearted 'immoral' support.

The rest of the evening was spent discussing the fact that we are running out of space in St Norbert's graveyard. Discussions revolved around the proposal that people who attend the church regularly should be given priority when it comes to allocating space for interments. The rest of the community, it seems, would have to lump it. Mr Wilberforce protested that this could lead to people only coming to church so that they could reserve the best spot in the graveyard. Miss Cranmer suggested that a minimum length of attendance should apply before anyone should be permitted to be buried there. The discussion raged on: should it be six months' attendance, a year, two years? What about people who knew they were dying? Would they be allowed to attend just so that they could be buried in the graveyard? Chrissie sat through the discussion with her head in her hands.

'Well, I'm blowed if I'm going to ask new church members if they have a better than even change of surviving more than six months! Perhaps I should insist on seeing a doctor's certificate before I let them join the electoral roll.'

'Good idea,' said Miss Cranmer. 'Have you got that, madam secretary?'

Chrissie rolled her eyes heavenwards. 'Give me strength!'

The discussion was postponed until the next committee and the meeting closed with a prayer.

'Did you manage to get all the important points down?' Chrissie asked me after the meeting.

'What important points? I don't think I noticed any.'

Chrissie's eyebrows creased until she realized that I was only joking. She gave me a friendly punch on the arm. 'Good one!'

Wednesday 15 March

Kevin and I both took the day off today and I finished packing. Although I am not moving out until next week, we decided to move all superfluous furniture and objects from my flat to my parents' house, the idea being that we can load the rest of my stuff into the van and do one final run next Thursday. Have just retained the essentials: bed, sofa, diary, television, fridge (for the storage of emergency chocolate rations – oh, and food, of course), computer and a few clothes and cosmetics. I feel like a hermit monk, alone in my austere cell.

Friday 17 March

Couldn't believe my eyes when I saw this week's local paper. The front-page headline read 'VICAR IN KNICK-ERS' and underneath was a photograph of the Reverend Christina Monroe wearing a bikini. 'No vest in *her* vestry' ran the sub-heading. 'Parishioners get an eyeful at even-song'. The article went on to be a groundless but vicious character assassination. I read on in sick horror as snide questions and double-entendres littered the article. It was all unjustifiable but nevertheless malicious. I was stunned. St Norbert's had always had a good relationship with the local press. What was the background to this article and, more importantly, where had the photo come from?

Then I noticed the name of the journalist who had written the article – Brian Wedgwood. There had to be some connection.

Saturday 18 March

I am in detective mode. Chrissie was more upset by yesterday's paper than she pretended to be. It was a classic case of making a mountain out of a molehill (or, in her case, two molehills). She wasn't doing anything wrong. Wearing a bikini on a beach holiday is hardly a cardinal sin. The article was designed to humiliate, and for all of Chrissie's brave talk about turning the publicity to her and St Norbert's advantage, I could tell it disturbed her deeply. The question of who dunnit seemed pretty easy to answer. There are not many Wedgwoods in the area, but how did Jeremiah get the photo and why should he want to degrade the vicar in this way?

Sunday 19 March

Strange service this morning. The worship unfolded much as it had for the last four months, but there was an air of expectancy that heightened as Chrissie climbed the steps to the wooden pulpit. It was one of those situations where everyone knew what everyone else was thinking but nobody said a word. Chrissie looked tired, and her smile didn't seem as natural as usual. But she did it. She preached from God's Word and the people listened.

At the end of the service Charity sidled up to me and whispered out of the side of her mouth, 'Have you seen the paper?'

'Of course I've seen the paper. Everyone's seen the paper.'

'Isn't it disgraceful?'

'Totally. I'm appalled.'

'But what can we do?'

'I'm not going to let it rest.'

'Good for you, Theodora. I'd never had you down for the campaigning type.'

'Oh, never cross a Llewellyn, so they say. I'm going to track down that journalist, and when I find him I'm going to stick that notebook ...'

'The journalist? Why do you want to take it out on him?'

'For publishing all that rubbish about Chrissie . . .'

'Good on him, I say, letting us know what our vicar is really like. And to think she's supposed to be our moral and spiritual leader.'

I couldn't work out what Charity thought Chrissie was supposed to have done. Wearing a bikini on the beach is equivalent to being found naked in the shower or in bed with one's spouse. Charity didn't know, either, except that she and Nigel didn't approve and she'd had to hide the paper away from the children.

Good job she didn't know about the night-club.

Monday 20 March

Chrissie phoned me at work today. She's never done that before. Apparently a tabloid newspaper had approached her.

'Good, I thought. A chance to put my case. Then they told me they wanted me to pose topless. Honestly, I'm a parish priest. That's all I've ever wanted to do. Now they're trying to stop me doing that. Oh Theo, it's not fair.'

Tuesday 21 March

I'm determined to find out who is behind this smear campaign to discredit Chrissie and get them to stop. The story is all round the village. People in spiteful little huddles, gossiping. I have watched enough *Inspector Morse* to know how this is done. I got a pen and a notebook and started to write down the facts.

Facts

The reporter is Brian Wedgwood.

He may be related to Jeremiah Wedgwood.

Jeremiah disapproves of female clergy and left after a disagreement with the defendant.

The photographs come from Rev. Monroe's personal collection.

The accused must have had access to her possessions.

Action

Find the link between Brian and Jeremiah Wedgwood.

Speak to Brian.

Track down Jeremiah and see if he has an alibi.

Confront the perpetrator and secure a confession followed by an apology to Rev. Monroe, preferably to include some form of public humiliation.

Habeas Corpus.

No idea what the last phrase means. Heard it in a detective film once and feel it gives my list a touch of legal credibility.

Wednesday 22 March

Tried phoning the newspaper but Brian Wedgwood was out, so I couldn't speak to him, and besides, the receptionist said that it would be 'unprofessional' for journalists to reveal their sources. At the word 'unprofessional' smoke started coming out of my ears. Unfortunately I couldn't think of what to say in time and the receptionist had hung up, leaving me opening and closing my mouth like a goldfish.

I tried to trace Jeremiah by going to his old flat and then to the post office to see if there was a forwarding address. Alfreda Polanski, who owns the post office, had of course seen the article and clucked with sympathy but turned out unhelpful when I asked for Jeremiah's new address, muttering something about 'client confidentiality'. She's hardly Coutts Bank.

Thursday 23 March

Chatted to Harry in Invoices today. It is common knowledge that after his wife left him and ran off with a double-glazing salesman, Harry became an expert in surveillance. I bought him a coffee and we sat in a corner of the canteen away from the windows (he still can't bear to be near sealed units), and I picked his brains as to how I could find Jeremiah Wedgwood.

'So, Harry, if I wanted to find someone, how would I go about it?'

'Right, what do you know about this person?'

'Well, their name. That's about it.'

'There must be more than that. Where do they work?'

'Retired, I think.'

'Good, so they probably draw a pension. If you have a rough idea of the district they live in, what you have to do is strategically stake out each post office in the vicinity on pension day. You're bound to come up trumps sooner or later.'

I had a mental picture of myself wearing a balaclava and sitting in a deckchair reading a newspaper with eyeholes cut in it. I didn't think this was quite my style.

'Er . . . I think he has private means.'

'OK. What about his hobbies? Does he belong to any clubs or societies?'

'He almost certainly goes to some kind of church.'

'Great! Then what you have to do is strategically stake out each church in the vicinity on Sundays . . .'

Friday 24 March

Harry was rather a waste of time. I have decided to draw Brian Wedgwood out of the woodwork and persuade him to print the truth. I'm hoping to get a lead on Jeremiah at the same time. Mrs McCarthy confirmed that Brian is indeed Jeremiah's nephew. She remembers Jeremiah talking about a journalist in the family. Told Chrissie my intention but she was all for dropping the whole plan. I found her scanning through this week's local paper, but there was nothing. It was as if the article had never appeared.

'Just let it go,' she said wearily. 'Today's news, tomorrow's fish and chip wrappers.'

But I am determined to put the record straight. I am on a crusade. I feel as if I've found my 'ministry'.

Saturday 25 March

Moved out of my flat today. We loaded my last few possessions, including the budgie, into the van and cleaned the flat. I cried buckets as I walked round saying goodbye to each room. That didn't take too long, as it is only a one-bedroom flat. The part that took the longest was Kevin dragging me out of the door by my ankles while I clung on to the hall carpet with my fingernails. Mrs Barrie stood at the front door and kissed me on both cheeks.

'Goodbye, dear. I shall miss our meals and discussions so much.'

What meals? She had once come up to me for a cup of coffee and a chocolate digestive. As I remember it, we discussed the weather, Prince Charles' tie and the exorbitant price of tap washers. Hardly stunning intellectual discourse. I had invited Mr and Mrs Barrie on several other occasions but Mrs Barrie had always declined on both their behalves 'on account of Mr B's veins'. I never found out what was wrong with Mr B's veins, only that he had them. Nevertheless, I hugged her fondly and said I'd be in touch.

8 p.m.

I am now back in the bedroom I inhabited as a child. Mum has just offered to make me a cup of cocoa. I feel rather like the Prodigal Daughter Returned, except that I am hardly prodigal. I have just realized that I still have the same pyjamas as when I lived at home. I bought them to match the wallpaper and bedding. The fact that the 'My Little Pony' pyjamas are still in existence stands alone as proof of my frugality.

Sunday 26 March

Kevin came to hear our banns read for the first time. It's a bit of a shock hearing your full name and status of spinsterhood read out to the congregation. It was even more of a shock to find out that Kevin has two extra middle names I didn't know about. I knew he was Kevin George, but I hadn't a clue about Gladstone and, of all things, Waterloo. After the service I asked him if his father had been a fan of great military campaigns. He replied that unfortunately he had acquired the name for less heroic reasons. His dad had told him that he'd been conceived in the waiting room of Platform 4 at the railway station during one very long and tedious delay.

I sighed with relief that nobody knew of any just cause or impediment to the marriage. I don't know why this worried me, I just had some vague underlying dread that somebody would bring up the fact that I had cheated in a spelling test when I was nine or that I'd kissed Jeremy Magellan at the school disco when I should have been with Martin Hudson.

It made it feel real. We're actually getting married in a few weeks' time. Kevin squeezed my hand and asked if I was happy. I smiled and nodded. I'd feel even happier if we'd got somewhere to live.

Monday 27 March

I anticipated that it would be difficult to settle back in with Mum and Dad after living on my own for so long. I'm really extremely grateful to my parents for letting me move back, but I just find some things soooo annoying. For a start, Mum keeps tidying up. I am used to putting something down and finding it days, weeks, even months later where I had put it. Now I'm lucky if anything stays still for five minutes! She uses different washing powder to me and fabric conditioner that makes me itch. And Dad *never* shuts the bathroom door when he's on the toilet. He thinks that singing is sufficient measure to ensure privacy. On the plus side, I'm getting my meals cooked and my parents have a far better stereo system than I do.

Tuesday 28 March

It is my birthday. I am thirty-one. I am now officially in my thirties. Mum says it is the age at which she started counting backwards. I have never understood why women lie about their age and claim that they are younger than they really are. It would make far more sense to add years on to their age. If I start telling people that I am thirty, or even twenty-nine, where will it end? By the time I'm forty-five I'll be telling people I am fifteen. I will have to start painting on fake acne. And by sixty-one, by my reckoning, I would be an embryo.

Besides, if I were to pretend I was younger than I really am, the person I am talking to might think, 'My goodness, she says she's only twenty-five, she must have had a hard life.' On the other hand, if I claim to be older than I actually am they will think, 'My goodness, you don't look a day over thirty-one. Haven't you worn well!'

Wednesday 29 March

I telephoned the local newspaper again today and asked to speak to Brian Wedgwood. I got the same less-than-obliging receptionist.

'Listen,' I whispered in my best conspiratorial tones, 'I've got some more information on that "Vicars in Knickers" story you printed and I could let Mr Wedgwood see something that is guaranteed to make his hair curl.'

'Really?'

I'd finally aroused her interest. 'Tell Mr Wedgwood to meet me at six o'clock outside the old cinema and I promise I will let him have the full unexpurgated details about Reverend Monroe.'

9 p.m.

I met Brian Wedgwood as arranged outside the derelict cinema. He's tall and thin, and I immediately recognized the Wedgwood features. However, without the Christian faith of his uncle, this Wedgwood was altogether a more acrimonious man.

'I haven't got much time. Tell me what you know about that woman vicar.'

'Er . . . would you like a coffee?' I indicated a nearby burger bar. It was starting to drizzle. He reluctantly agreed and we settled ourselves at a table.

'Well, show me what you've got,' demanded Brian.

'Just a minute. Tell me where Jeremiah is.'

'Nothing to do with you. Just give me the stuff. Stop wasting my time.'

'No address, no story.'

'I'll give you a phone number,' growled Brian. He was torn between curiosity and irritation.

'Fine,' I agreed and proceeded to tell Brian exactly what Chrissie was like, how she related to young and old people, how she helped and comforted those in need, how she lived her Christian faith rather than just talking about it. I showed him photographs of the children's Christmas party and the elderly folks' outing.

'Wasting my time,' spat the furious Brian.

'You wanted to know what she's really like, so I told you,' I said innocently.

'All Christian propaganda. You told the receptionist you'd show me something to make my hair curl.'

True to my promise, I reached into my bag and brought out a packet of home perm solution. 'This will make your hair curl – it says so on the packet.'

Thursday 30 March

Kevin took me out for a curry to celebrate my birthday. He was in a good mood; his team has just bought a new striker and one of their defenders has been pronounced fit after injury worries.

'Well, that's a load off my mind,' I said sarcastically.

'Yes, it's a huge relief,' agreed Kevin, totally serious.

It never ceases to amaze me how Kevin's moods are so dependent on the fortunes or otherwise of his team. I have to tune in to the football results to determine whether I will be greeted with a bear hug or morose indifference. His mood swings are so intense they are virtually hormonal. I'm sure he suffers from PMT – Post Match Tension.

With our wedding less than a month away, I wondered if this would be a good time to come clean and admit that I don't actually like football. Ever since I went to a European fixture in Italy last year and, I have to admit, got rather carried away with the excitement of the match, Kevin has been under the impression that I have undergone some kind of 'road to Damascus' experience and am now a keen aficionado of what he calls 'the beautiful game'. I really don't want to disillusion him but I don't feel I am being honest. Kevin is not the sort of person who can take hints. Even the occasion when I had invited him round for a romantic dinner and he had spent the whole evening reading his football programme so I had set fire to it had failed to communicate how I was feeling.

'Kevin, I want to talk to you about football,' I began.

'Brilliant, fire away,' he responded.

'No, it's not brilliant. That's what I want to talk about.'

'Oh.'

'The thing is – and this may come as a shock to you – I don't actually like football.'

'I know that.'

'You do? Then why do you spend so much time talking about it when you know I'm not interested?'

'Well, you spend hours talking about the things that interest you – your work, all those weirdos at your church, your diets – and I pretend to be interested. I thought you could have the decency to do the same for me.'

I opened my mouth to speak, then closed it again. Is this what marriage is all about, pretending to be interested in your spouse's hobbies for the sake of being civil?

We polished off the chicken tikka and lamb dansak and tried to find a topic of mutual interest to discuss over the After Eights.

11.30 p.m.

Aaarggh! I accidentally consumed an After Eight and broke my fast.

Friday 31 March

I rang Jeremiah Wedgwood today. He didn't seem pleased to hear from me.

'I expect you know why I'm phoning.'

'Delightful as it is to speak to you, I have no idea what you want from me. St Norbert's with its wayward congregation is now thankfully in my past.'

'But it isn't, is it? You are still finding ways to spread your poison.'

'Stop speaking in riddles. I can't waste my time in this manner. As it happens I'm awaiting a very important telephone call.'

'From the press?'

There was a kind of strangled gasp from Jeremiah that could have been indignation but I took to be an admission of guilt.

'Where did you get the photograph from?'

Jeremiah sighed, 'When that . . . that woman arrived, she asked me to help sort out and file some sermon notes. It was just blatantly lying there among the pages. That travesty, that harlot, just lying there betwixt God's Word . . .'

'So you stole it.'

'It was evidence.'

'Of what, the fact that the clergy go on holiday?' The truth is that she is an attractive, successful woman and you, in your warped, twisted little way, couldn't cope with that.

You wanted to destroy her ... a good woman who is trying hard to do what she feels God wants her to do.'

'You stupid girl!' Jeremiah spat. 'I was destroying evil – "Woe unto them that call evil, good and good, evil ..."'

I took a deep breath. Shouting back or fencing with scriptures would be no use. My voice was trembling but I continued as calmly as I could. 'You have every right to your opinion on the ordination of women, Jeremiah, but the only thing you have destroyed is your credibility. I feel very sorry for you, with all that bitterness inside. You are a very sad little man and St Norbert's is a much, much better place without you.' And I put the phone down.

Far from ameliorating my conscience, I felt soiled, contaminated. Jeremiah had dragged me down to his level of name-calling and personal insults, and Chrissie had been right. It had achieved nothing.

I got home to find the local paper had been delivered. I didn't really want to look at it; I wanted to burn it. I made Mum a cup of tea, and took my tea and the paper up to my room with the 'My Little Pony' wallpaper and flopped on the bed. In spite of myself, I couldn't resist flicking through the newspaper. There was the usual scintillating stuff about town planning and elderly patients competing as to who had been kept waiting on a hospital trolley for the longest. Then I came to the letters page. Instead of the usual complaints about vandalism and dog mess, there was a title: 'Massive Support for Lady Vicar'. I sat up on my bed. There were dozens of letters from St Norbert's regulars, other people in the parish, people outside the parish, people who never set foot inside a church and even people who disagreed in principle with the ordination of women. The

one common factor in all the letters was the universal con-
demnation of the despicable treatment of Reverend Monroe
by the newspaper. There were testimonies of her kindness,
integrity and good character from all over the area. The
paper even printed an apology – which was unheard of.
Even the time it had carried the 'Rat-Burgers in Local
Restaurant' story, when it had been taken to court, it
printed a retraction without an apology and embarked on a
campaign for 'the right to investigate'.

I ran downstairs and rang Chrissie.

'Isn't it fantastic?'

'It's reassuring to have that much support.'

'But . . . shouldn't we throw a party or something?'

'I just want to forget it and get on with my job. It's
hardly cause for celebration when a story with no sub-
stance, which should never have been written in the first
place, gets recognized for what it is.' She paused for a
moment. 'And everyone in the entire parish still knows
exactly where my cellulite is.'

April

Saturday 1 April

Dad thought it would be really funny to wake me up at seven o'clock on a Saturday morning and tell me how he'd just heard a news report about a sudden shift in the earth's magnetic field producing strange effects. While I forced open my bleary eyes, he waved a compass under my nose to demonstrate that what used to be magnetic north was now magnetic south. He then dragged me into the bathroom to observe how the water now rotates in the opposite direction.

'But I can't remember which way it went before,' I groaned sleepily.

'Well, now it goes the opposite way,' he announced. 'And the toilet.' He flushed it. It didn't look any different to me. 'Of course, you'll have to learn to stir your tea in the opposite direction if you want it to taste the same. And look at this.' He led me downstairs to the kitchen and opened the cupboards. All the jars and tins were in the cupboard upside down. 'Now we're in the southern hemisphere, we've got to think like the Australians.'

'But . . .' I began.

Then I remembered the date.

Sunday 2 April

Things seem to have settled down at church after Chrissie's 'fifteen minutes of fame'. Jeremiah never actually apologized but I don't think he'll cause any more problems. It seems that he is now attending a church that disagrees with the ordination of women to the extent that it has opted out of diocesan control and has a special bishop to oversee it. However, I have heard that it is not above having bingo sessions and barn dances in the church hall. I'm sure that will keep Jeremiah busy.

Even Charity, who was originally outraged to see the vicar showing her considerable assets, seemed to have changed her tune.

Two people I had never seen in church before sat in the back pews. I prayed that they were not reporters and afterwards I discovered that one was a teacher and the other was an ex-Baptist. They had read the newspaper reports, admired Chrissie's stance and had wanted to see her in the flesh, albeit rather less flesh than the picture in the newspaper.

Chrissie had regained her confidence and wore bright red lipstick, which clashed rather with her purple stole. Heard our banns again. I still can't get used to being a spinster. I suppose I won't be one for much longer.

Spent the afternoon e-mailing friends and acquaintances to tell them of my new (temporary) address and phone number.

Monday 3 April

Myrna has decided that what we need for the start of a new financial year is a sort of spring clean. We unloaded cabinets full of files to see what needed to be kept and what could be consigned to the shredder. Unfortunately, procedures dictated that most of it had to be kept. So it went back into the cabinets. At least we dusted. Today I understood why they pay me my exorbitant salary.

Wednesday 5 April

My e-mailing session on Sunday has resulted in a flurry of return e-mails. It was good to hear from Diana, who seems to be growing in leaps and bounds in her relationship with God. Declan, on the other hand, seemed very down. It sounds as if he still hasn't made many friends. I really must try to get up to Manchester to see him.

Friday 7 April

Woke up in a state of panic. I am getting married in three weeks' time and I still haven't got a dress or a house. Eloise has bought Kayla, Kevin's three-year-old penguin-loving niece who is a sort of miniature Boadicea, a frilly pink dress and matching hat. Ariadne, my matron of honour (ha!), refuses to consider wearing anything that remotely corresponds with Kayla's outfit despite Eloise's assertions that 'It comes in big sizes too.' I am going to check with the florist after work tonight to finalize the floral arrangements. Mum is already in a cooking frenzy and her large freezer is full to capacity with Greek delicacies for the reception. Charity and some of the other people from St Norbert's are bringing finger-food for the disco in the evening and Kevin has apparently booked Vague Dave from the market, who apart from being our chauffeur also works as a DJ, to run the disco. I wouldn't say that I didn't trust Vague Dave, just that even if the things he acquires haven't fallen off the back of a lorry, I have the sneaking suspicion they never quite made it on to the lorry in the first place.

Monday 10 April

Mum and Dad are going away for a few days to see one of my manifold great-aunts. Mum has left me a list of instructions, including locking the back door, when to put the rubbish out and how to answer the phone. With Mum's company depending on new contacts from a recent advertising campaign, she can't afford to miss any business while she is away. Apparently I am supposed to say: 'Good morning/afternoon/evening (depending on the time of day) Aphrodite's Greek Delicacies, Aphrodite's personal secretary speaking, how may I help you?'

I think there's something to cover this scenario in the Bible under the heading 'food sacrificed to idols'.

Tuesday 11 April

Horrible morning at work. Apparently the sales figures are so far down that the Managing Director has issued a statement about the future of the company. It was written in a way which was supposed to sound positive – 'weathering

the storm', 'retaining our competitive edge', 'some reduc-
tions through natural wastage' – but has had the effect of
sending the entire workforce into headless chicken mode.
Rumours of redundancy are ricocheting around the department. I am just trying to keep my head down. However, I
have reached the point with this job where redundancy
actually seems an attractive option. If only I didn't need the
money.

Went out for a walk at lunchtime to pray and to try to
cheer myself up a bit. I decided to walk in the opposite direction to my normal route, and before long found myself in a
tangle of back streets and alleys. There were antique shops,
Chinese restaurants and florists. I don't remember ever going
that way before. I stopped at a newsagent's to buy a sand-
wich and a drink. As I came out, I noticed a bridal wear shop
and hurried across the street. There in the window was the
most beautiful wedding dress I have ever seen. I pushed the
door open and stood on the rich red carpet. A young sales
assistant emerged from a back room and smiled.

'That dress in the window,' I stammered, 'could I see it,
please? What size is it? Is it sold?'

'There's a bit of a story behind that,' explained the assistant. 'Jean, our designer, made it for a young lady due to be
married next week. She'd had her final fitting and it was all
ready when she rang to say the wedding was off and she
didn't need the dress. Of course, she'd paid the deposit but
we are trying to sell the dress off as quickly as possible,
hence the price.'

She removed the dress from the mannequin in the window and held it out to me. It was gorgeous. I could see the
price label.

'Three hundred and fifty pounds, is that all?' I squeaked in amazement.

'We're on a very tight turnaround here. Jean's just keen to cover materials and cut her losses. Of course, if she needed to make any alterations, that would be extra.' She held the dress out to me. 'Would you like to try it on?'

With trembling hands, I took the dress and went to the curtained-off area to try it on. It fitted perfectly. I stepped out of the changing room and found an older woman in black trousers and top had joined the assistant. This was Jean, the dress designer and maker. They fussed and primped the dress, then the assistant went to a drawer and took out a veil with a sparkly head-dress and put it on my windswept hair. I looked in the mirror. In spite of the rather carelessly applied make-up, black office shoes and unkempt hair, I looked transformed. I beamed at them, then promptly started to cry. I told the two women about not being able to find a house or a dress and wondering if the wedding would ever actually happen. I couldn't believe I had finally found a dress and it was perfect. They clucked and patted and gave me tissues.

I thanked them, bought the dress, head-dress and shoes there and then and hurried back to work. Initially, Myrna looked rather sour-faced at me being a quarter of an hour late back from lunch, but her mood changed when she saw what was in my enormous carrier bag. We were soon surrounded by a gaggle of women all feeling the fabric, admiring the style and marvelling at the price. Lizzie from Accounts thought there might be some kind of jinx on the dress. Perhaps I should ask Covenant Blake to exorcise it for me. The other women were more positive. They even tried to persuade me to try it on, but I didn't want to spoil the surprise. I rang Ariadne, who squealed with delight, and later, on the way home, it was all I could do to dissuade her from making me strip to my underwear and try on the dress in the train carriage.

Wednesday 12 April

Received a bank statement today that included the cheque for the sale of my flat. I am officially loaded. I know it will have to go towards a house, *when* we eventually find one we can agree on, but there is a huge temptation to go and blow it on something extravagant like having my fingernails gold-plated or buying a new pair of pyjamas. Ariadne suggested spending the winter in the Caribbean. It's all right for her, she and Tom and Phoebe are off for a fortnight in a villa near Milan tomorrow. I have booked a couple of days off after Easter to help Kevin look for a shed. I pointed out to him that we don't even have a house yet.

On second thoughts, the way things are going we may end up living in a shed.

Phoned Mum about the dress. She was also stunned by the price. 'We'll make a businesswoman of you yet,' she said.

Thursday 13 April

The phone rang early this morning just in that crucial five-minute period between a quarter to eight and a quarter past. I was surprised to hear Declan's voice.

'Declan! Hello, how nice to hear from you. How are you?'

'I'm um . . . fine, just fine. How are you?'

'Fine, just fine too.' I gave a light laugh. 'Only I'm verging on the late side of fine, so is there anything I can do for you or can I ring you back tonight when the dragon lady is less likely to bite my head off?'

I hunted for my shoes. Now where did I leave my keys this time?

'Theo, there's something I want to tell you that just won't wait.' Declan's voice sounded thick and flat as if he had been drinking or crying.

'Go ahead.' Keys located. I just need to find my handbag.

'Theodora . . . I want to marry you.'

Handbag behind a sofa cushion. 'Well, that's very sweet of you, Declan, but I'm afraid the vicar's already booked. We've got a lady vicar now, Reverend Christina Monroe, she's very . . . different. Nice different, though. Have I told you about her . . . ?'

'No, listen to me, Theo. I don't want to marry you as a priest; I want to marry you as your husband. I love you. Do you love me?'

I stopped, one arm halfway down the sleeve of my coat. 'What?'

'Do you love me?'

The room started to rush away from me at great speed. I sat down hard on the sofa, still with my coat half on. I was no longer fine, in fact I was very much not fine and I was just about to be very late.

'I . . . I don't know, Declan. I'd have to think about it.'

'What do you mean you'd have to think about it? I'm asking you how you feel about me. What is there to think about? You can either tell me to get lost, and I promise I'll do that, if you really mean it ... or you can admit that you love me too and we can take it from there.'

After the initial shock, anger began to surge in me. How dare he spring a question like that on me?

'I'd have to think about it because I've never considered being in love with you as the remotest of possibilities until about ten seconds ago. First you were with Katherine and I was with Kevin. Then Katherine left you and Kevin and I broke up and you were my boss, then I was back with Kevin and you were about to become a priest! Being in love with you was never even on the agenda.'

'What do you want me to do?'

'Quite frankly, Declan, I don't care what you do.' The anger flared up inside me. 'What do you think you are playing at? In two weeks I'm supposed to be walking up the aisle with Kevin.'

'Oh, it's still going ahead, then. And what about Kevin, the fella you're to be married to? Do you love him or do you have to think about that one, too?'

I slammed the phone down before he could ask any more difficult questions.

6 p.m.

At work I sat in a daze. I couldn't honestly remember one piece of work or one conversation I had today. My head was spinning. My emotions ranged from fury to bewilderment to confusion and back again. I couldn't talk to anyone, not even Ariadne, because I could not have put the feelings and emotions into words. There was a storm inside me and it wasn't dying down. What about Kevin? What on earth am I going to say to Kevin?

Friday 14 April

3.07 a.m.

Whatever am I going to do?

Until yesterday morning, everything was straightforward; my life had a plan. I had a career, a fiancé, a future and a faith. Now I'm not sure I have any of those things. Declan has blown my world apart as surely as if he'd detonated an atom bomb. I would never have said I was ecstatically happy exactly, but there was a certain settled-ness to my existence. My life before 'That Question' had pattern, had order, had destiny. Now, 'That Question' has thrown it into utter chaos.

Why didn't I answer when he asked me if I loved Kevin? If I can't be certain a fortnight before my wedding, when can I be sure?

And my job! I realized that every day since Declan left I have hated my job. He was the only thing that made working in that horrible soulless place bearable.

What about my faith? I was sure, I was so sure I was on God's side, and now ... now I seem to be in direct competition with him over Declan. I'd have to admit that I had my doubts about Declan's 'vocation' from the first time he mentioned it, but I supported him. I backed him up to the hilt. If Declan was hearing from God about the direction his life was going, well, bully for him. I thought I was the only person who didn't seem to have a direct hotline to God's heavenly careers service.

What am I going to do, Jesus? What am I going to do?

Saturday 15 April

'Kevin, look, I'm really sorry about this but I can't marry you.'

'Ha, ha. Very funny! April Fool's Day was two weeks ago. You're a bit late there, Theo. Good joke, though.'

'I'm serious, Kevin. Look, I'll call round tonight and explain.'

'No way! You're not getting away with playing games with me like that, Theodora. You explain to me what you mean right now.'

'I'm sorry, Kevin, I can't. I'll come round tonight and we'll talk properly.'

'Women! I can't understand them.' And he hung up.

Sunday 16 April

I can see why Kevin reacted like that. I don't understand women either.

Or men.

Or God.

I don't understand anything any more. I'm not sure Kevin has taken me seriously. I think he's putting it down to pre-wedding neurosis. Even when I handed back the ring, he tried to persuade me to keep it, 'in case I change my mind'.

I tried to explain things to him last night, but missing out the bit about Declan left the entire situation sounding rather vague. The only thing I can do is go and see Declan and sort the whole mess out. Am I in love with him? I just feel very angry with him and extremely confused. All I know is that my heart gave a little skip every time I heard his voice on the phone and every time I found a letter or card from him on the doormat. I enjoyed his company and tolerated his sense of humour. But love?

I just can't believe this is happening.

Couldn't cope with church today. Strangely enough, all the hymns, prayers and liturgy which normally make me feel closer to God would have made him seem remote. All the friends I usually rely on so much for advice and support wouldn't understand. I shall sit here and rant at God for allowing everything to go so wrong.

11.30 p.m.

Kevin has rung four times today. I couldn't talk to him. When I disconnected the phone he came round and rang the doorbell. Fortunately Mum and Dad are still at Auntie Gladys's in the Rhondda so they couldn't let him in. He shouted to me through the letterbox when I wouldn't answer the door.

'Theo, I don't understand what's going on. Please let me in. At least let us talk about this. I'm not angry, Theo love, just very, very confused. Please . . . Please don't shut me out.'

Monday 17 April

The Managing Director came to our office in person this afternoon to allay our fears and boost staff morale. He had the air of a First World War general on a visit to front-line troops in the trenches. I can honestly say that I couldn't care less what happens to the office or its inhabitants. They could all be transferred to Outer Mongolia as far as I am concerned.

Tuesday 18 April

Called round to see Chrissie today to cancel the wedding.

'Is this some kind of joke? We only finished reading your banns on Sunday.'

'Couldn't be more serious,' I said. 'It's . . . complicated. I've got a lot of things to sort out. I just can't go through with it. It would all be a lie.'

'I'm sure it's just nerves.'

'I wish that it was,' I said, fighting back the tears. 'I just know that I can't get married. Will you do what's needed to cancel it? I'm really sorry to cause so many problems.' And I couldn't hold back the tears any longer. I picked up my coat and ran out of the vicarage.

'We need to talk . . .' called Chrissie to my back as I stumbled down the drive.

Wednesday 19 April

Mum and Dad came back today. I was sitting at the bottom of the stairs waiting for them.

'The wedding's off,' I blurted.

Dad put down his suitcase. 'Well, we can't leave you alone for five minutes, can we?'

'But I've bought a hat,' said Mum.

I ran upstairs, locked myself in my bedroom, ignoring their attempts to reason with me, and cried into my 'My Little Pony' duvet cover until I fell asleep.

Thursday 20 April

Spent a depressing evening phoning round all our guests to tell them that the wedding is off. Dad refused to help out. He doesn't like using the phone; he thinks phones have germs, so he says. Apparently he sees himself as a kind of poor man's Howard Hughes.

Perhaps Lizzie in Accounts was right and the dress is cursed. Looking at it hanging on the back of my bedroom door I hate it. It seems to be mocking me. I haven't heard any more from Declan. Kevin came round again last night but I still refused to talk to him. I can't think of anything that either of us could say which would help the situation. Instead, I heard him in the kitchen talking to Mum and Dad, no doubt trying to rationalize my behaviour. I think they all believe I will change my mind. As far as I know, they haven't told Ariadne yet. Part of me is glad she's not here. She would force me to talk and I can't tell anyone about Declan. I still don't know how I feel about him.

Friday 21 April, Good Friday

I went downstairs to find a letter on the doormat. The writing on the envelope was Kevin's. I tore it up without reading it and put it in the dustbin. What is the point?

Went to the Good Friday service. Listening to the account of Jesus' agony on the cross made me cry. In the prayer time, I added a few of my own troubles to all the ones he already had.

News that I had called off the wedding had raced round the church faster than a greyhound on steroids. People kept coming up to me, putting their arm around my shoulders and squeezing me. I think it was supposed to make me feel better. Actually made me feel like punching them. Charity had adopted an expression of sympathetic concern.

'It's probably for the best,' she said. 'I could never see you having the submissive heart necessary to be a good wife.'

It was then that I knew I had to get away.

Sunday 23 April, Easter Sunday

Couldn't face church today, everyone would be too happy and I would have to pretend. Instead, stayed at home and watched a television programme about the Easter Bunny. Realized I could eat chocolate again after Lent. Perhaps things are getting better after all. Life is possible if you have chocolate.

I have e-mailed Declan to say that I am travelling up to Manchester on Tuesday as I feel we have some serious talking to do. Seeing Declan face to face might help me to know how I really feel about him. If I decided that I did love him and wanted to marry him, he would have to give up his vocation to be a priest. That puts me in opposition to God, not a comfortable place to be.

Monday 24 April, Bank Holiday

Mum and Dad seem to be on some kind of 'Let's cheer up Theodora' crusade. I know they mean well but I feel as if I'm trapped in a *Wizard of Oz* film. We went for a family drive, followed by a family walk through the local park and down to the boating lake that has rowing boats for hire.

According to a notice by the lake, a 'Family Row' cost £2.50. A 'Family Row' was just what was brewing, but in our family we usually manage to argue for free.

We went to a local carvery for lunch. Although I didn't feel much like eating, Mum had offered to pay and I have never been one to turn down a free lunch. I munched my way through the dried-out roast beef, soggy cabbage and carrots that dissolve when you try to stick your fork in them. Trapped with Mum on one side of me, Dad on the other and *Save All Your Kisses for Me* on the juke box, the questions started.

No, we hadn't had a quarrel.

No, I wasn't pregnant.

No, Kevin hadn't run off with another woman.

No, Kevin wasn't gay, and neither was I.

Then they asked me if there was somebody else and I couldn't answer. *Your Cheatin' Heart* came on the juke box. They looked at each other knowingly and Mum ordered triple chocolate gateau all round.

In the car on the way home, Mum tried to probe me about the other person but I wasn't going to say anything. They wouldn't understand what was going on. After all, I'm in the middle of it and I don't understand. When we got home, Kevin had left five messages on the answering machine.

Tuesday 25 April

Mr Singh dropped a bundle of mail round this morning. Obviously my change of address hasn't quite worked its way through the postal system yet. Among the invitations to cheaper insurance, mail order catalogues and credit card applications was a postcard from Digger in Australia. On the front was a photograph of a surfer doing something utterly improbable on a surfboard. On the back were the usual greetings and a bit of news about how he is getting on in his new church. Unusually, he hadn't included a Bible verse. Instead he'd included a short paragraph which he headed 'Surfing Tips'.

> Always keep your eye on the waves. Never let them catch you by surprise.
> Never surf on your own. Make sure you're always surrounded by friends. If nothing else, they'll be bait for the sharks.
> Keep the leash firmly attached. If you need to leap off your board, it'll keep you fixed to something that can keep you afloat.

I wonder what all that is about. I think he's a couple of snags short of a barbie. The only surfing I've ever done is on the Internet.

After breakfast I packed my bag, put petrol in the car and headed off to Manchester.

11.48 p.m.

I am now sitting in a clean and tidy, if rather impersonal, motel room somewhere off the motorway just north of the Midlands.

I arrived in Manchester just after half past two. It took me another hour and a half driving round the one-way systems of Greater Manchester to eventually find Declan's lodgings. His flat was near the top of what must once have been a very grand residence but had long ago been divided into flats, which now seemed to house mainly students.

On the long drive from London to Manchester I had rehearsed many times what I was going to say to Declan when I saw him. I would be dignified, I would be composed, I would be assertive. But after tackling the one-way system and struggling to find the flat, I was red in the face and had steam coming out of my ears. I climbed the stairs and rang the doorbell. Declan answered, looking dishevelled as if he had just got out of bed.

'Theodora! What a surprise! How lovely to see you.'

'Don't give me that. You knew full well I was coming and I'd have been here a darned sight sooner if it wasn't for your bloody one-way system.'

'Now you can blame me for a lot of things, but Manchester's one-way system isn't one of them.'

I glared at him. 'Where's your toilet?'

Declan pointed to a beige door. The flat was dark and dingy and the curtains hadn't been properly pulled back. There was an unmade bed against one wall, a desk, an armchair and a television. A dining table covered in papers stood in the centre of the room. It had a half-empty whisky bottle and a dirty glass on it. I stomped off into the tiny bathroom. Towels littered the floor.

'Can I get you a coffee?' Declan asked when I returned.

'Glad to see you made the effort and tidied up for me.'

'Ah, Theo, sarcasm doesn't become you. Now do you want this coffee or not?'

'Yes please,' I said, sitting at the table.

Declan returned from the kitchen area with two mugs of instant coffee. I studied him as he sat across the table from me. He had lost weight, almost gaunt now, and he needed a shave. His eyes looked dull and his hand shook slightly as he handed me the mug.

'Are you well?' I asked, forcing myself to be polite.

'Not really. I've been eating too little and drinking too much and pining for you.'

'Oh,' I said.

'How about you?'

'Oh, pretty good really, considering I've lost my fiancé, I've got nowhere to live and my boss thinks I'm a moron. Oh yes, and did I mention that I'm spending most of my time trying to think a suitable way of killing the scum who has completely wrecked my life?'

'I'm sorry.' He reached across the table to take my hand. I snatched it away from him.

'You just have no idea, do you?'

'Look, Theo.' He stood up and ran his hands through his hair. 'God knows I never wanted to hurt you. I was really confused. I was questioning my faith, my vocation. I was lonely. I left all my friends, all the people whom I loved in London. I thought it would help to make a complete break ... but ... when I got here I knew I'd made a huge mistake. All the other candidates were all so sure, like they had a hotline to God or something, and there's me groping in the dark, trying to make sense of it all, to do my best, trying to do the right thing. The only good thing I could think about was you.'

'Will you carry on into the priesthood?'

'I don't think so. One thing this year has achieved is to show me what I can't do, and being a priest is one of them. I'm just not "holy" enough.'

❧ 254 ❧

I grunted. So I wasn't competing with God. God had already dropped out of the fight.

'Oh, come on, I'd have been a lousy priest. I love the women too much.'

'I thought loving people was what being a priest was all about.' I studied him across the table and tried to analyse what I felt. Pity; certainly; affection, possibly; and something else. Something I couldn't put my finger on.

I heard a key turn in the door. A slim girl with long dark hair came in. She put one arm around Declan's neck and the other around his waist, pulled him close to her and kissed him on the lips. Then, casually, she unwound her arms and began tidying the empty coffee mugs and whisky glass into the sink.

'Theodora, this is Scorcha.'

The girl turned towards me and smiled. I sat with my mouth open, unable to speak.

'I can see this isn't a good time,' she said.

She turned to Declan and kissed him on the cheek. 'I'll meet you in the pub.'

Declan nodded and patted her bottom as she left.

'And just who is she?' I spat.

'Would you believe the cleaning lady?'

I stood up and leaned on the table with both hands. 'You ... you tell me you love me. You wreck my life, my wedding, and when I come up here to sort things out ... this ... this girl ...'

'Scorcha.'

'... whatever her name is, has got her hands all over you. Declan, what is going on?'

'I've moved on.'

'In a fortnight?'

'Theo, you have to believe me, every word I said to you on the phone that morning was true. I do love you and I do want to marry you. It's just that I've had time to think, time to realize you're far too good for a lousy, slimy low-life like me.'

'Too right!'

'Theo, I only want the best . . .'

'So you just decide to leave my feelings in shreds and get it on with the first girl who happens to cross your path!'

'Come on, I've done you a favour.' He was shouting now.

'And just how do you figure that?' I shouted back.

'If I'd kept my mouth shut, you'd have gone ahead and married that Kevin and ended up regretting it for the rest of your life.'

I took a deep breath. My voice sounded as if it was coming from someone else. 'Well, thank you for saving me from that. You truly have missed your vocation.'

I shut the door quietly on my way out, saving my tears for when I got back into my car.

I intended to drive back home tonight but realized I was too tired and overwrought to do it safely. So here I am on my own in this motel. All on my own.

Wednesday 26 April

Aaaarrrgggghhhh!

Thursday 27 April

Got back to work to find Covenant Blake sitting at my desk. Threw down my briefcase, (Ariadne was right, it does give me an air of authority) and stormed into Myrna's office. She was on the phone.

'What's he doing at my desk?' I demanded, not waiting for her to finish.

'Sit down,' she said calmly, finishing her call. I stayed standing.

'The thing is, while you were away we've had a bit of a departmental reorganization. The Divisional Director asked for suggestions from staff for streamlining the running of the various departments within the London office. Covenant put in a proposal which at first surprised us all, it was so radical and audacious, but when we ran his projections past our long-term strategy team it all made perfect sense. A way to downsize, through relocation and redeployment, and save almost a third on next year's proposed budgets.'

'You still haven't explained why he is sitting at my desk.'

'Well, you see, dear ...'

She called me 'dear' again; I can't stand it when she calls me 'dear'.

'... while you were away, Covenant was deputizing for you ... and the long and the short of it is that he achieved your monthly targets in just two days.'

'Great, I get back from a couple of days' leave to discover that I'm completely superfluous. Where does that put me?'

'Rickmansworth.'

'Where?'

'Our Administrative Maintenance Support Department in Rickmansworth.'

'But ... but ... that's in north London.'

'Not that far from Watford, actually,' contributed Myrna.

'But I don't want to go to Rickmansworth, actually,' I said, close to tears.

There was a knock on the door and Covenant breezed in. 'Hello, Theodora, good to see you back.'

'The feeling's not mutual.'

'Now, now,' chided Myrna. 'It could be a great opportunity. I've been looking through your last couple of annual appraisals and, let's face it; you have been growing a little stale. A move to Administrative Maintenance Support could be just what you need to give your career a boost.'

'I don't even know what they do in Administrative Maintenance Support.'

'Classification and storage of documentation mainly,' supplied Covenant.

'Filing,' I said with contempt.

Myrna and Covenant exchanged glances without speaking. They didn't need to. As if I didn't have enough on my plate, I was now demoted to filing clerk in Rickmansworth.

I stormed out of the office, threw Covenant's belongings on the floor, sat down at *my* desk, at *my* computer and typed my letter of resignation. I claimed four weeks annual leave in lieu of notice, thrust the letter into Myrna's hand, put my contemporary cacti and picture of Phoebe into a cardboard box and left the office for the last time.

I am now a free woman.

Oh Jesus, help me, I'm scared.

Friday 28 April

Spent the day making phone calls and sending e-mails. I've just got to get away.

Mum and Dad think I've lost the plot completely since I informed them last night that I'd resigned my job.

'Great,' commented Dad. 'From being a homeless spinster this morning, by 'alf past six this evening she's made herself an unemployed homeless spinster.'

I stomped off to my room and started to pack.

Saturday 29 April

Am sitting on a plane on my way to Evia. I have been reading back through my diary. I had written that 12 January was the worst day of my life. I was wrong.

I'm tired. I'm going to sleep now.

Sunday 30 April

Today should have been my wedding day. Instead I am serving Australian beer to a group of German tourists in a Greek taverna.

Monday 1 May, Bank Holiday (England)

Phoned Mum and Dad to let them know that I have arrived safely and asked them to look after the budgie. Ariadne was there when I phoned. She started screaming down the phone at me. She berated me for being irrational, irresponsible and impulsive. That was rich coming from someone who was yelling like a banshee. Eventually, I had to hang up; I couldn't stand it any longer. I suppose it is understandable: she went away on holiday thinking her sister was getting married and returned home a fortnight later to find that not only has the wedding been cancelled but I've actually left the country. Poor Ariadne.

The journey to Evia did not seem quite so arduous this time. I was grateful for the space to be quiet and disengage my brain. I was so glad to get away from all the fallout from last week and was so pleased to see Diana waiting at the port to greet me in her grandfather's beaten-up van. She gave me a hug and handed me a bar of chocolate. It's at times like these that you know who your true friends are.

Wednesday 3 May

After my dramatic resignation from my job last Thursday, I had spent Friday morning phoning Diana then went straight to the nearest travel agent and booked a one-way flight to Athens. With the money from the sale of my flat and my savings, my bank account was more comfortably padded than I ever remember it being before. The temptation to blow it all on a new car or something equally extravagant still tugged at me, but my conscience tugged back. Sensible Theodora won but acquiesced to allowing me a few weeks in Eviä. I knew that Diana's grandparents rented out rooms in addition to running the taverna, and I had planned on leasing one for a while. When I arrived, Diana's grandparents greeted me like a long-lost family member. Diana told them of my plight and they made me an offer. They said I could live in one of the apartments rent-free, meals included, in return for waitressing and cleaning duties. They are just coming into their busy season and could do with an extra pair of hands. It would enable me to stay here as long as I wish and without eating into my cash too much. I kissed them all and tears of relief and gratitude ran down my face.

Saturday 6 May

Wrote to Ariadne, trying to explain my actions. She won't understand, I know she won't, but at least I've come clean. As I tucked it into the yellow post box, it felt as if I was posting the letter to a different planet.

Sunday 7 May

Went to church with Diana this morning. The small evangelical church, which is not really supposed to exist at all, met in a house belonging to a businessman from Athens. Most of the congregation of about fifteen were English, German or American, with only a handful of Greeks. Ninety-five per cent of the Greek population belongs to the Greek Orthodox Church and although other denominations are free to exist, provided that they meet the guidelines and have a permit, they are not allowed to proselytize, which makes life rather difficult for an evangelical church.

We sang choruses in Greek and English accompanied by Brad on the guitar. In the prayer time I found my mind wandering to Declan. How could I have got it so wrong? Either I was stunningly gullible or he was a complete shyster. Perhaps both. All I know is that my unwillingness to be happy with what I had has led to me losing everything.

Tuesday 9 May

My mother phoned this evening. It was very difficult to follow as she insisted in conducting the whole conversation in Greek. The way her mind works seems to be that I, her daughter, am in Greece, therefore I speak Greek, so it would follow that if she speaks to me in Greek I will (a) understand her and (b) be able to reply. After five minutes it was apparent to both of us that she was labouring under a misapprehension.

'Mum, I'm really sorry, I just can't understand you. Please speak in English.'

'I just wanted to see if you were all right and tell you we miss you.'

This time I heard the words and I understood.

Thursday 11 May

I am sitting here in the sunshine, looking at the sea, listening to it gently lapping. My friend Diana, who never asks any difficult questions, is sitting a few feet away from me. Kevin, Declan, Ariadne and all the people who cause me problems or want to know when I will come to my senses, when I will stop acting like a spoilt child and when I will return home and face up to my responsibilities, are hundreds of miles away. The truth is I don't feel like facing up to my responsibilities. I know I'm running away but I don't care. For once I'm doing something because I feel like doing it, not because my parents or my sister or my church say I ought to. Ariadne says I'm being selfish, I have been refusing to answer Kevin's phone calls, and after my visit to Declan, I don't think I'll be hearing from him again. How could I have been so stupid?

I like it here, just the sea, the sand, God and me. There is a man with a surfboard. He's doing his best to ride the waves even though there is hardly any surf. He is watching carefully for the waves, but a moment ago he was so busy watching a young woman walking along the beach that a wave knocked him off his feet. He's got a string attaching the board to his ankle, I think it's called a leash. Whenever he falls off (which is frequently) the leash means that he doesn't lose his board and he can lie on it and paddle back to shore. His friends are sitting on the beach and shouting whenever they spot a wave. Surfing looks great fun. I'll have to try it one day if I can ever pluck up courage to take the plunge.

I've been talking to God a lot in the last fortnight. Unfortunately he doesn't seem to be talking back. Perhaps he's cross with me too. And yet today, by showing me his glorious ocean, deep enough to swallow up all my worries, and his beach, wide enough for me to walk and walk, and his sunshine, warm enough to thaw the ice-block of resentment, anger, confusion and apprehension which seems to have formed around my heart ... Perhaps, in time ...

Sunday 14 May

Diana had disappeared by the time I woke up this morning. I made the guests' breakfasts and cleared the tables, refilling the oil and vinegar bottles for the new day. Then I helped to knead the dough for the bread. Most restaurants buy in their bread from the bakery but Diana's grandmother has always taken pride in baking her own, with poppy seeds or sesame seeds and glazed with egg and milk; her bread is reason alone to eat at her restaurant. Diana's grandfather, Dimitri, sauntered off to feed the chickens. I can hear the bells from the little Greek Orthodox church in the village. That must be where Diana's grandmother, Maria, is. A few days ago, when I was in the village, the door of the church was ajar so I peeped in. It was larger than it looked from the outside, and in contrast with the plain whitewashed exterior, the inside was ornately decorated with paintings and statues of the saints. As my eyes became used to the candlelit interior, I noticed a bent little old lady, dressed all in black. She said something in Greek that I didn't understand, and then she beckoned to me. I went inside. The inside of the church was cool and gloomy in comparison to the glaring heat of the day. The light that there was came from a myriad of small candles, hardly bigger than the ones you would find on a birthday cake, that were arrayed in holders at various points round the church. The old lady held out a box with bundles of unlit candles and some loose change in it. '*Efahristo*,' I said and took a couple, dropping a few coins into the box. I lit the candles and placed them in a holder, then I sat down and thought about St Norbert's and Kevin and my life at home.

Tuesday 16 May

I went to Halkida, the island's capital, with Dimitri this morning. He needed to buy catering and domestic supplies, and although he is as scrawny as a plucked chicken and as strong as an ox, he still needed an extra pair of hands to help with the fetching and carrying. The journey into town in his battered van was rather quiet. His English was far superior to my Greek. Nevertheless, he only spoke when he had something significant to say. He is not a man who likes to waste his words. We bought the supplies and loaded the van. He explained that he was going to have a drink with a friend and would meet me back here at four o'clock, and disappeared into the dark interior of a *kafeneion*. It was clear that I would not be welcome to join him.

The sun was high in the sky now, and whereas in my tourist days I would have donned my bikini and headed for the beach, I now hunted out a taverna to drink lemonade and escape the mid-day heat. I bought a map and guide-book from a newspaper kiosk, and in the shade of the taverna's awning I sipped my iced lemonada and read about this historic town. Like most things Greek, there is not one clear explanation or one accepted spelling or one style of architecture. There is even speculation about the origin of the name Halkida. It may come from the Greek word for copper, *halcos,* or from *halki,* a type of shell used to produce red dye. The town was built on the site of a very ancient city and contained temples dedicated to Zeus, Apollo and the goddess Hera. The mediaeval fortress contains a Byzantine basilica and there is a museum as well as shops, hotels and bars. Apparently there is a strange configuration of tides where the island is so close to the mainland. Legend has it that Aristotle was so perplexed by these mysteriously changing tides that he threw himself to his death. I can understand how he felt. I looked at my watch and thought, 'It is a pity there isn't more time to explore.'

At four o'clock I returned to the *kafeneion* to meet Dimitri. He was nowhere to be seen. I waited fifteen min-utes, half an hour, three-quarters of an hour. I know that Greek timing can be a little ... imprecise, but this was get-ting ridiculous. Finally I marched into the café and came to an abrupt halt. Inside were nine or ten Greek men of a sim-ilar age to Dimitri and apparently wearing identical clothes. My initial thought was to wonder if the island had been the location for a cloning experiment some time in the 1940s, then I spotted Dimitri half slumped over a backgammon board while his mirror image eyed me suspiciously from the other side of the table. Judging by the empty Metaxa bottle and glasses, Dimitri hadn't spent the afternoon drinking coffee. Although the *kafeneion* regulars were initially suspicious of this strange Englishwoman, they soon forgot their scepticism and helped me manoeuvre the close-to-comatose Dimitri into the passenger seat of the van. I retrieved the keys from his pocket. It was clear that I would have to drive back. I hoped that I could remember the way. Driving along the ribbon-thin path through the mountains, with pine trees on one side and a hundred-foot sheer drop on the other, I now understood why Dimitri didn't go to Halkida to get supplies on his own.

Thursday 18 May

The chickens escaped today. I have learned to shout, 'Come back, chickens!' in Greek. It still took us over four hours to round them all up. Perhaps they didn't understand my accent.

Tuesday 23 May

I have just realized that I haven't written in my diary for nearly a week. Perhaps it is that nothing happens here to write about. Actually that's not strictly true. Things happen, but in such a leisurely manner that there is nothing exceptional to report. Each morning I get up at half past six to help Maria with the breakfasts, then every other day I clean the guests' rooms and make beds. The afternoon is siesta, when I either take the opportunity to nap or go for a walk along the beach or borrow the van and go into the mountains. The evening is spent serving in the taverna. The number of diners varies between none, in which case we spend the time playing cards or backgammon and chatting, and forty, when we hardly get time to draw breath. Maria, bless her, is trying to teach me to cook. Last week I accidentally put salt in the Greek coffee. I am sure her hair has become even greyer in the last few weeks.

Thursday 25 May

Diana and I took a stroll along the beach tonight. The taverna wished its last customer *'kalinichta'* just before midnight and we cleared up more quickly than usual.

'Well, Theo, have you decided what you are going to do?'

The question sneaked up on me and stung like a wasp. 'I ... I ... haven't really thought about it yet. Is there a problem?'

'Not really. Yaya is quite satisfied with your help in the kitchen and even Grandpa thinks you work well – for an Englishwoman.'

I stared at her.

'Oh, don't worry, that's a compliment, coming from him. There's no problem in the summer, my grandparents need your help. But come winter ...'

'I know. I must decide soon. But I've blown it with Kevin, I'm unemployed ... I haven't even got anywhere to live.' All the insecurities began to well up in me again.

'It's a wonderful opportunity,' said Diana, her eyes shining. 'You are a free agent. You could go anywhere, be anybody and do anything ... you could ... be a painter in Paris, a writer in New York, an actress in Hollywood, anything.'

'Anything except Kevin's wife in Sidcup.'

'But is that what you really want?'

The realization hit me that it was what I wanted more than anything in the world – now that it was too late. I know that I called him 'spiritually degenerate' when the truth is that he is probably closer to God than I am. I know that I have constantly griped about his football when it fills just one afternoon a week. I know that I have taken the heart of this good, honest hardworking man who loves me and only ever wanted the best for me and ripped it out. I was wrong, so wrong. The tears were about to start again. I looked at the dark sea.

Suddenly, I heard a sound, a call, more of a whisper that tore me out of my daze. Diana, who had been walking with her arm linked through mine, detached herself and ran on ahead. A young man appeared from behind some rocks. Diana jogged up to him and took his hand. Her eyes were shining and she was slightly breathless. He slipped his arm around her waist.

'Are you all right to find your own way back?' she called, then added, 'Don't tell Yaya.'

Friday 26 May

Diana looked as bright as ever at breakfast. When her grandparents were safely out of the way I grilled her about the young man she met last night.

'Boyfriend, eh?'

'One of them,' she replied coyly.

'How many have you got?'

'As many as I like. Mainly Greek boys, they're very sexy, but sometimes the tourists. I can find you one if you want.'

'No, I don't want.' I felt angry with her. I had waited so long for Kevin. Now I had lost him, and here was Diana offering me sex without strings whenever I wanted.

I felt cheated.

I was also worried about her. If she has become a Christian, sleeping with a different boy every night is not on. But how can I talk to her? What makes me an expert in relationships anyway?

Sunday 28 May

Dimitri and Maria gave me the day off today. I hired one of the little mopeds which buzz around the towns like mosquitoes and took off into the mountains. I was a bit wobbly at first, and I had asked for a crash helmet, which completely threw the man who owned the bike shop. He was also called Dimitri.

There has been an increase in the number of foreign tourists, mainly British and Germans, since I was here in October. My knowledge of the Greek language is now sufficiently advanced that if I go into a shop to buy a loaf of bread, I don't come out with an aardvark.

I found a quiet spot and parked my moped. The silence and the smell of pine were overwhelming. I sat on a grassy area to pray and think. Part of me wants to stay here for ever – I love the climate, the people, the landscape – but it can never be home. This was only ever temporary.

In one sense Diana was right when she said I could be anything I wanted. I don't have to work in an office for ever. I once did a magazine questionnaire, 'Find Your Ideal Job'. I was surprised when I turned out to be 'creative and intuitive, a really gifted communicator who can adapt easily to most situations'. The trouble with being adaptable is finding an occupation that is really what you want. I sort of drifted into office work, but once I was in I didn't know how to get out. I'd considered nursing but the thought of dealing with blood and vomit and any number of other unspeakable bodily fluids put me off. Then I turned my hand to counselling; my first client is still on medication, and my run-in with Brian 'paparazzi' Wedgwood has put me off journalism for life. Perhaps I should take up a religious vocation, become a vicar like Chrissie or a missionary or an evangelist. My attempts at evangelism have usually resulted in me believing less about my faith than when I started, and more than once I've ended up trying to persuade the person not to come to church because they probably wouldn't like it very much. Maybe I should have a family and become a 'career mother' like Charity. What if I turned my hand to practical work? Except Kevin always says I've as much spatial perception as a short-sighted bat and I need help to assemble cardboard magazine holders ...

... Kevin doesn't say that any more because I don't see him any more. Perhaps I should write him a letter and explain everything. I feel as if I've treated him so badly ...

My bout of remorse and self reproach ended abruptly when my borrowed mobile phone rang. It was Diana.

'Er ... Theo, I think you'd better come home.'

'Why, has something happened?'

'It's just that there's someone here to see you.'

'Who?' I asked, fearing Dimitri of the bike-hire shop was coming to reclaim his moped before I did anything dreadful to it.

'Just come back and see.'

I rode back to the taverna as quickly as I could without either falling off or running over the goats and chickens that seem to wander freely in this part of the world. I arrived at the taverna to find it deserted, with a note on the table.

'Come to the beach.'

I sprinted down to the beach and found Diana sitting on the sand with a bottle of retsina and some of Yaya's bread.

'What's this all about?' I demanded. 'Who's come to see me?'

Diana pointed towards the sea. I shielded my eyes from the sun. All I could see were a few families paddling and making sandcastles. I got up and walked towards the water's edge. There was a young couple dangling a baby in the surf at the edge of the sea. The baby was laughing and kicking its feet in the water. The woman was laughing. She looked up, then handed the baby to the man and started running towards me.

I hugged Ariadne and spun her round until we both nearly fell over. I disengaged myself and hugged Tom and kissed Phoebe. I have never been so pleased to see anyone in my entire life.

'What on earth are you doing here?'

'Er ... we needed a holiday?'

'Liar!'

'Theo, come back, please. We miss you.' She held both my hands in hers.

I shook my head and looked down.

'We do. I miss you; Mum and Dad miss you. You miss her too, don't you, Tom?'

'Oh yes,' said Tom in agreement. 'I do.' He nodded vigorously at me as if to consolidate the statement. Phoebe just gurgled and ate sand. I suddenly realized that I had been so self-absorbed that I had forgotten her first birthday.

I introduced my family properly to Diana and we all went back and ate at the taverna. We talked late into the night and Phoebe fell asleep in her buggy. Diana offered Tom and Ariadne a room for the night but they were already booked into a hotel in Halkida. We hugged and I promised to go over and see Ariadne tomorrow.

'Oh,' she said, 'I nearly forgot, there was some post for you.'

She handed me a bundle of correspondence which seemed to contain a fair amount of 'You have definitely won a fabulous prize' letters and, I suspected, some unwelcome bills.

I waved to my family as they drove off in their hire car. Dimitri and Maria went to bed, and just as I was going to my room I saw Diana, with her bag over her shoulder and her shoes in her hand, creeping out of the entrance to the courtyard.

'Sshh,' she said, holding her finger to her lips. Going to meet another boy, no doubt. I shall talk to her in the morning.

I got back to my room and turned on my newly acquired mosquito-killer. The little pests have been having a tasty meal of plump pink Englishwoman for too long and now is the time to fight back. I sat on my bed and opened the letters. I was right; mostly junk mail which was destined straight for the bin. One letter in a very official white envelope was from 'Ashcroft, Miller and Steinbeck, Solicitors'. I was puzzled, as they weren't the solicitors I had used to sell my flat. A pang of guilt shot through me. Perhaps Kevin was suing me for breach of contract. I opened it with trembling fingers. The letter was from the solicitors acting on behalf of Miss Chamberlain, or, to be more precise, Miss Chamberlain's great-niece. The letter apologized for the delay in informing me and explained there had been some 'uncertainty' over the instructions for the disposal of property in the will. I blinked and read the letter again. It seemed that rather than leaving her cottage to her great-niece, she had left it to me! I couldn't believe it. I wanted to tell somebody, to shout it from the rooftops. I had a house! It would explain why the cottage was taken off the market so soon after Miss Chamberlain's niece had put it on: it had never been hers to sell. I couldn't imagine her giving it up without a fight, although the implication at the time was that Miss Chamberlain had left her a substantial sum of money.

I can't wait to tell Ariadne. Roll on morning.

Monday 29 May

I was woken up at half past two by the sound of crying. I opened the door of my room and a shadowy figure jumped like a scalded cat.

'Diana?'

'Sssh. Go back to sleep.' Her voice was shaking.

'Come in here.' Reluctantly Diana came in and sat on my bed. She was trembling and her make-up was streaked from crying.

'Diana, what happened?'

'It's all right, I just need to go to bed.'

'OK, but first tell me what happened. I need to know that you are all right. Was it a man?'

She nodded.

'Did he hurt you?'

'It's nothing. He was a bit rough, that's all.'

'Did he force you?'

'No, no, nothing like that ... As I said, he was a bit rough.'

I felt that Diana's dismissal of the incident hid something deeper. Perhaps now would be the right time to talk to her.

'Diana, I'm worried about you.' She opened her mouth to speak but no words came out. 'I'm going to tell you something that you probably don't want to hear, but I'm going to say it anyway because I'm your friend... I think you are putting yourself at a huge risk.'

'I'm always careful.'

'I don't just mean getting pregnant or catching a disease, although even with the best-laid plans ...'

'I know, I know.'

'I think you are risking your self-esteem, and you could be jeopardizing long-term relationships. I mean, if a man just wants to be with you for one reason ...'

'But I want it too.'

'Do you really? I know I'm hardly one to pontificate in how to succeed in relationships because I've just quite successfully blown my best chance and lost the sweetest man ... Oh dear.'

I stopped talking. This was supposed to be about Diana, not me.

'Do you think this is God's way of telling me that I'm doing the wrong thing?'

My mind started racing. 'Well, I'm sure God doesn't hurt people to "teach them a lesson", he's not like that, but if circumstances and things that happen to us make us think about what we're doing, I believe he will use those opportunities to speak to us.'

'But if I did meet a nice man now, someone trustworthy who would value me, someone like your Kevin, I . . . I don't think he'd want me, after . . .'

'You can't change the past, but the future's up to you. Like you said to me, "You could go anywhere, be anybody and do anything." It's up to you.'

Diana hugged me. 'Thanks,' she said.

'Would you like me to pray for you?'

Diana nodded.

'Our loving heavenly Father, thank you that you care so much about Diana that you only want the best for her. Please help her to hear you speaking to her and help her to do what she knows in her heart to be right. Amen.'

'Amen,' agreed Diana.

She stood up to leave. 'Theodora, I just need to ask you something.'

In the glow of our friendship I was ready to assist with any problem, solve any enigma, assuage any fear. 'Fire away, anything I can do to help,' I said humbly.

'You are thirty-one years old. Why on earth are you still wearing "My Little Pony" pyjamas?'

Tuesday 30 May

After Diana's visit in the early hours yesterday morning, I overslept and arrived in the kitchen of the taverna just before eleven. Maria had to do the breakfasts on her own and was now in the middle of preparing lunch. She didn't seem too pleased with me, nodding her head towards a large pile of potatoes that needed peeling. I couldn't explain why I was late (I didn't want to betray Diana, besides I didn't know the Greek word for 'overslept') so I thought the best policy was to get on with my work as quickly and with as little fuss as possible. Although I'd arranged to see Ariadne today, I didn't feel I could ask to have time off, borrow the van and drive over to Halkida. I would ring as soon as I got a break.

Ariadne's voice on the phone sounded irritated. 'Where are you?' she snapped.

'I'm really sorry, I have to work today and tomorrow but Wednesday's my day off. I'll get the van and I'll come over then, I promise.'

'Can't you get here any sooner? Only there's something important . . .'

'Oh, talking of important,' I interrupted, 'you know that solicitor's letter which was in the bundle of mail you brought?'

'Yes.'

'Well, you won't believe it but I've inherited a house. Miss Chamberlain, that old lady who died last year, left me her cottage in her will.'

'Was she deluded? You didn't dupe her, did you?'

'Of course not.' I tried to sound offended. I'm sure she was joking.

'Does that mean you're coming back to England?' asked Ariadne in a small voice.

Wednesday 31 May

I can't believe it!
I'm getting married!
I can't believe it; I'm engaged again.
Whoopee!

June

Thursday 1 June

I worked extra hard on Monday and Tuesday so by Tuesday night, when I asked to borrow the van for the next day, Dimitri and Maria were quite amenable to the idea. I set off early and found myself almost singing as I drove across the pine-scented mountains in the sunshine. It is the first time I've felt really happy for weeks. I'm sleeping better, feeling fitter from all the hard work and have a light tan from the sun that seems to shine all day. On the downside, I can't do my jeans up because of all of Maria's fabulous moussaka.

I arrived at the hotel just before ten and went to find Ariadne by the pool. Tom had taken Phoebe for a walk. I bought us both a drink and sat on a sun-lounger next to Ariadne.

'What did you want to tell me that was so important?' I asked, sipping my frappé.

'Well, you know that Tom and I love you very much, and the last thing we'd want to do is interfere ...'

'Yeah, right.'

'Hear me out. If you could change one thing about your life, what would it be?'

'Apart from the size of my bottom?'

'Apart from that.'

'To have Kevin back, of course. I'd do anything not to have hurt him the way I did.'

'Theo, it wasn't just the three of us who came out here. There's someone else who can't wait to see you.'

My mind raced. It couldn't be Mum; I'd phoned her yesterday. 'It's not Jeremiah Wedgwood, is it?'

'Of course not.' She handed me a key. 'Go up to our room.'

I went up the stairs to room 302. I turned the key in the lock, not knowing quite what to expect. As I went in, there, sitting on the bed, was Kevin. I wanted to leap on him and hug him and kiss him. Instead I gave a half-hearted little wave and said, 'Hello.'

'Hello,' replied Kevin.

'How are you?' I asked.

'Mustn't grumble,' said Kevin.

I couldn't hold back any longer. I threw myself at him and wept and said I was sorry and wept some more. After that we had a long talk when I told him everything. To my astonishment he understood – and he still wanted us to get married. He took the engagement ring out of his pocket and replaced it on my finger.

'Just don't wear it in the swimming pool,' he said.

We went back down to the pool. Tom had returned with Phoebe, who was wearing arm-bands and a sun hat and was covered in white slimy sun cream. We broke the news and stood hand in hand, grinning like idiots as Ariadne insisted on photographing the moment for posterity. I drove back to the taverna for my evening shift and to break the news to Diana and her family. This time I did sing.

Today has been a whirl of phone calls and arrangements. Kevin drove over in a hire car and was treated like a lord by Maria and Dimitri. They actually seem sorry to see me go and have started searching for my replacement. Our flights back to England are booked for Saturday.

Friday 2 June

Phoned my parents to tell them the wedding was back on. Dad answered.

'I'll go get your mam, I think she's just roasting something.'

'No, Dad, I want to tell you. I'm getting married again.'

'Who to?'

'Kevin, of course.'

'Right-o. There goes the old credit card again. Thought I'd got out of that one a bit lightly. I'll go and tell your mam to get her hat out. Hold on, she'll probably want to speak to you.' Dad put the receiver down on the table, I could hear muffled voices, then a scream. Dad's voice came back on the line.

'Er . . . I'll get your mam to ring you back in a while, when she's got over the shock.'

Saturday 3 June

After a rush of goodbyes and the offer of a room for our honeymoon, we arrived in Athens and boarded the plane back to England, back home. We arranged to meet up with Ariadne and Tom at the airport and have the prospect of flying back next to a fractious baby.

We have left most of the practical arrangements about the wedding until we get home. I don't even know if we can just carry on from where we left off. I hope we don't have to go through all that banns stuff again.

Sunday 4 June

Back to St Norbert's today. Kevin came back too and held my hand and fetched me a coffee at the end. It was wonderful to see the astonished, delighted faces of all our friends after we broke the good news to them. It was even good to see Charity Hubble again. Charity is enormous. I have never seen a human being so vast. When it came to hugging her, I didn't know where to start. You would need to charter an aircraft to circumnavigate her. The triplets are due in about three weeks although everyone will be surprised if she lasts that long.

'Have you thought of any names yet?' I asked, dreading the answer.

'We thought Shadrach, Meshach and Abednego if they are boys and Faith, Hope and Charity if they are girls.'

I succeeded in not pulling a face. 'And what if they are a mixture?'

'Oh, I hadn't thought of that.' Charity looked perplexed. 'I'll have to ask Nigel. Oh, by the way, I believe congratulations are in order, I hear the wedding's on again.'

I grinned sheepishly. 'That's right.'

'Only I hear the choir are taking bets as to whether you'll actually make it up the aisle this time.'

Monday 5 June

Kevin and I have spoken to Chrissie and the date of the wedding has been fixed for Saturday 17 June. Unfortunately the church hall is booked on that date so we will need to search for a new venue. As it will be within three months, the banns don't need to be read again.

Chrissie has offered me a part-time job as church secretary until I find something else, although to be honest I am going to be so busy rushing around preparing for the wedding, I'm not sure I'll have time to work.

Tuesday 6 June

I collected the keys for Miss Chamberlain's cottage from the solicitors today. Kevin asked if I wanted him to come with me but I think it is something I need to do on my own. Besides, after taking time off to pursue me across Europe, he needs to work. Chrissie has offered to come and pray around the house and she is meeting me there at eleven.

I pushed open the garden gate. The roses are all in full bloom but the border has become overrun with weeds and the lawn is waist high. I turned the key in the front door lock. A faint musty smell greeted me, so I went around from room to room opening the windows. There was a little dust and a few cobwebs, but otherwise it was pretty much as Digger and I had left it last year. I don't know what I expected to feel when I thought about living in the cottage – haunted, I suppose. But there were no ghosts here, how could there be? There were just memories, and most of them good ones. St Norbert's clock struck eleven. Chrissie would be here soon. I felt peaceful, as if the waves had finally stopped crashing. I had ridden the surf, I had kept my leash firmly attached and my friends had protected me from the sharks.

Friday 9 June

Have spent the last few days decorating and moving my stuff into the cottage. The electricity, gas and water are now on and most of my belongings have been transported here from Mum and Dad's. Chrissie slept in the spare room last night, so that I wouldn't spend my first night in the cottage alone. Ariadne came over for the evening and we had take-away pizza, a bottle of wine and a giggly girlie night in. Better than any hen night. Just as we were settling down to go to sleep Chrissie called, 'Oi, hired hand, have you typed my *Church Organ* yet?'

'Er . . . it's in the pipeline,' I replied. I have been so busy that I had forgotten all about it. I know Chrissie is only joking, but after she's been so good about the wedding and everything, I feel it's the least I can do. I'll start first thing in the morning.

Saturday 10 June

Without a secretary, *The Church Organ* is in danger of falling by the wayside. Then what would the congregation do during the boring bits of the sermon?

I arrived at St Norbert's at half past nine, settled myself in the little office at the back of the church next to the vestry and started work. The file was full of the usual scintillating notices from the nursery school, Ladies' Guild and Over Sixties' Club. Sadly, Ernest Dexter, a popular local window cleaner, died in an accident last week. However, I hesitated about including the obituary written by his window-cleaning companions.

Each day he climbed his wooden ladder
With chamois and bucket and cloth in hand.
He never left a mark behind him
Now he's cleaning windows in the Promised Land.
A builder on the roof was working
And called, 'Look out, you'd better duck it,'
But when the slates came tumbling downwards
Ernest Dexter kicked the bucket.

I typed out the times of the services for the coming week and an invitation to everyone to the wedding. It took hours because people kept interrupting me. Most came to congratulate me on the wedding or ask what presents we would like. I tried closing the heavy oak door but the populace still found its way in. By half past twelve, I had only finished the front page and three of the notices. However, I was fully acquainted with Mr Wilberforce's theory on copper mining in the Old Testament, Mrs McCarthy's television aerial and how, instead of *Countdown*, she seems to be receiving strange Swedish programmes featuring people with no clothes on, and Miss Cranmer's hysterectomy. At four o'clock I was still there, having typed one more page and listened to Charity Hubble telling me all about eight-year-old Priscilla and Aquilla's school assembly about Siddhartha Gautama and how she was worried that they are thinking of becoming Buddhists.

'Where do I go from here?' she moaned.

I felt like saying, 'Anywhere away from me so that I can get on with this wretched magazine,' but I just shrugged, tutted and tried to sound perplexed.

Shortly after Charity had left and I thought that I could finally 'put it to bed', as they say in the printing trade, Kevin arrived. He'd spent the afternoon trawling around trying to find a venue for our reception. He had a shortlist of two, the scout hall, which would be fine if it doesn't rain, and the lounge bar of the Rose and Crown. He had also been listening to the away match on the radio and his team had been losing heavily. I think he'd come to me expecting sympathy.

'Oh, what do you want? I've been slaving away over this thing all day. All I need is yet another disturbance.'

'Thanks! I'll go away again.' Kevin looked crestfallen.

I was stung with guilt. 'No, please stay. You can help with the collating if you like. It's just that every time I get going, some well-meaning soul comes and tells me their life story.'

'Promise I won't disturb you,' said Kevin and sat down to read his newspaper quietly.

I heard a noise in the nave and peered out of the office window into the car park. There was a Citroen 2CV with a bumper sticker that read, 'Opticians make spectacles of themselves.'

'Get down,' I whispered to Kevin.

'Who is it?' he whispered back.

'Mary Walpole, the optician. She must be finishing off the flowers. If she gets talking, I'll be here till midnight.'

'You get under the desk, I'll hide in this cupboard.'

I flicked the computer on to stand-by and scrambled under the ancient oak desk. I watched an arm come out from the old stationery cupboard, snatch up the newspaper and disappear back inside. I could hear footsteps coming up the aisle.

'Yoo-hoo, anybody here?'

I held my breath. The office door swung open.

'Anybody he-ere?'

The door swung shut again and there was a click. Footsteps and a tuneless sort of humming grew more distant until I heard the main door close and lock. A few moments later, I saw the Citroen drive away. I started to breathe again.

'Has she gone?' whispered Kevin, peering out from among the choir robes.

'Yes, thank goodness.' I crawled out from under the desk and brushed the dust off my knees. 'Just get these printed out and we can go.'

It was starting to get dark so I flicked on the light switch and the neon strip buzzed and spluttered into life.

'Just nipping to the loo, then I'll help you with the folding.' Kevin flapped his newspaper down and went to the door.

'It's locked. Have you got the key?'

'Yeah, in my coat pocket,' I muttered, trying to work out which way round to put the originals in the new photo-copier.

'Where's your coat?' asked Kevin.

'On the coat rack.'

'Where's the coat rack?'

'Just outside the door, next to the hymnbooks.' I ran off a test copy. One side was upside down and the front was where the back should be.

'Just outside this door, the one that's locked?'

'Mmm, that's right.' I stopped and turned round. 'She's just locked us in. Mary Walpole must have locked the office when she thought it was empty . . . and my keys are outside.'

'I'll try to force it.'

Kevin twisted the handle back and forth. He tried to slip a credit card behind the latch. He tried to shoulder barge it, but the solid oak door, designed to withstand marauding Saxon invaders, wouldn't move an inch.

'There's no phone here. That's why so many people call in person,' I said. We sat in silence for a few moments.

A brainwave – I pointed excitedly at Kevin. 'Phone . . . you've got your mobile. Let's ring Chrissie and she'll nip down and let us out.'

'Brilliant!' Kevin handed me his phone and I dialled the vicarage number.

'The signal's terrible, it keeps cutting out.'

'Try walking around – sometimes the signal's better in a different place . . . or try holding it up in the air.'

I paraded up and down the tiny office, holding the phone first high, then low. Finally, I discovered that the only way I could get a good enough signal was by standing on the desk, facing into the corner of the room with my head jammed into the cornice. I must have looked like some kind of insecure gargoyle. It would seem that the Norman church builders didn't make many mobile phone calls either.

'Hello, Chrissie?' I called into the phone.

'Hello. You have reached St Norbert's Vicarage. I'm afraid that Reverend Monroe is not able to take your call at the moment. Please leave a message after the tone. Beeeeep.'

I left a message, hoping that she wouldn't be long.

'There must be another way out,' said Kevin, surveying the office. He dragged a chair over to the window, stood on it and tried to lever the small leaded pane open. It opened a fraction on its ancient hinges. Kevin stuck his arm through.

'It's got bars,' he said dejectedly. 'Even if I could get it to open any more, we wouldn't be able to climb through it.'

I sighed and slumped into the office chair.

'Somebody else must have an office key.'

'Well,' I said, 'I've got the secretary's key. Chrissie's got one. Mary's obviously got one, because she locked us in, and Jeremiah had one. I've no idea what happened to that.'

'Do you know Mary's number?'

We checked the phone directory and the parish records but her number wasn't listed.

'Oh well,' I said resigned, 'we'll just have to sit tight until Chris gets the message.'

I ran off the rest of the copies of *The Church Organ* for the morning and Kevin and I sat in silence, folding them.

By 10 p.m. it was starting to get cold. As I hadn't heard from Chrissie I rang again, and again got the answering machine. I left another message and yawned.

'*Match of the Day* soon,' muttered Kevin.

'Is that all you can think about? I'm hungry.'

'Haven't you even got any chocolate?'

'In my coat pocket which is ... the other side of that door. Aarrgh!'

'Shall we do the crossword? Take our minds off things.'

The crossword in Kevin's paper whiled away three-quarters of an hour. My eyes were beginning to close.

'You look tired,' commented Kevin. 'Shall we snuggle up and try to get a bit of kip?'

I was a bit concerned that 'snuggling up' might turn into something else. I haven't hung on for all these years just to blow it a week before my wedding night. Kevin had made a sort of nest on the office floor out of the choir robes. I stood about four feet away from him, leaned over and gave him the lightest of perfunctory pecks on the cheek and retreated back to the squeaky typist's chair by the desk.

'What's the matter? I'm not going to eat you, you know.'

'It's not eating that I'm worried about.'

'All right then, I won't "molest" you. Trust me.'

'It's me I don't trust. Two people, him dark and hand-some, her exotic and vulnerable, thrown together by cruel fate, trapped for who knows how long, sharing body heat to keep warm. Passions are inflamed and the next thing you know they're writhing together on a fur rug, the flickering flames of the open fire fuelling their fervour ...'

'You watch too many James Bond films.'

'But you understand what I'm saying.'

'Let me tell you a story. In my family, it was the tradition that on our birthday, all our presents, the ones from Mum and Dad plus the ones posted from grandparents and uncles and aunts, would be gathered up and put on the dining-room table the night before. Then on the morning of their birthday, the birthday boy or girl could go down, collect the presents, take them up to Mum and Dad's room and open them with everyone watching.

'It was the day before my tenth birthday and I decided to have a nose around inside Mum's wardrobe while my parents were out. I happened to find a bag of presents. Some were wrapped; some were still in carrier bags. I decided to have a little peep. I saw a drawing set, some goalkeeper's gloves and a football. I thought, "Wouldn't it be nice if there was a football shirt to go with it?" so I had a feel. One present felt as if it could be a shirt so I just peeled back a bit of sticky tape and peered under the wrapping paper – and there it was. There was another one that felt a bit like a book so I had a peep at that, too. It was a *Match of the Day* book. After that I couldn't stop. I peeped at all of my presents, then carefully pressed the tape back in place so nobody would know.

'The next morning I didn't rush downstairs, there was no point. Eventually I thought I ought to open my presents, but it just wasn't the same. The presents themselves were perfect, just what I wanted, but there was no surprise. That was my worst ever birthday. And that is why I won't let anything happen tonight.'

We snuggled up on the choir robes and both kept our wrapping paper on. We didn't even peep under the sticky tape.

Sunday 11 June

We were woken up by a scream. It was Chrissie, come to prepare for the early communion service.

'You frightened the life out of me. What on earth were you two doing there, or need I not ask?' She winked and tapped the side of her nose.

'Don't you listen to your answering machine messages? We were locked in,' I said icily.

'Ooh, my back,' groaned Kevin, shuffling to his feet.

It was not possible to continue the discussion any longer as both Kevin and I secured a hasty exit to the toilets.

Wednesday 14 June

Charity had her triplets yesterday. They came two weeks early, and to her disappointment she had to give birth in hospital in case of any complications. There weren't any. Charity seems perfectly adapted to having babies.

I have just been round to see them at home. Charity is beaming but is looking more tired than I have ever seen her before. The triplets were two girls and a boy. They are called Martha, Mary and Lazarus. Poor child – Lazarus. That will cause some consternation when it comes to filling in his birth certificate ... and even more so in the future, when it comes to filling in his death certificate.

Friday 16 June

Bridesmaids, cars, food and wine, photographer, decorations for the scout hut. Rang Diana, flights booked for the

24th, bought rings, dress still fits, suits hired, football shirts relegated to back of wardrobe. Hair cut and coloured (me), trimmed and re-styled (Kevin), manicure, pedicure and make-up (me), rowdy night at the pub and Alka-Seltzer (Kevin). Outfits co-ordinated (Mum and Eloise). Shoes fit but feet cold.

This time I'm really going to do it.

Saturday 17 June

This is my last diary entry as a single woman. I have been forbidden to record details of our wedding night and banned from taking my diary on honeymoon. Oh well, I'll just have to find something else to keep me occupied.

Everyone else is at the church already except Dad, in his best suit with a carnation in his lapel, who has just gone outside to see if the car has arrived yet. He has left me in my wedding dress sitting on a straight-backed dining-room chair in the middle of the lounge, holding my bouquet ... He has left a small glass of brandy on the table 'to steady my nerves' ... I keep catching sight of myself in the mirror. It doesn't look like me at all, in my white dress, with my veil and my perfect make-up and hair ... I hope Kevin will be there. Wouldn't it be ironic if I arrived at the church expecting to see him smiling at me from the front pew and he'd changed his mind? Perhaps I will have a sip of that brandy ... I have looked forward to this day for so long. I thought it would never happen ... I can hear Dad coming back.

'Come on, love, the car's here. Better go ...'

**The Hilarious, Sparkling and Endearing Diaries of a
Thirtysomething Christian, Theodora Llewellyn**

Theodora's Diary
Faith, Hope & Chocolate
Penny Culliford

Saturday 8th May. Emergency!

It is 11:30 p.m. and I am suffering from an incredibly intense chocolate craving that will not leave me in spite of prayer, distraction activities and half a loaf of bread and butter. Got out of bed and searched the house. No luck. Not even a bourbon biscuit. Not even a cram egg left from Easter. All the shops are closed so no nipping out to replenish supplies. Nothing else for it. I'm reduced to the chocoholic's equivalent of neths — cooking chocolate.

It's been one of those days for Theodora. Her mother has become the Greek equivalent of Delia Smith, her boyfriend would rather watch 22 men kick a ball around a field than go shopping with her, and chintzy Charity Hubble wants to pray for her. And of course, the crowning insult is her utter lack of chocolate. Join in her daily life with all of its challenges and joys, tears and laughter.

Softcover: 978-0-007-11001-8

Pick up a copy today at your favorite bookstore!